Mitakuye Oyasin
(We all are Related)

Wicahpi Win
(Star Woman)

Bonnie J. Hunt
Lou Ann Hunt

THE GREAT POWWOW

Copyright 2003 by Bonnie Jo Hunt and Lawrence J. Hunt

First Printing, 2004

Library of Congress Catalog Number: 2003113739
International Standard Book Number: 1-928800-08-4 (Vol.IX)

Cover designed by CYBERDESK Solutions,
Ricardo Chavez-Mendez and Michelle Marin-Chavez
visit their website at www.orofineart.com
Medallion features arrival of Nez Perce Indians at the
Walla Walla Treaty Council grounds May, 1855
sketch by Gustavus Sohon courtesy of
Washington State Historical Society

Published by:

Mad Bear Press
6636 Mossman Place, NE
Albuquerque, New Mexico

THE GREAT POWWOW
(THE DAY MOTHER EARTH WAS STOLEN AWAY)

THOUSANDS OF INDIAN PEOPLE ARE PROMISED A NEW LIFE IF THEY WILL GIVE THEIR HOMELANDS TO THE GREAT WHITE FATHER

by

Bonnie Jo Hunt

and

Lawrence J. Hunt

This country holds your father's body. Never sell the bones of your father and mother. . . .
Dying words of Tuekakas, father of Chief Joseph, Nez Perce

A LONE WOLF CLAN BOOK, VOL. IX

Words of Appreciation

The Lone Wolf Clan historical series is the work of many talented people. As usual we are indebted to our fine editorial staff without whose assistance we would be lost. The comments, corrections and suggestions of Barbara Lee Hunt, Juyn Krumm and Susan Shampine are invaluable. For this publication we also were fortunate to have the additional editing help of Kiki Bastle, Punky DePuy, and Betty and Vern Hunt.

We announced in Volume VIII, <u>The Cry of The Coyote,</u> was the last book of the Lone Wolf Clan series. So many readers expressed disappointment we reconsidered. The result is <u>The Great Powwow</u>, Volume IX, which takes up the saga of the Lone Wolf clan from where it left off in <u>The Cry of the Coyote</u>. We are delighted we continued the series as <u>The Great Powwow</u> gave us the opportunity to present more crucial events of Northwest history and the impact they had on Indian people.

Among the special people who contributed extraordinary help in the promotion of the Lone Wolf Clan series are, Harriet Braden, Jim and Phyllis Gilbertson, Betty and Vern Hunt, Dee McLaughlin and others too numerous to relate. Technical and research help as been generously tendered us by Lawrence "Larry" Dodd, Archivist, Northwest and Whitman College Archives, Penrose Memorial Library Whitman College, Vivian Adams, Yakama Nation Librarian, Lydia French Johnson, Confederated Tribes of the Umatilla Indian Reservation and Elaine Miller, Curator of Photographs Washington State Historical Society. Pilamayaye (thank you) so much.

Mitakuye Oyasin (We all are related)

Bonnie Jo Hunt and Lawrence J. Hunt

A VISIT TO LONE WOLF COUNTRY

A goal of the Franklin Pierce administration was to link the Atlantic seaboard with that of the Pacific by transcontinental railway. Isaac Stevens, Governor of newly created Washington Territory, took on the task of surveying a northern route. News that the "iron horse" spewing smoke and cinders soon would come steaming through their lands, sent fear into the hearts of every Indian man, woman and child of the Pacific Northwest. How did one fight this terrifying monster with a voice 10 times louder than the mating call of a bull moose?

It quickly became evident Indian people had more to lose than their pristine and peaceful environment. "Iron horse" trailblazers wanted land -- not just the amount necessary for the path of this steaming monster -- but great chunks of territory, no matter who presently occupied them. In the spring of 1855, fears of the Indian people were realized. Governor Stevens called a council -- the site, the Walla Walla Valley. Here, in late May, 5,000 to 6,000 Indian people arrived to meet with Governor Stevens and government officials.

From the land of the Nez Perce, the talkative leader named Lawyer arrived with 2,500 or more followers. The venerable Peu-peu-mox-mox came with several hundred Walla Walla, as did Young Chief of the Cayuse. Kamiakin and Skloom led the band of Yakama. In less than two weeks these Indian nations were shorn of most -- in some cases, all -- of their homelands. Peace held for a while but when government promises went unfulfilled, war clouds began to appear. . . .

*This is the ominous background in which the saga of the Lone Wolf clan continues. Readers will find **The Great Powwow**, Volume IX of the Lone Wolf Clan historical series, an exciting and gripping tale.*

NORTHWEST TERRITORIES
1853

BUFFALO COUNTRY

SCALE OF MILES
0   50   100   150

DOMINION OF CANADA

Boundary to Rocky Mts. established 1818.

Boundary line of 1846

112   116   120

108

PACIFIC OCEAN

VANCOUVER I.
Strait of San Juan de Fuca
C. Flattery

Astoria
Vancouver
Columbia R.
The Dalles
Willamette
Des Chutes
Ft. Henrietta
Waiilatpu
Old Fort Walla Walla
Walla Walla Council
Lapwai
St. Joseph Mission
Flathead L.
Clark's
Marias R.
Yellowstone
Snake
Fort Hall
BOISÉ
Christmas Lake

THE GREAT POWWOW

I

The Great Spirit Chief made the world as it is, and as he wanted it, and he made a part of it for us to live upon. I do not see where you get the authority to say that we shall not live where he placed us.
Chief Joseph, Nez Perce

It was a windy, whispering, moonless night. The sound of thundering hoofbeats came echoing off the high bluffs. Like approaching thunder, louder and louder the drumming wafted over the sleeping village. The night guard jerked awake and reached for his Hudson's Bay musket. Dogs crept from their lairs. Instead of barking they tucked tails between legs to seek hiding places. No creature, two-legged, four-legged or winged, traveled the river trail at this hour.

Like a tall black phantom, the galloping horse burst out of the darkness. "Hoh!" the night guard yelled but the rider paid no attention. The black steed splashed through the creek to mount the far bank. The guard started to give chase, but held back. Only foolish people ventured up that trail at night. It led to the haunted lodge built by the mountain man called Little Ned. The thundering sound of hoofbeats began to recede, finally to die away.

"Hairy face," the guard thought scornfully. "Like messengers of death, they come whenever they please."

The guard's thought was not far from the truth. The horseman carried tidings that soon would strike fear in the hearts of every Indian on the Great River plateau. In later years storytellers would call it, "Night of the Black Horse". Perhaps if the rider had realized the terror that rode with him, he would not have come. In the end it would make little difference, for if he had not brought the news, others soon would have done so.

**

It was a reunion of sorts that brought the Lone Wolf Clan

together the spring of 1853. They met at the Nimpau village of Lapwai, a most fitting place for the occasion. Locust trees were in full bloom. The cool, fresh air was redolent with their fragrant perfume. A brilliant blue sky looked on. The surrounding bluffs were dotted with wild flowers of every hue. Dew on new spring grass made pasture fields gleam like acres of emeralds. High overhead circling hawks resembled thin, black undulating lines drawn by the stroke of an artist's pen.

Here, within a stone's throw of the swift running Kooskooskie, the last living members of the Lone Wolf family had assembled. Some were linked together by blood, others by marriage. The patriarch, Vision Seeker, had the look of a man much younger than his position suggested. But age had not been kind to younger brother, Running Turtle, who as a youth had been somewhat stout and now resembled a bloated toad. Incredulously, Father Time had been extra kind to the brothers' sister, Raven Wing. Her black wing of hair and bright flashing eyes were as striking as ever.

Among the youthful present were Michael Two Feathers, Raven Wing's half blood son, and his wife, Morning Star, also a half blood, but of the Cheyenne. Bashfully sucking a thumb and pulling on her skirt was the couple's two year-old son, One Who Kicks. Keeping somewhat apart from the others was a tall slender Indian man with the name Young Wolf. He was Michael Two Feather's half brother and second son of Raven Wing.

The last member of the group was aged hairy faced mountain man father of Morning Star, Deacon Walton. He, too, stood to one side as if he didn't belong.

**

The mystery rider who came in the dark of night was returning home after three years. Actually, he could not say returning home as for half his life he had drifted from place to place. But, it was the log cabin lodge the locals called haunted that drew him. His mountain man father had built the cabin and lived there with his Indian family. The rider had wanted to arrive before dark but had underestimated the distance. Rather than disturb Indian relatives in the black of night, the rider made cold camp and planned to appear in the morning.

At first light, uncles, brother, mountain man Deacon, and a boy child who tugged on the tassels of his buckskins, greeted him.

"This is my son, One Who Kicks," Michael Two Feathers said proudly, lifting the boy to his shoulder.

"Ah!," the newcomer uttered in surprise. He glanced at Michael's mate, Morning Star, who he once nearly asked to be his own wife. For a split second their eyes met, then the brown limpid pools of light quickly looked away. The brief emotional encounter left the man wordless. Was she having the same thought? If they had married, instead of Michael, he would be the father of this stocky boy child.

Food was brought out. They sat on the sunlit porch and ate their fill. Yet, what should have been a happy occasion appeared strained. The only one who seemed at ease was the boy child who scampered beneath everyone's feet. Not until late in the day did the black horse rider reveal why he had come. He was the advance scout of a survey party searching for the route of a proposed transcontinental railroad.

At first only Michael Two Feathers who had traveled on the iron snakelike monsters, seemed to understand. His mind went back to the journey his brother and he had made on the hissing, smoking, crawling creature. With great clanging of bells, the iron horse had leapt forward. Faster and faster the smoke belching monster sped, hurtling over shiny tracks that stretched to the horizon. It was like riding a wild steed without bridle or halter. There were no reins to guide the iron horse and no bit to pull it in. One had to ride it until it ran itself out.

In big villages called "cities" the iron monsters disappeared into great badger-like holes where they met with creatures of like kind. Seeing them crouched in these dark, smelly pits, hissing like snakes in a den, was a sight so unnerving he wanted to jump off and flee. To have such things in the homeland of the Nimpau was too horrifying to contemplate.

"When are they to come?" Michael finally asked.

"Many things must happen first," the messenger of the news replied, avoiding the accusing eyes. "How could you be a part of bringing such smoky, dirty things to this clean beautiful land," the eyes seemed to say.

This is bad news," Vision Seeker said. "How are we to tell the people? We must carefully think before we do."

The strain the rider sensed during the morning increased. It was more than the news he brought that made these people uneasy. He covertly studied each family member. Why were they troubled? With Morning Star's help, his stepmother, Raven Wing, busily began to clean the lodge. She glanced his way. Strangely, the scar on his temple began to throb, and no wonder. The last time he had visited Lapwai she nearly had put out his eye. The scene was so vivid it could have happened yesterday.

"Joe Jennings!" she had shouted his name like a curse. "You have stolen my first son." Her voice had risen in volume like that of Ko-hoh, the trumpeter swan. Then, without warning, she leapt, slashing at him with a knife that seemed to come out of nowhere. Joe involuntarily shivered. Did she remember that terrible day? Of course she did. How could anyone forget a murderous incident like that?

Hardly a day passed that Raven Wing didn't remember the time she stabbed her stepson. The sight of the victim brought it back like a slap in the face. The meeting place also increased her discomfort. The log cabin had been built especially for her by the youth's father. Every board, rafter, shingle and post had been lovingly prepared by his hands. The final touch was the flower bed in the front yard.

"I want this place to be as beautiful and pleasing as the lady of the house," Little Ned had said. Thanks to the care Running Turtle had given them, the flowers were in full bloom, looking as resplendent as that long ago spring when they first were planted. As hard as Raven Wing tried to prevent it, tears sprang forth, blurring her eyes until she could not distinguish one flower from another. "If only . . ." a small voice within her began to cry.

Michael Two Feathers' thoughts were as emotional and distressful as those of his mother. At a time when he needed love and understanding most, Raven Wing had ignored him. She had allowed Francois, his stepfather, to treat him worse than the camp mongrel. Then, she had claimed that he was responsible for Francois' death and cast him from the log cabin lodge.

Michael's bride, Morning Star, had been against this family reunion from the start, and it was turning out worse than she had expected. The sudden appearance of Michael's Boston half brother had made her heart pound until she thought she would faint. The past came rushing back. For years her father, Deacon, had told her Boston Joe and she would wed. Then one day her father had brought Joe's brother home, saying waiting for Joe Jennings was hopeless. Joe's Nimpau half brother, Michael Two Feathers, was the mate she should take. She had yielded to her father's wishes. Now, to meet her first love again was torture beyond belief.

Deacon, Morning Star's father and Joe Jennings' long time friend and former trapping partner, was apprehensive for a different reason. Morning Star and her boy were the apples of his eye. He had come to the family reunion to guard them from harm. Raven Wing was the one he feared. Twenty-five years ago he had encouraged Little Ned to take her for his wife. He also had known Francois, Raven Wing's cruel second mate. Actually, he knew too much about Raven Wing's love life. Would she hold it against him -- take it out on her daughter-in-law and baby grandson? He thought not, but unless she had changed, Raven Wing was as unpredictable as the spring breezes, blowing warm one minute and cold the next.

Young Wolf felt entirely out of place. He scarcely remembered brother Michael or uncles Vision Seeker and Running Turtle, and had laid eyes on half brother Joe only once. Except for a few hairy faced traders, he had little contact with people who came from beyond the River of Many Canoes. The presence of half

brother, Boston Joe, and the old mountain man, Deacon, made him
nervous.

Vision Seeker breathed an imperceptible sigh. It was the
news that Joe brought that distressed him. Already two groups of
men were on their way to prepare a trail for the steam driven iron
horse called "locomotive". The voice of this iron monster was
said to be 10 times greater than the mating call of a bull moose.
To have these iron horses hooting and snorting across plains and through
the mountains would be devastating. The animals Indian people de-
pended upon for their livelihood would find migration trails cut, confusing beasts of both the forest and plain. The iron tracks the iron
monster ran upon would muddy streams. Fish would die -- salmon no
longer would find their way home to spawn. Trees would be destroyed, leaving no nesting and roosting places for the winged ones.

Vision Seeker sighed again. He long had known great changes
were in the offing, still news of the proposed railroad caught him unawares. Coming on top of the recent deaths of his parents, Lone Wolf
and Quiet Woman, the threat of the iron monsters was almost impossible for him to comprehend.

Lone Wolf's life had ended on the hunting grounds of Sun
River, where he now lay buried beside his firstborn, Many Horses.
Soon after Lone Wolf's death, Quiet Woman went to join her
mate. She, too, was not buried in Lapwai, but in the land of the
White Birds, her parental family's homeland, a day's journey to
the south.

In a way Vision Seeker was glad his parents had left Mother
Earth when they did. They had lived during the best of times.
Lately one disaster after another seemed to befall Indian people:
the terrible plagues of diseases that decimated villages and encampments; and the bloody tragedy at Whitman Mission when
the Cayuse avenged the deaths of their loved ones by killing 13
hairy faces, among them missionaries Marcus and Narcissa
Whitman. These tragic events still haunted Indian people.

Following the Whitman Mission killings came the invasion of volunteers under Colonel Gilliam who lived by the creed,

"the only good Indian is a dead Indian". For months his army had
harassed plateau tribes, even though several had no involvment
in the savagery. Finally, five Cayuse surrendered to stand trial for
the mission killings. All five men were judged guilty and hanged
even though at least one was believed completely innocent.

Now, three winters later, without consulting with Indian
people, or taking them into consideration -- and guided by White
Chief President Pierce -- armies of Easterners were marching west
to force what they called "civilization" upon the natives. Soon
the wonderful homelands Indian people had known since the beginning of time would be gone forever. The peaceful quietness
of the forest would be no more. The clear water of streams would
be tainted. The clean fresh air would be filled with the acrid
smell of railroad and factory smoke . . . not even sacred places
and burial grounds of the forefathers would be safe.

The sharp cry of the child, One Who Kicks, jerked Vision
Seeker out of his meditations. The poor boy was unhappy and
hungry, and no wonder. The long faces of the adults would distress even the happiest of folk. Vision Seeker stepped up and
clapped his hands.

"What is the matter with everyone? We make this young
man unhappy. Let us give thanks to The Great Mysterious and
eat of the bounty that has been prepared. Deacon, you know the
words of your Christian God. Lead us in prayer. Thank the Lord
for bringing us together on this beautiful day."

The child grew quiet. The prayer was said for blessings received. Raven Wing turned to give Morning Star a warm hug. Croon-
ing a lullaby, she lifted the boy and cradled him in her arms. "What a
wonderful gift you have given us," she said to the youthful parents.

Michael was so startled by the change in his mother's attitude,
he didn't know how to reply. Instead, he merely smiled. Morning
Star was more composed. She liked this dark-eyed woman. She
had a horrendous reputation and had suffered greatly because of it.
Like herself, Raven Wing had married one man and loved another.
The bitter pain they suffered made them sisters. She gathered her

baby and mother-in-law in a fierce hug. Otherwise, she would have burst into tears.

Covertly, Joe Jennings had been watching the two women. When they came together, his mood of gloom brightened. The two-year old boy made the difference. Raven Wing couldn't resist demonstrating her love for her lively, bright-eyed grandson. Again he felt a tremor of envy. All along he truly had loved Morning Star. Because of her youth, he had kept it buried in the recesses of his heart. Now it would have to remain there forever.

All through the past three years Michael and Morning Star had been foremost in his mind; and they had been the principal reason for his return west. He had gone east to enroll in Harvard College but couldn't keep his mind on his studies. His heart was in Indian country, riding alongside Michael and his black and white pony. Then came news from the nation's capitol that newly elected President Franklin Pierce, in his inaugural address, had pledged to link east with west. To accomplish this, two parties of men were given authority to survey routes for transcontinental railways. From then on Joe Jennings had been absorbed by thoughts of what this might mean for his Indian relatives.

He said good-bye to teachers and classmates and sought out those in command of the surveying parties. The top man hired him as a guide. His first assignment was to travel west and prepare Indian tribes for the surveying parties' arrival. He had been so delighted to be returning to the region he loved, he had given little thought to the awesome impact the news he carried would have upon his Indian relatives and friends.

Although he knew the news he brought would cause consternation, Joe reported it as agreeably as he could. Even so, every group of Indian people he met with turned away as though he had spoken words of doom. No wonder the Lone Wolf clan reunion had the semblance of a wake. Unfortunately, his job was not done. He had to carry the same terrifying message to the Cayuse, Walla Walla, Palouse and Yakama. What kind of reception could he expect -- not a good one, he feared.

THE GREAT POWWOW

II

My people, the Great Spirit has his eyes upon us. He will be angry if, like cowardly dogs, we give our lands to the whites. Better to die like brave warriors on the battlefield, than live among our vanquishers, despised.

Kamiakin, Yakama

Vision Seeker loved solitude. In his youth he had gone off alone to study Mother Earth's many mysteries. His father, Lone Wolf, often sent search parties thinking this prized, but strange, son of his had met with misfortune. Sometimes he would be found sitting by a pond watching tadpoles turn into frogs and larvae into mosquitos, or merely enjoying the antics of skaterbugs. At night he studied the stars, giving names to special constellations: Dove, Fish, Running Fox, Flying Horse . . .

In later years a favorite place was high on the Lapwai Valley hillside where he had a view of the village, Spalding's mission compound, valley pasture grounds and the bluffs overlooking the Kooskooskie. Here, entertained by the lulling whisper of pine needles, choruses of cheery crickets, drumming of flickers and rustling sounds of squirrels and chipmunks, he found peace. In this special place on the hillside many a worry had been cast aside and numerous nagging problems had been solved. After receiving the devastating news that Boston Joe brought, it was here Vision Seeker came to think things out.

He scanned the horizon. Messages often came to him from a flying bird, a cloud formation or the blue sky itself. Far up the valley a wisp of smoke appeared, thickening, it became a gray spiral. Vision Seeker shaded his eyes for a better look. That could come only from one place, mountain man Red Craig's farm. He was clearing land for spring planting. "Oh-hah!" Vision Seeker exclaimed. The problem of spreading the news Boston Joe brought was solved.

As they rode up the valley, Vision Seeker explained to Joe, "Our people are fragile. They are like head-beaten horses. When one approaches, they shy away, fearing another blow. Only someone they trust will they believe -- too many untruths by hairy faced ones. That is why Red Craig will tell them of the news you bring. His heart is good. They know his tongue is straight. He will help."

They found Craig plowing. When he saw them, he hooked the harness reins around the plow handle and strode across the fresh furrows to greet them. His square face broke into a smile.

"Howdy! Joe Jennings! Ain't seen you in a coon's age. Maybeso, not since your stabbing. I shouldn't have mentioned that. Sometimes my tongue works before my brain. Anyhow, step down and rest yourselves. Since you fellows came all this way, you must have something on your minds. Let's sit over here in the shade, and you can tell me all about it."

Taking great care to make his report thorough but succinct, Joe related the news. When he finished Craig thoughtfully ran his fingers through his short beard. "I knew something like this was in the wind. Those politicians can't keep their noses out of a thing, especially if it draws attention to themselves."

Craig turned to Vision Seeker. "I think it best to call a council. If we discuss this business intelligently, the people will understand and manage it without undue alarm."

**

No one urged Joe to stay when he announced he was under orders to continue west relaying the news of the surveyors' pending arrival. Yet, the parting was exceedingly painful, especially for Joe. His brother, Michael, carrying his baby son on a shoulder, walked with him to the pasture and helped catch and saddle his horse. When they returned to the log cabin lodge, Morning Star had a pouch of food prepared. For the second time during the visit her dark eyes looked straight into his.

"Good-bye," she said. Without waiting for an answer, she seized her baby son and disappeared within the cabin walls.

"My wife is shy," Michael, who also was uneasy, explained. He knew better than anyone of the love Morning Star had for his handsome Boston brother. She had not slept the night before, turning and twisting, finally getting up to see to their son. He had heard her pacing the porch, repeating prayers her ex-preacher father had taught her.

Joe busied himself tying the food pouch to his saddle. He wanted to be friends with both Michael and Morning Star, but he feared always there would be a barrier keeping them apart. He was saved from the difficult situation by his old friend and trapping partner, Deacon, who slapped him on the back.

"Headin' west, are yuh? Who do yuh plan ta visit next?"

"Probably Stickus and Young Chief of the Cayuse. After that Peu-peu-mox-mox of the Walla Wallas and wind up in the land of the Palouse and Yakamas."

"Well, now, I hate ta see yuh goin' off 'mongst those peoples by yer lonesome. Do yuh mind if I tag along?"

Joe studied his longtime friend and former cohort. The fringe of hair that circled the bald head had turned white as snow. Beneath the gray, tobacco stained beard, his mouth had collapsed into a thin line, making it obvious he had lost most, if not all of his teeth. Face lines above his beard were so deep and numerous they resembled harrow marks in a field of grainy sand. His former upright stance had turned into a semi-crouch.

Joe's first inclination was to turn the man down. Isaac Stevens, Joe's boss, was an ambitious person, anxious to make a name for himself. He had trained at West Point and therefore ruled by military spit and polish. He certainly would not like to have official messages delivered by his representative accompanied by a scraggly, aged mountain man riding a floppy-eared mule. Yet, Joe Jennings hesitated. Deacon and he were the last members of Buck Stone's trapping brigade. The camaraderie built up during lengthy trapping seasons was a tough thread to break.

But there was another reason to leave the man behind. His presence would be a constant reminder of Morning Star. Joe had no desire to live with that. He glanced at Deacon. The plead-ing look in his eyes was like a dagger thrust to the heart.

"Of course, partner," Joe said abruptly. "I'd love to have your company. It'll be great to reminisce about the old days."

"Yeah," Deacon said gratefully. "The older I git the more I 'member back when we had the world by the tail." Deacon turned to untether his mule, which Joe noticed was saddled with bedroll and gear securely in place. All the time the old fox had planned to go, regardless of whether or not he was wanted.

Vision Seeker and Running Turtle came to wish them safe journey. Taciturn Young Wolf, standing on the porch, lifted his hand in a farewell salute. Only Raven Wing remained hidden from view. They reined away, threading through the village, only stopping where the trail plunged into the fringe of trees bordering the Kooskooskie to look back. Everyone, including Raven Wing, was waving a last good-bye.

For a long while they rode in silence, each one sobered by the thought they might not pass that way again. Deacon, because he knew his end was near, didn't need a medicine man to tell him the grim reaper, sharpening his scythe, was close on his heels. Any day he could be cut down like a harvest ready stalk of corn.

Joe's thoughts were equally somber. He kept berating himself for the mess he had made of his life. He had quit the west when he should have stayed and helped his Indian friends and relatives. Instead, when things got tough, he went east and lived a life of leisure. Upon returning, he had made an even greater error in joining the gang bent on penetrating Indian country with iron rails and steam-driven monsters.

Near dusk Joe pulled up before a likely camping spot on a bend in the River Snake. "What do you say, partner, don't you think it's time to give the animals and ourselves a bit of rest?"

"Yep, I'll be agreein' ta thet," Deacon replied readily. "Joggin' on this ol' mule critter's like ridin' a knotty fence post. Me backsides're feelin' worse than a tom turkey thet's had its tail feathers jerked out by the roots."

For the first time it struck Joe his old trapping partner was far from well. Deacon slid from the mule's back with an unintentional groan and barely was able to stand straight. When he loosened the cinch to remove the saddle, its weight almost pulled him to the ground. Instead of rustling around helping make camp, the old timer sat leaning against a clump of brush, blankly looking on, something he never would have done in the past, while Joe made a fire and began to cook.

However, the next morning Deacon was cheerful and alert, scurrying around gathering wood for the fire and breaking into his kit for breakfast makings.

"I say, it's good ta be on the trail again," he said. "Sorry 'bout last night. I was thet tuckered I couldn't barely lift a finger. Guess it's the climate. Livin' in the mountains like I've done, I ain't used ta these flat, treeless plains."

Even so, Joe could see through all of his companion's bright talk and sprightly actions. The poor fellow was making a tremendous effort to cover up for aches and pains. To assist his old trapping partner he brought in their mounts and saddled both of them before Deacon could object. Silently, they ate, mounted up and continued west. There was little said. Partly because a stiff breeze began to blow into their faces, bouncing dry weeds across the trail like live creatures fleeing before a storm, it took all of Deacon's strength to keep his fur cap from flying away. Joe kept his eyes averted. How long could his old friend keep up?

They crossed the Tucannon, Touchet and were on the banks of the Walla Walla when Deacon suddenly seemed to gain new life. He pulled his gray mule up and pointed to the south.

"I say, ain't thet hill yonder the one thet guards the ol' Whitman Mission? We're in Cayuse country fer certain. Look at the band of horses grazin' on Tiloukaikt's ol' pasture grounds. Many a time I've wondered if'n ol' Joe Meek did right by hangin' the rascal. The ol' chief only was tryin' ta save his people from extermination by diseases homesteaders was bringin' in.

"Yer brother, Michael, keeps sayin' all five Cayuses Joe

Meek hanged should've been allowed to live. I'm thinkin' he's right. What did it gain? Ever since then the Indian people hev been as nervous as a swarm of wet wasps. Michael, who' been talkin' ta some of his Lapwai friends, says young braves're chompin' at the bit ta take ta the warpath. He's fearin' no matter how easy Craig breaks the news yuh brought, it's gonna stick in ther throats like cockleburs."

Deacon's utterances increased Joe's gloomy state of mind. Even his own brother believed he had landed on the wrong side. Agh! While gaining an education at Harvard College, he had lost touch with reality. He should have known his Indian friends still would be suffering from the aftermath of the Whitman Mission tragedy. The execution of the five Cayuse men who were charged with the crime, some of whom were considered innocent, was not easily forgotten or forgiven.

He certainly didn't blame them. The white man's system of justice was merciless. Indian people felt defenseless against it. Now, to add to the people's fear of the white man's ways, he was bringing a new threat to their existence -- a new wave of ruthless invaders into their homelands. What resistance could they give? None whatsoever. If they did they would be trampled underfoot like ants.

Immersed in thought, Joe was unaware that three mounted and armed Indians blocked the trail ahead, stolidly watching them approach. Deacon alertly pulled his gray mule to a halt. "Tarnation!," he uttered. "We got company, an' they ain't lookin' perzactly friendly."

Chagrined at his carelessness, Joe also reined his mount to a stop. Deacon was right. The horsemen did not appear pleased to see them. Except for the absence of war paint, they looked downright warlike. Nevertheless, Joe made no move toward the booted rifle. Instead, he held his hand up, palm forward with index and middle finger upright, the traditional sign for friend.

The horsemen made no response. Although the shaggy

ponies they rode pawed and pranced impatiently, the riders sat stiffly upon their native made saddles as though waiting for the white men to make the first move.

"We ain't gittin' nowhere starin' at each other. Let's mosey up an' see if'n we cain't do a leetle powwowin'," Deacon suggested. "Unless we find out what these folks're up ta, we ain't likely ta go very far."

The two white men rode within six horse lengths of the three Indians and stopped again. The horsemen who blocked the way continued watchfully to sit their mounts. Suddenly, the middle rider thrust up a hand. "White man, what brings you here?" he asked in surprisingly good English.

"We have a message for your people," Joe replied promptly. "Let us sit and smoke, then talk."

The three horsemen glanced at each other, mumbling a few words.

"They're tryin' ta decide whether to take our horses or our scalps, maybeso both," Deacon observed glumly. "Perhaps we kin buy our way outta this mess with a few twists of tobaccy."

"No smoke, no talk," the spokesman of the group said abruptly. "You come." He made a curt motion with his hand, pointing to the north.

"He wants ta take us ta his chief," Deacon said. "If we wanta keep our hair we'd better do as he asks."

The spokesman reined his shaggy mount about and again motioned for them to follow. Joe and Deacon rode by the remaining two horsemen who then reined onto the trail behind them. For a long while they traveled in silence. Joe shook his head in disgust. He had been so sunk in memories of the past that he had failed to keep alert. He had been over this track a dozen or more times and knew it well. This was Cayuse country, the homeland of the people who had perpetrated the Whitman massacre. But who were these horsemen? They didn't have the look of the Cayuse, and where were they taking them? Were they renegades determined to avenge those who had been hanged for the murders of Marcus and Narcissa Whitman and others at the mission?

They rode over a ridge and looked down onto a pleasant meadow. Along the bank of the river a dozen or more graceful tipi lodges loomed above a fringe of willow trees. On the opposite bank grazed a sizeable herd of horses. A covey of barking dogs and shouting children ran to greet them. Both dogs and children fell silent as they saw the two strangers. The dogs crept forward to sniff and growl. The children sidled away, their dark round eyes watching suspiciously.

The lead horseman dismounted and motioned for Joe and Deacon to do likewise. A sharp order was given. A boy dashed up to take the reins of Joe's horse and those of Deacon's mule, and led the animals away. From the lodges came a stream of staring people. The apparent leader of the group, an upright elderly man, strode forward.

"Welcome, white men," he said through an interpreter. "What brings you to the land of the Walla Walla?"

Joe was dumfounded. He knew this man. He was Peupeu-mox-mox, prominent leader of the Walla Walla tribe, often called Yellow Serpent by the whites. His son had been murdered by an American who never had been made to answer for the crime. The loss of his son had embittered the Walla Walla leader. For a long while he had vowed to avenge his son's death by taking the life of a member of Whitman's mission. Was he, at this late date, still planning to take his revenge?

Whether or not revenge was on the Walla Walla leader's mind, he certainly was not going to be happy to learn that soon chugging, hooting iron horses, as the Indians called them, would penetrate his homeland to race up and down the bank of the great river called Columbia.

THE GREAT POWWOW

III

We will not have the wagons which make a noise in the hunting grounds of the buffalo. If the palefaces come farther into our land, there will be scalps of your brethren in the wigwams of the Cheyenne. . . .
Roman Nose, Southern Cheyenne

The departure of his brother and father-in-law did not provide Michael Two Feathers with relief. He felt it necessary to keep close watch on his bride and son. He well remembered how unpredictable his mother, Raven Wing, could be. His fear was she would revert to periods of stormy meanness like he had suffered through during his youth. If that should happen he had to be on hand to protect his family. Day by day he hung around the log cabin lodge. Nothing untoward occurred except that he felt increasingly useless and frustrated. Idleness was an implacable enemy.

Vision Seeker, always attuned to the inner being of his fellow man, watched Michael with anxious eyes. He encouraged him to work among the horses. Many of the animals, still shaggy from the long hard winter, were as wild as mountain goats and needed gentling. Mares were ready to foal and needed watching. All animals should be examined for sores and injuries.

There also was the danger of losing colts to night prowlers. Wolves could be heard howling in the hills. They, too, had spent a hard winter, probably had not recovered from the great hunger that had reduced them to devouring the carcasses of their own sick and weak. Newborn colts would be tasty morsels.

Unlike in the days when meat came from hunting grounds, the tribe had turned to raising the white man's cattle. Grazing among the horses were scores of these cloven-hoofed animals. During the Season of New Grass, cows, like mares, began to deliver their offspring. They, too, needed watching and protecting from carnivorous predators.

Both Running Turtle and Vision Seeker spent long hours with the herds, often one or the other remained in the pastures all night. Although Michael was well aware of his uncles' long hours and diligent attendance to the livestock, he did not offer to help. This was so unlike him, that Vision Seeker wondered what could be wrong. Did the youth think he was too important to work, or was it something else?

Michael barely let Morning Star and One Who Kicks out of his sight? Did he fear someone or that something might happen to them? Surely, he had overcome his fears of Raven Wing. She had been as warm and friendly to Michael's little family as any mother and grandmother possibly could be. Vision Seeker knew from long experience his sister was one who could not hide her emotions, at least not for long. Was Michael waiting for his mother to revert to her former self?

Vision Seeker grimaced. What was the matter with him? Just because he was head of the family, he did not need to run everyone's life. For a short while he concentrated on the work at hand, then Running Turtle called to him for help. One of the mares was having difficulty dropping a colt. After a painful struggle, the newborn, gasping for breath, caught its first sight of Mother Earth. When the newborn's nostrils were cleared and coat wiped clean, it looked up at the two brothers as if to ask, what kind of creatures are you?

Running Turtle laughed. "Look at the little thing. It can't believe what it sees. What do you suppose it thinks?"

"I'm here on Mother Earth. What am I to do now?" Vision Seeker promptly answered.

When Vision Seeker left the pasture grounds at the end of the day he walked by Michael's black and white pony frolicking with one of the local mares. Michael loved this colorful Appaloosa nearly as much as he did his wife and child. He stopped to scratch between the pony's ears. It responded by nudging Vision Seeker with its muzzle. Suddenly, Vision Seeker knew how to lure Michael to the pasture grounds. He swung up on the pony's bare back and rode toward the log cabin lodge. As he approached Michael bounded down the porch steps.

"Why do you ride Magpie?" he asked, a little put out. He seldom allowed anyone to ride Magpie, not even Morning Star. "Is something wrong? There are many other animals in the pasture you could have ridden."

"Yes, but I thought Magpie would like to be with you," Vision Seeker responded. He patted the silken neck of the pony. "You never come to visit him. He must miss you. Since Lone Wolf gave him to you, the two of you have been like brothers."

Michael gave his uncle a strange look. "That is true. Perhaps Magpie should be kept close to the lodge."

This was not at all the answer Vision Seeker had hoped to hear. "Would that be good for Magpie? Like people, horses love their freedom. Besides, a mare in the pasture has taken a liking to Magpie. Horses get fond of one another just as do people. You wouldn't want to breakup a friendship?"

Michael stared at his uncle. "Magpie is gelded. He can't be interested in mares."

"I am telling you what I see. Why should gelding an animal take away the desire to have friends? Perhaps they need them more than ever. See how he nudges you. He is showing his love for you much as he did the mare in the pasture."

Michael kept Magpie tethered close to the lodge overnight and in the morning rode him down to the pasture. Vision Seeker, who already had arrived, saw him coming and signaled him over. Now that he had lured Michael from the cabin and his family, he had to keep him away.

"Come and take a look at this animal," he shouted. "It just limped in from the hills, perhaps a snake bite victim."

Reluctantly, Michael came over. He had no intention of remaining in the pasture. Magpie could have a love affair with a mare if he wished. He was not going to stand in the way. For some reason Vision Seeker was having fun with him, but why?

His uncle was not one to engage in frivolous behavior. Michael lifted the horse's lame foreleg and studied the hoof. It was plain as day what was wrong. The horse had a damaged frog, probably caused by stepping on a sharp rock. He pointed to the wound that appeared painfully infected and glanced up at Vision Seeker.

"Looks bad," Vision Seeker said. "I have many things to do. Would you take care of it?"

Michael was appalled. In the old days his uncle would not let a minute pass without tending to a wound like this. Yet, here he was acting as though it was of little consequence. Glumly, Michael studied the injured hoof, deciding what to do. Much of the morning was spent cleaning the wound, gathering mullein leaves, pounding them into paste for a poultice, which he applied to the injury with strips of rawhide. From time to time Vision Seeker came to cluck his approval.

When Michael completed the task Vision Seeker asked his advice on how best to heal some grievous saddle sores; then a calf had the staggers and a cow grazing on clover fell on her side, bloated with gas. Michael became so engrossed in the task of curing and helping the animals in distress, hour after hour slipped away unnoticed.

During the past few years the thought had come to him that he had greater ability to get along with animals than he did humans. At the end of the day it suddenly dawned on him, this was true. Even the mate he loved so dearly, often left him uneasy. Morning Star was everything a good mate should be, but never was he sure of what she was thinking. He had the gnawing belief she continually compared him to her first love, brother Joe, with himself coming out second best. Now that he had seen Joe and Morning Star together, he had the distinct feeling his fears were justified, another reason that kept him close to his mate and child. Without them he was nothing. They were as important to him as the air he breathed.

Vision Seeker, who had been keeping a constant watch on his nephew, almost could read his troubled thoughts. At the end of the day he walked alongside Michael. "You lessened the pain of many four-footed friends," he said as encouragingly as his passive nature permitted. "That is good. A learned man once told me that those who heal others are above all the great of the earth. You are blessed by a natural talent for helping the sick and troubled. Have you ever thought of studying doctoring?"

Vision Seeker's words of praise pleased Michael, but with wife and family the idea of studying medicine was absurd. He had no intention of becoming a medicine man, and to be a proper doctor meant years of study in eastern colleges. However, Vision Seeker's compliment set him to thinking -- made him want to accomplish great things. He was further gratified when Morning Star and One Who Kicks ran down the trail to greet him. His son grasped his hand and his mate clung to his arm. Talking at once, they began to tell him about the many things they did while he was gone. Why had he been worried? he wondered. This was his family. Never would they let him down.

As was his custom, Vision Seeker was up before dawn to greet Father Sun. He said morning prayers and left to tend to the livestock, chewing on a piece of dried meat, the only breakfast he allowed himself, except for a drink of water. He looked forward to the day's work. Surely, Michael would join in helping with the herd.   However, Michael made no move to return to the pasture grounds. He sat on the porch, bouncing One Who Kicks on his knee, waiting for the womenfolk to serve him the morning meal. Morning Star brought him a bowl of mush and sat down beside him.

"Vision Seeker told me of your wonderful healing powers," she said. "Your uncle says you merely can place your hand on an animal, and it feels better. What a wonderful gift to possess. Vision Seeker says this wondrous ability came straight from the Great Mysterious."

Michael made no comment but continued to eat his mush, from time to time offering spoonfuls to baby son. He was not quite certain how to take this sudden praise.

"Your mother agrees with Vision Seeker," Morning Star

continued. "She says when you were a youth she knew you were
destined to be an important medicine man."

Michael frowned. Why was everyone suddenly so interested in his healing ability? First it was Vision Seeker, then Morning Star and now his mother.

"Raven Wing told you of these things?" he mused.

"Yes, she said you studied with Thunder Eyes, the Lapwai
medicine man."

Moodily, Michael shoved the bowl of mush away. His
thoughts went back to that long ago morning when he awakened
on the last morning of his vision quest. Laying beside his blanket
were two feathers. At that moment he knew *Wyakin,* the spirit
that would guide him through life, had come to him. When he
came home and told Raven Wing the exciting news, she scoffed.

"Two Feathers! That is not a *Wyakin.* People will laugh.
You must return to the mountains and try again."

He took the sacred feathers from the protective pouch and
showed them to her. His mother seized them and raced to the
long lodge shouting at the top of her voice. When he arrived
Grandfather Lone Wolf held the feathers in his hand with a look
of awe. "Never has a young man returned from a vision quest
with more powerful medicine than this!" he exclaimed.

Yes. That day had been a turning point in his life. Everyone, including Thunder Eyes, believed the feathers he brought
back were sent by the Great Mysterious -- through them he had
received a power reserved for only the mightiest of people. For a
while he attempted to live up to these great expectations. He did
away with childish things. He studied with the *tewat,* Thunder
Eyes. He kept his pony near the lodge as important members of
the tribe were expected to do. He became so wrapped up in his
newly gained importance his friends, afraid of the great powers
he was supposed to possess, deserted him.

It took Vision Seeker to bring him back to reality. The
feathers had not come from the Great Mysterious. They came
from the scalp of his dead uncle, Many Horses. Through the

years Vision Seeker had guarded them, finally bringing them out to lay them beside Michael's blanket as he slept.

Michael uttered a deep sigh. He had played the fool. All along he had known the feathers did not come from the spirit land -- he was not blessed by the Great Mysterious, and he was no great healer. But when his mother, grandfather, Thunder Eyes and others made such a fuss he had not wanted to disappoint them.

Yet, perhaps the Great Mysterious did deliver a message. He did seem to have a way with animals. He loved to care for them. And, there were the many times he had gone with Dr. Whitman to call on the sick. He would interpret for him, hand him instruments during operations, and when necessary, hold the patient's hand. When the treatments were successful often the patients would thank him rather than the doctor. Their gratitude gave him great pleasure. It made him feel he had played an important part in easing their pain and lengthening their lives.

There also were moments not so enjoyable, as during the days when one plague of disease after another swept through Indian villages -- children desperately trying to catch their breath or burning with fever; tragic groups gathered around sickbeds or by gravesides . . . the agonizing mourning cries of loved ones who had lost family members. . . . There was no satisfaction in those days. Death cries were accusations. "You treated me, but you took my life away." Days after days those agonizing cries had drifted across the fields from the Indian villages to the mission compound.

Michael forced the grim thoughts from his mind. Why did all this come back to him now? It was Vision Seeker's fault. Why was his uncle suddenly so determined to keep him in the pastures working with animals? There was no one in the tribe who took better care of a herd than did Vision Seeker. Many believed he knew the language of his four-footed charges. He sat in council with them, listening to what each had to say. It also was said he liked them better than humans. He once had heard a woman whose daughter fancied Vision Seeker say, "Don't waste your time on him. He's wed to his four-leggeds."

In spite of his efforts to wash these thoughts from his mind,
the idea persisted. Perhaps he should follow in Doctor Whitman's
footsteps, try and make up for those disastrous times when death
hung over Indian camps and villages. The best place to decide
his future was in the pasture surrounded by horses and cattle.
When he appeared, Vision Seeker waved a greeting. "There's a
mare that needs the help of your healing hands and a newborn
calf that does not look well."

Vision Seeker, who merely had wanted to draw Michael
out of his malaise, would have been amazed at the tumultuous
thoughts he brought to his nephew's mind. As it turned out
Michael's presence in the pasture fields came at a very good time.
Arrangements for the council meeting Red Craig had suggested
were underway.

Already Lawyer from Kamiah had arrived to acquaint himself with what would be discussed. Always anxious to let it be
known he was a man of consequence, and had hairy faced friends
of authority, the man from Kamiah wore a stovepipe hat with
three fluffy feathers bound to it by strips of buckskin. If it weren't
for his strong nose, long flowing hair and piercing eyes, he would
have had the look of a clown. His voice also set him apart. Behind his back some of his detractors called him Caw-Caw, or
Talk-Talk. Regardless, he was treated with respect. When it came
to negotiations with hairy faces, he always was in the forefront.

To prepare for the meeting Vision Seeker and Red Craig
met with each leader separately. During a break in one of these
meetings Vision Seeker was called away. Running Turtle came
in from the pasture to report a group had ridden in from White
Bird country.

"Why are you bothering me with news like that?" Vision
Seeker said, somewhat sharply.

"White Bird man insists he must speak with you, alone --
a family matter. As patriarch, you are the one he must see. There
he is waiting." Running Turtle motioned with his lips and chin.

Vision Seeker turned to look. His mouth dropped open in surprise. Before him stood the largest man he ever had seen. His mount beside him was also large, but alongside the rider looked a mere pony. In three strides the stranger stood towering over him. Vision Seeker stood his ground but felt overwhelmed. A hand as wide as a frying pan was thrust out. Vision Seeker involuntarily winced, but the thick fingers that folded over his own were surprisingly gentle, as if the giant knew his strength and did not want to do him harm.

"I am called Tall Horse," the man said, his voice as large as his body. The sound echoed as though coming from a deep well. "My woman is in the Great Beyond. My lodge is empty."

Vision Seeker glanced up at the face that was as broad and long as that of his horse. What an unusual introduction, he thought. How did one respond?

"You have sister," Tall Horse paused as if searching for words. He pondered so long Vision Seeker felt sorry for him.

"Yes, I have a sister," he said. Suddenly it dawned on him. This man was looking for a replacement for his dead wife. Raven Wing was the one he had selected.

The big man seemed to recognize the gleam of recognition in Vision Seeker's eyes. "Yes, you see, I seek your sister. She needs a mate. I need a mate. We make bargain?"

Vision Seeker was so stunned he could not think. This was the last thing he ever expected to happen -- have someone ask him for Raven Wing's hand in marriage. If Raven Wing fancied this man she would go with him whether he approved or not. The White Bird was following tradition, speaking to the patriarch to arrive at an amicable marriage settlement. He glanced at Raven Wing's suitor and inwardly grimaced. He could not imagine them together. It would be like mating a dwarf with a giant.

"Yes, you see, five horses and your sister and we have bargain?" the big man said as though everything was settled.

Vision Seeker stared at the big face. Not only did the man want Raven Wing but horses, too. "No horses," he blurted.

"Ah, you are like your father, make hard trade."

"You knew Lone Wolf?" Vision Seeker asked in surprise.

"Ah, yes, we trade, steal horses many times."

"Hmm!" Vision Seeker grunted. Not only was this man huge, if he had gone on raids with his father he must be ancient. "Before we make any bargain, I must speak to my sister," he said.

The big man accepted the decision with good grace. "Yes, everything must be done in good manner."

Raven Wing did not look on the proposal with good grace. "Don't talk nonsense," she stormed. "Tall Horse! He's old enough to be my father. He doesn't want me. He wants to add to his horses. Besides, I've had two mates and look at what happened to me! Then there was Toohool . . ."

"Toohool? He was not your mate."

"He would have been if I hadn't been so cruel. You could have saved him, but you didn't. You are to blame as much as I."

Feeling tarnished by the exchange, Vision Seeker glumly returned to the meeting. No wonder Raven Wing nearly had driven Lone Wolf mad. She never forgot a slight or a misadventure with a knack of always bringing up something distasteful. Yes, perhaps during the skirmish with the Blackfeet he could have saved Toohool, the son of Weasel Face. But the youth had been warned the pony staked in the field was a trap. Yet, he went straight into it and was killed.

Tall Horse took the news amiably. "Yes, perhaps now is not the time to seek a mate," the big man said and turned away.

Still feeling unsettled, Vision Seeker entered the lodge where Red Craig waited. The former mountain man gave him a questioning look but said nothing. They resumed their discussion as if nothing untoward had happened. That was what Vision Seeker liked about Red Craig. The man understood the customs of Indian people. Actually, he had adopted many of their traits. A sudden bright thought occurred to Vision Seeker. If all hairy faces would be like Red Craig, Indian people and white people surely could live side by side, peacefully and harmoniously.

IV

We did not ask you white men to come here. The
Great Spirit gave us this country as a home. You
had yours. We did not interfere with you.
Crazy Horse, Oglala Sioux

Peu-peu-mox-mox studied the two hairy faced horsemen. They did not appear to be up to mischief as his scouts suggested. The heavily bearded one was obviously an old timer who knew the ways of Indian people. There was something familiar about the tall young man. He searched back in his memory. Ah, yes, there was that youth and his half brother of the mountain tribe, Nimpau. When the tribes came together 10 summers ago to meet with Indian Agent Elijah White the two brothers had turned the council gathering upside down.

The memory of the incident almost made the impassive face break into a smile. Somehow the brothers had cut loose Buffalo Horn's dappled gray stallion. The animal had stomped the Cayuse leader's tipi lodge into bits and then galloped off as though in the clutches of evil spirits. Since that day Buffalo Horn never had been the same. For that matter, neither had he. At the time his people were all for peace. They had no wish to offend the hairy faced ones. Realizing this, he had agreed to accept Agent Elijah White's cruel code of laws.

What a mistake that had been. He should have known the laws were trouble, not worth the talking paper they were put upon. Shortly afterward he had made that terrible cattle buying trip to California where a hairy face murdered his precious son. When he turned to Indian Agent Elijah White and demanded justice be done, the pompous agent would have nothing to do with him or the blatant crime. Enforcing the code of laws was the responsibility of the tribes that had accepted them, the agent had said.

How could he, Peu-peu-mox-mox, go into the lands of the hairy faces and bring the murderer to justice?

"Aagh! He had to put aside thoughts of that terrible time and deal with present problems. Why were these intruders here? What business did they have riding into the lands of the Walla Walla, Cayuse and Umatilla as if they belonged? For certain they did not know the dangers they faced. The old days were gone when wise leaders like Tiloukaikt, Stickus, Young Chief, and Teukakas ruled the land. No longer did tribal elders have control of their people. They could establish rules and give orders, but getting people, especially the youth, to observe them was something else. Youthful tribesmen had to show their coming of age by going on hunts, raiding the enemy, stealing horses -- making coups any way they could. With the world going mad, how was anyone to keep this wellhead of energy from running wild?

The Walla Walla leader motioned for his visitors to dismount. He ushered them into his tipi lodge and raised a hand for his mate to bring the pipe. Joe Jennings watched the preparations with a feeling of relief. Before discussing the reason for Deacon's and his presence, they would take part in the time-honored ceremonial smoke. Perhaps these few moments of respite would give him time to collect his thoughts.

From what he had been led to believe, the support of Peu-peu-mox-mox and Kamiakin, the leader of the Yakama, was necessary to successfully carry out Stevens' plans for the continental railway. Land for the roadbed and for railway workers' living quarters had to be acquired. Also there was the matter of cook houses and commissaries to take care of the workers' needs, and acreage was needed for storage facilities for the vast amount of materials that would be required. Arrangements had to be made to supply timbers for building lumber and to support steel tracks. This meant logging and sawmill operations. . . .

The needs were endless and complicated -- far too great to comprehend for these people who feared for their beloved homelands. Joe still was grappling with these thoughts as the In-

dian leader put away the pipe and turned from prayer to face his
guests. He raised a closed hand to his lips and flipped out two
fingers, the sign it now was time to speak.

Joe glanced at Deacon. Perhaps he should speak first.
These people paid great deference to their elders. Deacon understood, but shook his head. "This is yer funeral," he growled. "I
ain't a party ta this dirty business."

"We are honored to be invited to your lodge," Joe said
finally. "I have traveled many days from the land of the Bostons.
I come as a friend and a messenger from the new father in Washington. He sends his greetings to you and all of your people. He
is proud of this land called the Northwest. He has given the territory above the great river, Columbia, a new name, Washington,
the same name as that of the beautiful capitol city in the east."

Joe paused. From the impassive look on the Indian's face
the words that he had so carefully chosen and spoken would have
had more impact on a blank wall. Deacon shattered his confi-
dence further by hoarsely whispering,

"What's the matter with yuh? Yer blowin' more wind
than a Rocky Mountain williwaw. Quit thet fancy gabble an' talk
plain sense."

Before Joe could compose himself, the Walla Walla leader
spoke. Joe was surprised that he could understand every word.

"What name the white father in Washington gives this
land makes little difference. It still is the homeland of our people.
All our people wish for is to live in peace. Does the white father
send words that he will keep our homelands safe?"

Joe attempted to ignore the sinking feeling that suddenly
gripped him. He should have remembered from that long ago
day when Peu-peu-mox-mox addressed the crowd in Waiilatpu,
he did not beat around the bush. This was particularly true when
it came to protecting his herds and his fellow tribesmen. It was
said he was called Yellow Serpent because of his protective nature. Some said he should be named Rattlesnake as he usually
gave warning before striking.

"This new territory will have a governor chief named Stevens. He is now on his way to council with you and other tribal leaders. He wishes to have your help in planning the future of your homelands. Among his plans are ways of protecting and improving your homelands."

Joe paused, appalled at himself. He was getting as glib as a politician running for office. Had he said enough or too much? His orders were to pave the way for the survey parties that would soon arrive: one from the east and one from the west. He would be shirking his duties if he didn't break that news.

Peu-peu-mox-mox broke the silence. "Will the new governor chief speak of the steel trail that brings iron lodges on wheels?"

Joe gasped. "How did you come by that information?"

"In the land of the Yakamas there is a black robe that knows many things. He says soon white men will make an iron trail over the plains and through the high mountains. This passageway will carry wagons that live on steam and have a voice greater than that of a bull moose. Black robe says these things called "trains" move faster than a galloping horse, yet hug the ground like a snake and are strong enough to carry great loads of people and things. Black robe tells Yakamas, Palouses, Walla Wallas . . . all Indian peoples to make ready for its coming. He says our people's lives will be changed forever." The Walla Walla leader folded his arms and fell silent. His face took on such an expression of sadness it made Joe avert his eyes.

The same three horsemen who escorted Joe and Deacon into the Walla Walla camp, escorted them out. For a long while after the escort turned back, the two white men rode in silence, each of them mulling over what had taken place. The visit with Peu-peu-mox-mox had been civil and polite. At the same time the air was thick with tension. The camp was silent, hardly a child, dog or female was heard or seen.

"Thet camp has the smell of trouble," Deacon said finally. "An' what's happened ta all the Cayuses? The last time we was in these parts Injuns was poppin' up over every ridge like prairie dogs comin' out ta feed."

"Seems to me a lot has happened in these past three years that I've been away," Joe mused. "What about this black robe? Where did he come from? Perhaps we should ride over and visit with him. From the way Peu-peu-mox-mox speaks he must know everything that's going on."

"Yeah, I reckon thet might be a good move," Deacon said, "'cept I don't know a thing 'bout these Yakamas. I've been told they's peaceful folk but in these times they could be as jumpy as turpentined cats an' not take kindly ta visitors."

In a grassy meadow near the north bank of Mill Creek the two riders stopped to make camp. Little did they know in two years time on this very location what would become known as the Great Powwow would occur, and later a college named Whitman would make this place its home.

**

The following morning the former trapping partners began the search for the knowledgeable black robe. The only information they had to go on was that he lived among the Yakamas. Even that wasn't much help. During their sojourns in the former Oregon Territory neither Joe nor Deacon had traveled among the Yakamas. They did know their homeland was centered on the Yakama River, which entered the Columbia nearly a day's ride north and west of Fort Walla Walla.

"Me thinks we'd be wise ta drop in on ol' Factor McBean. If I 'member kerectly, he was a follower of the Roman pope?"

"That's right. The Whitmans disliked him -- accused him of helping priests establish missions among the Cayuse."

Joe fell silent. His thoughts were of Narcissa and Marcus Whitman. If they had one failing it was their narrow religious belief that Protestants, especially Presbyterians, had the true faith. They spoke ill of the Catholics, as did Reverend Henry Spalding who chose to spread the Gospel among the Nimpau. Ironically, it was a Catholic, Bishop Brouillet, who saved Spalding's life and was one of the first white people to come to the aid of the Whitman disaster survivors. He persuaded the captors of the survivors to give the victims a proper burial, and took it upon himself to conduct the funeral services.

Ever since the terrible Whitman Mission tragedy, thoughts of the missionary couple and their adopted children had weighed heavily on Joe's mind. How well he remembered the last time he had seen them, especially Narcissa and the children. It was a crisp fall day in '44. Early that long ago morning he had packed up to make the journey to Lapwai. Before leaving he stopped by the mission house to say his good-byes. Narcissa invited him to take breakfast. Her doctor husband was absent, tending to a sick child at the nearby Cayuse village. Narcissa had insisted he wait to bid farewell to Marcus.

Joe had waited, but the doctor did not return. When he felt he could wait no longer, he said good-bye to the couple's adopted children and Narcissa. It was obvious the missionary lady hated to see him go. She had walked outside with him, wrapping her arms around herself to keep out the morning chill.

"I have a fear of this season," she said, looking toward the hazy clouds that hid the Blue Mountains. "Autumn brings the chill of winter. It kills plants and makes leaves fall. It's a time of death and decay. . . ." Three years later, in the fall of '47, Narcissa, her husband and two of the couple's adopted children were slain by members of their Cayuse flock. Two others had taken sick while held captive, and died.

Forcibly, Joe swept thoughts of the past from his mind. It was the present he had to worry about. From all indications, the decade of the fifties appeared even more threatening to Indian people than any of the previous decades.

When the riders arrived at Fort Walla Walla, instead of encountering McBean, they found that a new man named Pierre Pambrun was the trading post factor. They quickly discovered Pambrun was a Catholic and knew a great deal about Catholic missionary work among the Indian people.

"Yep," he said when Joe asked about Peu-peu-mox-mox's black robe informer. "He probably meant one of the Oblate missionaries at St. Joseph Mission, quite likely Reverend Father Pandosy. He's taken to our red brethren like no one else, maybeso 'cause he's French. These people get all misty-eyed when they think of the plight of the red man."

"Seems like yuh don't 'specially hanker fer his attitude," Deacon observed.

"Trouble is you have to draw the line somewhere. From what I'm told this Pandosy fellow has become more Indian than the Indian. When he first arrived he traveled with them wherever they went. Recently he seems to have settled down."

"And where would that be?" Joe asked. "We'd like to meet with the fellow, talk to him."

"They have established a mission called St. Joseph's on the Ahtanum, a good day's ride from here." The fort factor dug around for a scrap of paper and drew a rough map. "Your best bet is to cross the Snake, follow the Columbia to where it meets the Yakama. Follow the Yakama. Soon you hit Ahtanum Creek. A trail along the bank'll take you to the mission. You'll know when you get there. Its the only sign of civilization in those parts."

Joe studied the map. This part of the territory he didn't know well. Were the Indians friendly or hostile? He wanted to ask but thought better of it. For some reason he did not trust this fellow, Pambrun. He worked for Hudson's Bay. They were British and probably resented the influx of Americans. Certainly they would not approve of the coming of railroads. It would mean competition. The reason Hudson's Bay continued to operate in the region was that their trading posts were needed. Soon Americans would erect mercantile establishments in the territory. When that happened Hudson's Bay would be forced out of business.

"Ah!" Joe thought, the departure of Hudson's Bay would be another blow to the Indian people. For two or more generations they had looked to these trading posts as buyers of their goods and furnishers of needed supplies. They became dependent on Hudson's Bay not only for their physical needs, but for advice and assistance in maintaining peace in the region. No one had been a better friend to Indian people than White Eagle John McLoughlin, who for years had been the head man of Hudson's Bay's Northwest trading post empire.

Late in the second day after departing from Fort Walla Walla, Joe and Deacon came upon a small group of log buildings, the mission of St. Joseph. Upon close inspection they found the small compound consisted of a chapel, living quarters, a corral for livestock and some distance away an enclosed garden. Hardly did they dismount before a native worker came to take their horses, and from the mission house two black clad figures emerged. They raised their hands in greeting. "Welcome to our humble home," they said almost in unison.

The priests introduced themselves as the Reverend Fathers Pandosy and D'Herbomez. They invited the newcomers to partake of a simple meal that consisted largely of bread and cheese served by a lay brother who moved around on moccasined shod feet as silently as a ghost .

Deacon, who, without teeth, had difficulty eating the hard cheese and bread crusts, combed the crumbs from his beard and thanked their hosts. "Mighty decent of yuh ta take in us sinners an' feed us as though we was part of yer flock."

"It is our pleasure," Father Pandosy replied. "I assume you have made the journey to St. Joseph Mission for a purpose. Pray tell what it may be?"

"Well, it's this way," Joe began, not at all sure how to approach the subject. "From the reports we get you may know as much about our business as we do. I have been sent ahead by the governor of Washington Territory to apprise Indian tribes of his pending arrival. A group of surveyors accompanies the governor, exploring possible routes for continental railways."

Joe paused. Both priests remained as stony faced as any Indian. "The governor's hope is to conduct the surveys without causing affront to the Indian people . . ."

"Hah!" Father Pandosy interrupted. "Pray tell me, how that will be accomplished? These surveyors will comb through tribal lands like a pack of hounds on the heels of a fox. After the survey the governor will want to acquire land upon which to lay the track. The trouble with you Americans is, you decide to do something and plow ahead regardless of the consequences. Have they given any thought to what this will do to the natives?"

The priest stopped to mop his face, so agitated his hand trembled as he reached for a handkerchief. Joe motioned to Deacon that it was time to depart.

A short distance from St. Joseph Mission, Joe and Deacon stopped to make camp on the north bank of Ahtanum Creek. On both sides of the gurgling stream brown hills rose up to block out the horizon. Although early evening, already dusk was beginning to fall. Suddenly the sound of hoofbeats came drifting up the valley. Nearer and nearer the pounding sounds approached.

Deacon, who had been tethering his mule, reached for his rifle. "Peers ta be someun ridin' hard." Soon, out of the fading light three horsemen emerged.

Deacon slid back into the shadows, laid out his hand gun, and cocked the long-barreled Hawken. "I say," he muttered. "Those fellas look perzactly like the three Walla Wallas thet stopped us on the trail."

Although the horsemen glanced their way, they made no attempt to stop. Instead, they galloped by so near the horses' hard breathing could be heard. In front of the mission buildings the riders pulled up, slid off their mounts and disappeared inside the priests' living quarters.

"Uh, oh! Look't thet, would yuh?" Deacon uttered. Out of the hazy dusk from the northeast came another group of horsemen. They, too, were riding at a gallop as though in a hurry to reach their destination. "What yuh 'spose's goin' on? These folks're stirrin' 'round worse'n a swarm of bees. Maybeso thet flunky fella kin tell us what's goin' on."

Joe and Deacon strolled across the grassy meadow to

where the mission worker was tilling the garden. He stopped work to watch them approach. Deacon held out his hand in the traditional greeting of the Cheyenne. "Yuh speak the English?" he asked.

The dusky face broke into a smile. "Yes, the fathers teach. I read Bible book."

"Good man," Deacon said. "I'm Christian, too. Did not the Good Book say, 'Have we not all one father? Hath not one God created us'?"

The smile on the dusky face grew broader. "'He loveth God, loveth brother'," he quoted.

Deacon shook his head. "Brother, yuh sure know yer Scriptures. Tell me, are the fathers holdin' prayer meetin' tanight? I see these people ridin' in like they was fixin' ta do somethin' important."

"No prayer meeting. People come for talk." By this time the horsemen from the northeast had circled the mission compound and slowed to a trot. "Important Yakama men come -- Skloom, Owhi, Kamiakin. . . ."

The former trapping partners walked thoughtfully back to camp. "If I 'member kerectly, the names thet fella mentioned 're Injuns of considerable consequence. If I was tryin' ta push this railroad thing, it'd make me plumb nervous ta see these Injun chiefs an' those French black robes actin' thick as thieves. 'Twouldn't surprise me none if the bigwigs of this new territory were ta give 'em the heave-ho. Catholics ain't especially welcome, an' these birds ain't helpin' their cause."

Deacon's prognostication was on the mark. Two years later, in 1855, a column of 700 regular soldiers and volunteers, pillaged St. Joseph Mission and burned the buildings. The temper of the despoilers was such that if priests had not fled, they, too, could have suffered greatly.

THE GREAT POWWOW

V

*... Can you stop the waters of the Columbia River from flow-
ing on its course? Can you prevent the wind from blowing?
Can you prevent the rain from falling? Can you prevent the
whites from coming? You are answered No!*

Joel Palmer, US Superintendent of Indian Affairs

The distress of Father Pandosy and his Indian flock un-
doubtedly would have been far greater if they had witnessed Governor Isaac I. Stevens prepare for the journey west. It was soon
evident this was a man who did not wait for opportunities to come
to him; he went in search of them. At 35 years of age Stevens had
advanced from a graduating second lieutenant at West Point to
the rank of major in the Engineer Corps. For the most part, his
promotions came as a result of cleverness and hard work.

There was no detail too small or unimportant for Major
Stevens' attention. Topography, zoology, botany, ecology, eth-
nology, mineralogy, meteorology -- he felt it his duty to explore
every aspect of the lands he would traverse. He interviewed countless authorities in the natural sciences and, where possible, in-
duced them to join his survey party. Among his prize recruits
was John Mix Stanley, noted western artist.

To further prepare himself for the journey and the gover-
norship, Stevens studied every report he could get on the land
and its people. He read Lewis and Clark journals, the writings of
Father De Smet, Washington Irvings' travels and reports written
by George Simpson of Hudson's Bay. He even sent an officer to
Canada to meet with the Hudson's Bay official.

Major Stevens also demanded the best available equipment and workers. He insisted on having his men armed with the
new Sharp's rifle, considered more accurate than other models.
To ascertain the capabilities of his men, he gave them a shake-

down march from St. Paul to Camp Davis on the Sauk River. There he paused long enough to sort out the bad apples -- 25 officers, enlisted men and civilians were dismissed or voluntarily departed. He judged all men by the same standards. First of all, could they stand the rigors of the journey? Secondly, did they have a commitment to the task at hand? Thirdly, were they competent? There was no place for the unfit, inefficient or lazy, and those without a proper attitude.

Even after the shakedown at Camp Davis, a dozen or more men were dismissed on the second leg of the journey. In the place of those who were eliminated, Stevens hired French-Canadian woodsmen and voyageurs, most of whom barely could read or write. At last, when satisfied with the personnel, a goodly portion of the major's party resembled a pack of raffish pirates rather than orderly, law abiding surveyors and map makers.

If there was a flaw in Major Stevens' character, it was the tendency to set his sights too high. He demanded too much of himself and those under his command. Also, he had trouble delegating authority. When the men were faced with critical situations, he encouraged them to use their own judgement. Often when the men acted independently, however, Major Stevens was quick to find fault in what had been done. It got to the point where many capable people refused to take initiative, making the journey more demanding than necessary.

The mules ridden by the men and carrying the packs acted as wild as the piratical French-Canadians looked. Riders were bucked off, pack saddle cinches busted, supplies and equipment sent flying. Some animals took off as if shot out of a cannon while others stubbornly stood stock still, bracing against their lead ropes. Once on the trail, for several weeks the animals continued to act as if possessed by demons.

To make the trip even more vexing and frustrating, Stevens issued strict travel instructions. Cook fires had to be started by two A.M.; cooks and teamsters had to be on the job at three; officers arose for reveille at four; the whole camp was served breakfast shortly after four; tents were struck at four-thirty and the column on the march by five.

Among late replacements receiving Governor Stevens' approval was outspoken, rotund, carrot-topped Patrick O'Flanigan, an Irishman who had ridden in on a mule he named Donahue demanding to see the officer in charge. When interviewed by Stevens and questioned about his fitness to survive the difficult passage ahead, his face turned the same color as his reddish hair.

"I'm tellin' yuh man, I been over these prairies an' mountains goin' an' comin'. In '46 I followed the trail of Jessie Applegate through Black Rock Desert an' inta Umpqua Canyon, two hell holes of the universe. I stepped off a bit of acreage in the valley of the Willamette an' started abuildin' me a home, but bless me, I got awesomely lonesome livin' alone. I sashayed back ta the ol' country only ta find the lass of me heart with kids hangin' ta her skirts, married ta me best friend. Wagh!" He spat on the earth in disgust. "I'm tellin' yuh, I knows how ta deal with trouble the likes yuh've niver seed."

"Well, I guess you'll not fall by the wayside, but what can you do?" Stevens asked.

"Do, man, there's nothin' I set me mind on I cain't wrestle with an' best. Fer instance these hee-haws of yers need a stern but kindly hand. Turn 'em over ta me an' in a week's time I'll hev the lot of 'em as tame as this crowbait of mine, Donahue." He patted the nose of his long-eared mount that stood patiently by his side switching flies.

In spite of Stevens' careful attention to detail, the surveying party with its 100 plus members, made only fair progress. Muddy ground and swollen streams plagued them for the first week. In the lands of the Dakota huge herds of buffalos crossed their path, holding them up. Stevens estimated one herd contained between 200,00 and 500,00 animals. So thick were they, hunters were sent ahead to clear the way.

Carrot Top O'Flanigan's valiant attempts to tame the remuda of mules and keep them from straying, were far from successful. A number of the animals were swallowed up by the buffalo horde. This loss was the final blow to the Irishman's good nature.

"These blinkin' dumb critters got the brain capacity of hummin' birds. I train 'em, mother 'em like a brood hen, pasture 'em in knee-deep buffalo grass, an' still they act as mean as corn-crib rats," he ranted.

"Thought yuh tol' the boss yuh could do anythin' yuh set yer mind on," reminded a raunchy gray bearded teamster named Rankin. "I'm thinkin' yuh sure was blowin' hot air when yuh tol' him yuh could tame these critters. Look at 'em; they's still as wild as new-sheared sheep. When yuh mention mule, the major looks like he's bit inta the back end of a skunk. Fer sure, if he ever stops long enuff ta count his mules an' find 'em short, he'll be comin' after yuh with one of those fancy Sharp's huntin' sticks."

"Let him come," Carrot Top grumbled. "I've wrestled with better men than him."

Teamster Rankin clamped down on a plug of tobacco and spit. "Me thinks thet ain't all yuh'll be wrestlin' with. Afore yuh kin say Jack Sprat, these buffaloes're goin' ta start drawin' Injuns ta 'em like buzzards ta dead meat. The next thing yuh an' yer mules'll be facin're bands of red men."

The teamster's predictions were correct. Boutineau, one of the French-Canadian voyaguers, came upon a large Indian camp. It was a war party of Sioux, Boutineau claimed, nearly causing the Stevens' party to panic. Instead, it turned out to be a Meteis hunting party on their traditional spring buffalo hunt. Later an encampment of Assinibones also was encountered. Stevens smoked with them, ate with them and sat in council with them. Assinibone elders had signed the Treaty of Fort Laramie in 1851 but complained it had not been observed -- invading hunters came to slaughter game on their lands at will, taking skins and tongues and leaving good meat to spoil.

"And what will happen to our game when the 'iron horse' come?" an elder asked.

Stevens, prepared for questions of this kind, glibly replied, "Whites who settle along the railroad will bring goods to replace the game. The father in Washington will give plows and hoes so you may obtain food far easier than you do now."

"I niver seen nothin' like it," Adams, a farm youth who had witnessed the meeting between the Assinibone and Stevens, announced. "There they was, actin' like ol' friends, smokin', eatin', an' talkin'. The major must hev the constitution of one of these ornery mules, diggin' inta the vittles the way he did. Those women ladlin' out the buffalo stew wasn't a bit keerful. Dogs were sniffin' it, kids were pokin' fingers in it, an' great gobs of fat floated on top like scum on a stagnant pond. Aagh! But the major didn't blink an eye. Chewed an' swallowed -- chewed an' swallowed . . . yuh'd thought he'd growed up on the stuff."

"He was probably glad ta hev a change from the slop our cooks hev been throwin' at us," Carrot Top O'Flanigan, who gobbled his food like a starving dog, observed sourly.

On the Little Muddy River the surveyors encountered a hostile party of Blackfeet. A man who had married a Blood, a division of the Blackfeet Nation, was able to persuade the hostiles that the surveyors only were passing through and would do them or their lands no harm. Although most of Blackfeet country was out of his jurisdiction, Stevens promised to return the following year and sit in council. The purpose of the council would be to assure peaceful relations between Americans and the Blackfeet as well as other tribes in the region.

"It is my desire to have all peoples live in peace," Stevens declared. However, keeping peaceful relations among the surveyors almost was more than Stevens could manage. The party, made up of military personnel and civilians, often were at loggerheads. Upon setting out Stevens had declared that everyone in his command was to be considered equal. To set an example the governor pitched in, working alongside teamsters, herders, cooks, interpreters and scouts. Yet, someone had to issue instructions, maintain schedules . . . keep the column moving and on

track. Irritations soon emerged. A civilian gave an order to a
military medico officer.

"Damned if I'll take orders from you," the doctor stormed.

Similar incidents occurred. Men who had worked agreeably together got into bitter quarrels and refused to speak to one
another. Stevens' plan of equality ultimately was in shambles.
Regardless of the troubles, he saw to it the party steadily continued westward. A painful hernia that, at times, prevented him
from horseback riding, did not stop him. The knowledge that
soon he would enter the domain over which he would rule, kept
him plowing ahead. Nothing was going to keep him from making a name for himself in the new territory of Washington.

**

Soon after Joe's and Deacon's visit to St. Joseph mission,
a delegation of Yakama, Walla Walla and Cayuse made a trek to
Fort Dalles on the Columbia River. There they met with Captain
Benjamin Alvord, commandant of the post. News of the approaching survey party weighed heavily on the Indian leaders' shoulders. They rode in silence, unaware of the pleasant surroundings
that came with early summer.

One awesome question after another battered their be-
numbed minds. What did the coming of this new governor mean
for their people? What did he expect of them? Would he ask
them to give up their precious lands? Would they see the surface
of Mother Earth torn by plows and harrows? Would the people
be forced from their villages, face a march to strange lands like
their fellow man had been forced to do in the east? The future
looked so grim for Indian people, it was painful even to discuss
these torturous questions around campfires.

Captain Alvord greeted the Indian contingent civilly. He
could see by their expressions they were troubled. Like an invis-
ible cloud, a feeling of tension hung over the meeting place.
Alvord had a good idea why the Indian leaders had sought an
audience. News of the pending survey party's arrival was the
major topic of barrack gossip. What his Indian guests did not

know was that not only one, but two survey parties were on their way into Indian lands. George B. McClellan, commandant of the second survey party, had crossed the Panama isthmus and soon would be disembarking at Fort Vancouver to lead his surveyors over the Cascades and into the valley of the Yakamas.

After the preliminary niceties were performed, Captain Alvord indicated it was time to speak. "I know you men have made this journey to speak of what is in your hearts," he said through an interpreter. "Will you speak now?"

"Your tongue is straight. We do come to speak of what lies heavily in our hearts. We are told the iron horse that runs on tracks of steel soon will cross our lands," the spokesman of the Indian group said. "We fear what this iron horse may bring. We have no fear of the Red Coats of Hudson's Bay or the Blue Coats of your American army. We know them. For many winters we have seen them come and go. Now, we hear that this thing you call 'railway' brings with it many people armed with axes, plows and shovels. The steel tracks will cross hunting and pasture grounds. The people who will come will tear at the skin of Mother Earth, cut down her forests and build immovable lodges of sticks and stones. How can our people allow this?" The speaker fell silent.

Captain Alvord cleared his throat. For days he had tried to prepare for a meeting like this. But what could one do or say? The Indian situation was bad and only could get worse. From the eloquent way these people spoke, they had to have been coached. That pesky French priest on Ahtanum Creek was up to his old tricks. He had drilled these Indians on what to say. Alvord had heard the Yakama chief, Kamiakin, was like a brother to Father Pandosy. The only reason the Yakama leader did not wholeheartedly accept the Catholic faith was that once he was baptized he would have to give up his multiple wives.

The interpreter cleared his throat loudly. Aware of the Indian delegation that impassively waited for him to speak, Captain Alvord jerked his thoughts back to the present. "Your tongues also are straight," he said, playing for time. "Your message is clear and heard. Your words will go to the father in Washington. He wants no harm to come to Indian people. . . ." The captain paused. To these worried folk what else could he say that would put their minds at rest -- at least for a while?

The interpreter cleared his throat again. And again Captain Alvord wiped his mind clear of troubling thoughts. He had to be careful. The man Stevens expected everyone to toe the mark. What was said and done here would be gone over with a fine toothed comb. He had to appear positive -- end the meeting on a high note.

"Give each of these men a packet of tobacco and can of molasses," he instructed his aide. He stood up and stiffly saluted the Indian delegation, waiting for them to leave, inwardly cursing himself for the niggling way he had handled the meeting. He had given no assurances and had received none in return. The whole business might as well not have occurred.

Yet, there was one gain. He now could say he had met with the troubled Indian leaders. He had listened to their fears and sent them away reasonably happy. Of course, whatever he said would not alter the course of history one iota. From the commander-in-chief, President Franklin Pierce, down to the lowest private soldier, the official word was out, "we're going to civilize the west or bust a gut in the process".

THE GREAT POWWOW

VI

*When I looked for good, then evil came unto me: and when I
waited for light, there came darkness.*
Job 30:26

While tribes on the Columbia plateau stewed and fretted,
life in the land of the Nimpau went on much as usual, especially
for the occupants of the log cabin lodge the mountain man Little
Ned had built. The men went daily to the pasture grounds to work
with horses and cattle. The womenfolk collected kouse roots, berries
and other edibles from hillside bushes and plants. The weather was
warm but pleasant. Vision Seeker, who felt responsible for the family,
continued to keep close watch on everyone, but the days slipped by
without incident. The family appeared happy and well.

Except for the initial flurry of alarm over the approaching railway surveying party, life in Lapwai village also returned to normal.
Gradually the elders looked on the surveyors' arrival as an event that
would do them little harm. After all, 50 winters previously, the Lewis
and Clark expedition had passed through the Nimpau homeland. Yes,
for a short while the people were perturbed but the explorers were
friendly, doing no more damage than buying up and eating all the camp
dogs.

Deep in his heart Vision Seeker knew the coming of the
surveyors was a far different story. These people had their minds
set on "civilizing the west". They would not come and leave like
the early explorers, but stay to build villages and cities and mul-
tiply. The native people would be forced to live side by side with
these invaders or be driven into enclaves in lands where they would
not get in the way of white father President Pierce's policy of
Manifest Destiny.

The encounter with the big man, Tall Horse, continued to

bother Vision Seeker. He had the distinct feeling that there was a
great deal more about his interest than either he or Raven Wing
revealed.

Raven Wing strengthened the belief when one day she
said, " I can't imagine why that big man came all the way to
Lapwai to bargain with you. What does he think I am, one of
your mares that you wish to trade?"

Another time, while beating the dust out of a woven mat,
she gave it an extra hard whack and broke out with the words,
"The gall of the man, why doesn't he stay home and look for a
mate in the White Bird camp."

Vision Seeker kept his thoughts to himself. Other than
Raven Wing's occasional bursts of temper, the family was getting along so well he did not want to unsettle them in the least
way. He especially was pleased with Michael. His nephew, who had
planned to visit a short while, was now a stalwart in keeping family life
pleasant. Every day he worked with the horses and cattle. He had
practically every animal in good health. The Lone Wolf clan herd was
the prize livestock in Lapwai Valley. Even Old Joseph (Tuekakas),
Nimpau leader from the far away Wallowa Mountains came to inspect the herd and speak with the caretaker, Michael Two Feathers.

"Ah-hoh!" the leader of the Wellamotkin band of Nimpau,
uttered. "What is it you do to make your animals the finest in the
tribe? Come to Wallowa country and tell us what we can do."

The invitation pleased Michael, but instead of taking pride
in his successes, he felt humbled. If he was to become a great
healer he had to learn much, much more. He began to experi-
ment with herbal plants, roots and tree barks. He sought out local
healers and asked their advice. Everything he learned he set down
in a journal. At first none of the family members paid him much
mind. Then one day Michael saw his mother intently watching.

"What are you doing?" Raven Wing asked.

"What I learn, I write down. Some day I may have enough
words to make a book. Perhaps what I learn now will serve to
help others."

"Hmm!" Raven Wing grunted and turned away. Michael

decided his jottings did not interest her, so he offered no further explanation. Actually, he got the idea of taking notes from his work with missionary Doctor Whitman. When encountering an unusual ailment, the doctor consulted one of his thick books.

The few words Michael said to his mother had a far greater impact on her than he realized. It brought her back to the days when she carried this young man in her womb -- the grim winter she lived with her trapper husband on the trap lines. At the end of almost every day Buck Stone, the trappers' leader, picked up a pad and pen and began to write or sketch. His sketches of birds and animals were so real it looked as if they would step off the page and walk or fly away. Raven Wing tried her best to put memories of those days behind her, but every evening when Michael sat down to write, thoughts of that long ago winter returned to haunt her.

It was not until midsummer that troubles loomed on the horizon. One bright sunny day One Who Kicks stumbled and crawled up the hillside where Raven Wing was picking berries. Waving his short arms he frantically gestured toward the log cabin. Raven Wing dropped her basket, grabbed the boy, and rushed down the hillside to find Morning Star, pale and peaked, languishing on the porch bench.

She pulled the slack figure to her feet and walked her into the log cabin lodge and laid her on the sleeping pallet. Always healthy herself, she hardly knew what to do. As soon as she made the sick woman comfortable, Raven Wing called for Second Son, Young Wolf, and sent him to the pasture to fetch Michael, but Michael could not be found. He had gone to collect fresh herbs in the nearby hills.

Vision Seeker, who was in the pasture, answered the call of distress. He arrived at the log cabin lodge and listened to Raven Wing's agitated description of Morning Star's ills. He studied the sick woman's pallid face, for she had fallen asleep. There were questions he wanted to ask, but they were of such intimate nature he felt it was not his place to bring them up.

"Let her sleep," he said to Raven Wing. "Leave it to her medicine man mate to discover what's wrong. Let him get some doctoring practice on his own kind."

"Oh-hah," Raven Wing uttered and said no more. Vision Seeker returned to the pasture and upon seeing Michael started to speak, then changed his mind. He couldn't run to his wife every time she had a twitch of pain. Raven Wing was up to handling the situation. When Michael appeared at the log cabin with his collection of herbs and heard his wife was unwell, he hurried into the back room. By that time Morning Star was awake, looking almost normal, delighted to see her husband.

"Young Wolf said you were ill," Michael blurted.

"It is a good illness. You are to be a father again."

"Oh-hah," Michael uttered, glancing at his mother who sat with her back to him cleaning the berries she had picked that morning. She also was thinking of a second grandson. The first one was always underfoot. A second one . . . !

On the morrow and the day after, Morning Star remained in bed late, finally to arise feeling unwell. Raven Wing, who was busy collecting and preparing berries and roots that would take them through the coming winter, had to put aside her work and care for One Who Kicks. Then she began taking him with her to pick chokecherries. The boy, who still was learning to walk and run, found the rough ground difficult to negotiate. Easily tired, he plopped down anywhere that took his fancy. One day he dropped near a coiled rattlesnake that buzzed its deadly warning. Raven Wing grabbed him up and ran screaming for the cabin. She still had not recovered when Michael came in that evening.

"The hillsides are no place for your son," she burst out, shivering as though she had the ague. "From now on you must take him with you to the pasture grounds."

Day after day the arrangement went well. Michael loved to have his son nearby. The big horses did not frighten the child and, after the first sniffings and eyeing the little man, the animals resumed grazing and switching their tails as if it was normal for the little man child to be there. Then one afternoon Spotted Badger, Michael's one time friend who had turned enemy, rode by. He saw the youngster and reined to a stop.

"You are a strange one," he said to Michael, "bringing your girl child to teach her the ways of horses."

"Girl child!" Michael turned on the horseman with such fury it made Spotted Badger flinch. "This is my son."

"Son? But he looks female." Spotted Badger quickly rode away, leaving Michael steaming. He swung his son upon the horse and studied him. The boy's hair had an unusual tendency to curl and fell to his shoulders. His olive skin with its healthy rosy glow, was a thing of beauty. The mischievous glint in the large brown eyes made Michael's heart turn over. Spotted Badger was right, Michael ruefully realized. Put his precious son in a dress and One Who Kicks would be the picture of an enchanting woman child.

Right then and there, Michael decided to remake his firstborn. He took the shears he clipped manes and tails with and trimmed off the locks that were the pride of mother and grandmother. He draped his buckskin jacket over the boys small shoulders and took from his bag of belongings a wide brimmed hat that he acquired while serving with the Regiment of Mounted Riflemen. He had to stuff it a bit with horse hair to bring it down to size and trimmed off some of the brim. He set it on the boy's head. That was better. If one didn't inspect him too closely, he looked like a miniature mountain man. Michael placed his son on Magpie's back, swung up behind him and rode toward the log cabin lodge. The little boy scrambled down and up the steps, one hand clutching the jacket and the other the oversized hat.

Raven Wing stopped in her tracks. "*Soyappo*," she screamed. She snatched the hat off the boy's head and sent it sailing on the wind. "Aiee! What has your father done to you, cutting your beautiful hair." She glared at Michael, her eyes flashing fire. "If this is the way you want your boy to look, I'll not have him in the lodge."

Michael stared at his mother, shocked by her ferocity. "Do not glare at me like that. This is my lodge. Do not darken it again." Raven Wing whirled around, entered the cabin and slammed the door so fiercely it made the window glass that Little Ned had gone to such expense to acquire, vibrate like a pounded drum.

The situation had not improved when Vision Seeker came back from the pasture grounds. The three members of the Two Feather family were sitting on the porch. Morning Star looked wan and pale, the expression on Michael's face was as dark and foreboding as a thunder cloud, and little One Who Kicks, hopped around in his new outfit as chipper and bright-eyed as a squirrel.

Vision Seeker did not have to be told what had happened. It was clear that Raven Wing, whose good behavior had surprised everyone, had reverted to her former belligerent self. He sat down on a porch step and stared into the distance. What could be done about his beautiful sister? She goes from happiness to viciousness at a snap of a finger. "What happened?" he asked finally.

"I dressed the little one like a boy," Michael explained. "She took one look at him and began to scream . . . *soyyapo* . . . grabbed his hat and threw it away."

"*Soyappo*," Vision Seeker mused, "the name given to the first white men." He glanced at Raven Wing's grandson who had retrieved his hat and had it pulled down nearly over his ears.

Vision Seeker grimaced. Of course, it was clear as day. Dressed in fringed buckskin and with that wide-brimmed hat on his head, the little man was a small-sized twin of his grandfather, Little Ned. Raven Wing never had gotten over the despicable way she had treated Little Ned who had been so kind and considerate. To save her sanity she had to rid herself of everything that reminded her of the big trapper and the terrible things she had done to hurt him.

VII

I have recommended . . . the early extinguishment of Indian titles to all lands belonging to these three tribes (Cayuses, Walla Wallas, and Nez Perces), lying within this Territory as a measure important to the preservation of peace.
Joel Palmer, Superintendent of Indian Affairs in Oregon, 1854

On July 18th a column of men under the command of a Blue Coat officer named McClellan marched away from Fort Vancouver toward the northern Cascades. The scouts that watched the party depart reported that they wandered around like lost dogs, sometimes following existing trails and at other times striking out into the unknown. They trekked through almost impassible forests and over terrain that even the natives avoided. As a result animals and men soon became exhausted. In 12 days it was estimated they had traversed a mere 78 miles.

It seemed as though the gods were against them. They encountered all sorts of unanticipated problems. Forest fire smoke hung heavily overhead, obliterating landmarks. Horse flies as large as humming birds, attacked the animals. The resulting bucking and thrashing about broke flimsy pack saddles, scattering supplies helter-skelter. The problem became so severe the party was held up while riders returned to Fort Vancouver to fetch additional saddles.

Ultimately, the McClellan command arrived at the foot of the Cascades where it again paused to regroup and gather reinforcements. A number of Klickitat guides were recruited. A short time later several scouts were sent east to investigate mountain passes. Eventually an elderly white recruit with a nose like a fox searched out Joe with orders to report to McClellan.

Joe, who only had recently arrived from Yakama country, received the summons with apprehension. Ever since he had ac-

companied Colonel Gilliam on the disastrous 1848 campaign to
apprehend the Whitman Mission murderers, he had a distaste for
the military. Gilliam had marched into Indian country with the
intent of capturing the culprits regardless of who got hurt or what
property was damaged in the process. His callous treatment of
prisoners, his stubborn belief in the righteousness of his actions,
and his complete disregard for the dignity of humanity, had left
Joe sickened and feeling sullied. At the end of the campaign
when Gilliam accidently shot and killed himself, it seemed an
appropriate climax to the whole unfortunate affair. Someone on
high had witnessed the colonel's disgraceful behavior and had
smote him down -- justice had been rendered.

Later, Joe had marched across the continent with the Regiment of Mounted Riflemen. The officers behaved decently but
the enlisted men were lazy, incompetent and uncontrollable. Before the end of the journey a fifth or more of the troop had deserted, the officers helpless in their attempt to discipline them.
Thus, when asked to report to Captain McClellan, Joe did so dubi-
ously. Was the officer narrow-minded and insensitive like Colonel Gilliam -- a weak commander like the officers of the Mounted
Riflemen, or an eager beaver like Major Stevens?

"What's this all about?" Joe asked the elderly fox nosed
messenger.

"I don't perxactly know, but I'm told the captain likes ta
size up his men afore sendin' 'em inta the field."

"Hmm!" Joe grunted. Where had he been if not in the
field? Was the Gilliam silliness beginning again?

McClellan was seated in front of a tent above which flew the
stars and stripes. The captain, who had been reading a sheet of paper, glanced up and motioned for Joe to take a camp chair. While
waiting, Joe had time to evaluate the officer, who in the future would
command the Army of the Potomac -- defenders of the nation's capitol during the Civil War. A young man, still in his twenties, McClellan
made a good impression. It was said he was an engineer, and apparently a good one, having taught the subject at the US Military Acad-

emy on the Hudson.

"Sorry to keep you waiting," the captain said. "There is the saying the army runs on paper. That must be true. It certainly follows me wherever I am. Now, let's see . . . Your name is Joe Jennings. I'm told you know this country and its people about as well as anyone. You certainly will be of great help. I must admit I have had little experience in dealing with Indian people so I must ask your forbearance." He searched through the papers, finally had to call for a map.

The captain's modesty and willingness to learn boded well, Joe thought. It was an entirely different attitude than the plateau people could expect from their new territorial governor.

"Here we are on the western slope of the Cascades. As I see it, perhaps the first people we will contact are the Yakama. Tell me about them. How should they be approached?" McClellan asked.

Joe moved near to better view the large scale map. At first glance it appeared extremely sketchy -- even hard to locate where they were. But, of course, that was the purpose of the surveying party, to map out the land for the passage of the proposed continental railway.

"The heart of the Yakama homeland is just beyond the mountains," Joe said finally, getting himself oriented. He jabbed a finger at the eastern slope of the Cascades. "It is said the Yakama's most trusted leader is a man named Kamiakin, an intelligent person who keeps careful watch over his people. As most tribes on the plateau, the Yakamas are quite uneasy about this railway survey. They feel the government will take their land and leave them homeless.

"Kamiakin is a special person. By marriage he is related to the Spokan, Klickitat and Nez Perce. Also, he is a close friend of Peu-peu-mox-mox of the Walla Walla and the priests at St. Joseph Mission. It is said he hardly makes a move without first discussing it with the Oblate priest, Father Pandosy. My suggestion is to visit St. Joseph Mission and speak with Father Pandosy before approaching any of the Indian chiefs. If anyone can get us on the good side of the Yakamas, this man can do it."

"Hmm!" McClellan grunted thoughtfully. "I guess those in Washington wouldn't take it amiss if we ask for the help of the Catholics. Goodness knows, from what I've heard these priests have isolated themselves in these wilds until they're more Indian than the Indians."

Down Ahtanum Creek McClellan's force marched, rather straggled, as the party included civilians, Indians and a great herd of horses and mules. The Yakamas were astonished at the size of the approaching group that now numbered in excess of 200 men, uncountable horses and mules and mountains of supplies. These people were either planning on a long journey or to settle in for a long stay. Either one was not to the liking of the locals.

Watchers also were surprised to see the Blue Coat leader and his entourage make straight for the lodges of the black robes. Not far from the mission the cumbersome column stopped to make camp in a park like meadow. On one side brown bluffs loomed against the skyline while on the other side gurgled Ahtanum Creek. The following morning, McClellan accompanied by Joe, went to visit St. Joseph Mission. The Oblate fathers were out front to receive them.

Joe hardly had slept the previous night. What kind of reception will we get? he kept asking himself. The fathers certainly could not be happy to see the large McClellan contingent cross the mountains and descend into the valley practically unannounced and without invitation. But Joe's worries were quickly put to rest. The Oblate brothers graciously greeted them.

"Welcome to St. Joseph Mission," Father Pandosy said, introducing his guests to the household. A slight dampening of the cordiality came when a tall, large, and very dark man emerged from the mission house. His unsmiling, massive square face reminded Joe of a grizzly bear he once had encountered. Would the Indian man draw a weapon from beneath the voluminous coat he wore and cut them down where they stood?

"Come, my friend. Meet our visitors," Father Pandosy said to the man. "These folks come in peace. Gentlemen, this is Kamiakin, a trusted, loyal member of my flock." The big Indian's expression immediately changed. He smiled and stepped forward to shake hands. Joe could feel his mouth drop open. The smile changed the face of the Grizzly Bear to that of a friendly St. Bernard. Yet, he radiated dignity and self-assurance. Joe could not help but be impressed. Here, indeed, was a man who demanded respect and should receive it. He was no fool and would be a wily but honorable foe.

McClellan and other members of the surveying party were jubilant over the warm reception. "Perhaps, the good fathers are the key to the success of our railway venture," McClellan confided to George Gibbs, an artist who had been recruited to make sketches of the flora, fauna and personalities encountered.

"Yes, indeed, their knowledge will be most helpful," Gibbs replied. "I doubt if there's a single white man who knows the local Indians better than Father Pandosy. I'm told he's even working on a Yakama language grammar and dictionary, truly a most challenging endeavor."

"Hmm!" McClellan grunted thoughtfully. "The good father is certainly to be commended, but knowledge of Yakama grammar isn't going to help us a wit. What we need to know is if there are there any passes through the Cascades that will make a transcontinental railway feasible."

That evening as Joe and Deacon prepared their evening meal, a dusty column of pack mules plodded into camp.

"From the way those mules're strainin', they're sure enuff carryin' powerful heavy loads," Deacon observed.

"Probably the quartermaster outfit," Joe surmised.

"Hey, thet mule handler's an odd lookin' duck, 'peers ta be all arms an' legs. Look't his elbows. They stick out like wings on a picked chicken. I'll be blessed if'n thet fella don't remind me of Beamer's ol' sidekick, Grasshopper Stillin's . . . By gum!

'tis him. Hey, yuh skinny galoot . . . what's the matter with yuh, pullin' in late like this? Don'tcha know, these sojer boys been waitin' fer those supplies? Didja git lost in the forest?"

Startled by the shouted greeting, the lanky teamster pulled his mules to a stop. "I must be seein' things," he exclaimed. "If I didn't know better, I'd say thet's the unfrocked parson who calls hisself Deacon. If I'd a know'd yuh was waitin' I'd sure enuff took another trail, not thet I chose this 'un. Anyhow, if yer cookin' vittles put on another helpin'. I'm as lank as a fastin' greyhound."

After pulling the packs from the mules and staking them out to pasture, Stillings came and plopped down beside the campfire. He stretched a long arm for a tin cup and helped himself to coffee as though they'd been fellow travelers, when, in fact, more than three years had passed since they had laid eyes on one another.

"Yep, I sure likes coffee an' vittles ready-made at the end of a day's journey," Stillings said gratefully. "Makes one feel right at home. Anyways, what're yuh birds doin' heya? Last I seen of yuh, yuh was moseyin' east toward the lands of the Blackfeet, intendin' ta mark Beamer's son's grave."

"Yep, thet's where we was goin'," Deacon replied. "We found the place an' marked it good an' proper."

"Well, whatcha been doin' since? Thet was three summers ago, mighty long ones at thet. I cain't tell yuh how much I miss thet ol' pal of mine. Beamer was as windy as a colicky baby but had a heart as large as all outdoors."

Stillings paused to swallow a lump in his throat. "I'm sure happy ta see yuh galoots, brings back those good ol' days when things was good. What fun usn's had whilst marchin' with thet misfit batch of Mounted Riflemen. Yuh 'member Sarjent Coombs? Well, thet ol' snappin' turtle's 'round heya somewheres, ornery as ever, acts like somebody's chewin' on his tail. I ain't sure but what he's sorrowin' over Beamer, too. Yuh know he was the cause of Beamer's death, sendin' us off on thet goose chase after supplies up thet muddy track called Barlow Road."

The mention of Sergeant Algeron Coombs made Joe grimace. The last time he saw the irascible soldier was in Oregon City, right after the trial and execution of the five Cayuses accused of perpetrating the Whitman Mission killings. Coombs had come galloping in, pulled his pregnant wife off her father's wagon and carried her away draped over the saddle like a sack of meal. The memory still made him furious. If it hadn't been for Deacon holding him back, he would have gone to her rescue.

Hardly did the thought enter Joe's mind and there he was ... Sergeant Coombs -- as unbending as the barrel of a Hawken -- emerging from the shadows. For a moment he stood glaring at Mule Skinner Stillings.

"Might have known you would be up to your old tricks, lolly-gagging as if you had nothing to do," Coombs snapped. "There is still work to be done."

"Sajant, why dontcha take a load off yer feet an' visit a bit," Deacon affably invited. "We ain't seen yuh since yuh was guardin' prisoners in Oregon City. Whatcha been doin' since? An' how's yer wife an' family?"

Surprisingly, the sergeant, after glowering at Stillings, hunkered down by the fire. His expression gradually turned from one of belligerence to that of congeniality. Before leaving Fort Vancouver Captain McClellan had stressed the need for spreading good will. Besides, somehow the old mountain man reminded Coombs of his father who had recently passed on. He hadn't seen his old man for more than four years and now never would see him again, at least not in this world. The news of his father's passing had sent him into a blue funk that he could not shake.

One of his greatest desires had been to take his little family east to meet the old man. He would have been delighted to see the sturdy boy, his only grandson. Probably the sight of the child would have extended his father's life, giving him reason to live. He, the elderly Coombs' only son, had done little to make his father proud. His hope had been that his handsome offspring would make up for his own shortcomings, but it had yet to come to pass. "Aagh!" Coombs inwardly groaned. The life of a career soldier was full of disappointment and heartbreak.

Sergeant Coombs accepted the cup of coffee Deacon handed him and took a sip. "Yep, a lot of water has flowed under the bridge since we last met," he said finally. "The family is well. Lucille and I have a son going on four, sprightly as a spring robin."

Sergeant Coombs glanced at Joe and quickly looked away. A little worm of worry began to bore away in his brain, reminding him that this man still could be a threat to his marriage. He and Lucille were now getting along well but . . . He dismissed the distressing thought. As he just had said, a lot of water had flowed under the bridge since Joe Jennings and Lucille had last seen each other. Perhaps the romantic feeling they had shared was dead. He certainly hoped so.

"The in-laws are doing well," Coombs continued. "We don't see them much any more. Our home is in Fort Vancouver and, thank goodness, they have remained in the Willamette Valley."

The sergeant gulped down the last of the coffee and abruptly got to his feet. "As I was saying, Stillings, there still is work to be done. We have to unpack the supplies. The captain is going to visit St. Joseph Mission again and wants to take along some gifts."

"I'll be hornswoggled," Deacon uttered, as the two soldiers strode away. "What came over the sajant? He turned from a snappin' turtle ta a friendly house cat. Maybeso thet wife of his mellowed the fella . . . more likely it's the son thet did the trick."

"Yeah, he doesn't seem like the same man," Joe agreed, his thoughts going back to the march of the Mounted Riflemen in '49. Sweet and bitter memories crowded his mind. Did he, Joe Jennings, still love Lucille? Did she still love him? If everything had worked out as he once had dreamed, Sergeant Coomb's sprightly boy could have been his own son. Would the lad have changed him as much as he apparently had Sergeant Coombs?

The thought made him scowl. There he was, thinking of what could have been. He, too, brushed memories of the past from his mind. He'd had his chances to settle down and start a family and flubbed every one. First there was Melody Abernathy, then her sister, Bithiah, then Lucille Morgan and then Morning Star . . . he stood up and shook himself like a water soaked dog.

"Yep, those fleas're sure hard ta unseat," Deacon observed. "They say there's a powder thet kills 'em deader than a landed fish. Maybeso, next time we're in a tradin' post, we should git a passel of it."

At the same time Captain McClellan was leading his surveying party through the Cascades and into the land of the Yakamas, another group of men journeyed up the Columbia River heading east under the command of a Lieutenant Saxton. Saxton's party carried supplies for the eastern arm of the railway survey led by Isaac Stevens.

At Fort Walla Walla the Saxton party stopped to visit and ask for directions. Hudson's Bay's factor, Andrew Pambrun, suggested they journey north, across Cayuse country and on to the lands of the Spokan. The appearance of 50 or more Blue Coats and dozens of pack animals, increased unease among the Cayuse, Walla Walla and Palouse. They watched as, like flood waters during the Season of Melting Snow, hairy faces came from every which way, carving trails wherever they fancied.

A party of Walla Walla sent by Peu-peu-mox-mox arrived at the St. Joseph Mission with the disturbing news. Father Pandosy called on Captain McClellan to ask for an explanation. When the captain told the priest the purpose of Saxton's 50 man column, Father Pandosy was not comforted.

"You and your large force coming across the mountains from the west, another body of men skirting the southern edge of the territory, and a major expedition approaching from the east makes these Indian people nervous. I don't blame them. Seems to me this survey effort could be managed more discreetly and with more consideration."

Father Pandosy paused, clutching the black and gold cru-
cifix that hung by a black cord that encircled his neck. For a
moment the priest appeared to be repeating a prayer. "You men
are playing with these peoples' livelihood," the father declared,
breaking the silence.

"I pray that the actions of your surveying parties do not
lead to bloodshed. I'm not so concerned about the Yakama, but
the Walla Walla and Cayuse really have suffered greatly at the
hands of you army people. Remember the Whitman Mission
murders? Something just as bloody very well could happen again.
I can calm the Yakama and probably the Walla Walla, but that
leaves the Cayuse . . ."

The father's blunt words disturbed Captain McClellan.
To have Isaac Stevens arrive to find himself involved in an Indian uprising would be disastrous. It could result in the recall of
them both. The railroad project would grind to a halt. The white
people in the region would be placed at risk. It was possible the
British, fearing their trading posts and citizens were endangered,
would step in and the whole territory could be lost.

Captain McClellan gritted his teeth in exasperation. Peace
had to be maintained at all costs. He summoned his aide. "Have
that scout, Joe Jennings, sent for immediately," he ordered. When
Joe arrived the captain immediately got to the point.

"Father Pandosy believes there is danger the Cayuse and
Walla Walla may go on a rampage. He will speak to the Walla
Walla leader but has little contact with the Cayuse. . . ."

Shortly after the meeting with McClellan, Joe and Deacon,
who miraculously had regained new vitality, packed up and left for the
land of the Cayuse.

VIII

The man from Europe is still a foreigner and an alien.
And he still hates the man who questioned his path
across the continent.
Standing Bear, Oglala Sioux

Major Stevens swore. The railway survey was going nowhere. He had sent riders to the north, south and west and yet not
a one of them had returned. There had to be a route through the
Rockies that would allow the passage of locomotives, but where
was it? It had to be found soon. The way his surveyors were
proceeding, snow would fall and they still would be floundering
about like blind mice at the bottom of an empty coal pit.

Not only time, but money was running out. From all indications he would be hard-pressed to get more. For certain, it
would take an act of Congress. Getting molasses to move in Janu-
ary was quicker than it took some of those senators to make up
their minds. The Southerners, especially, were against a northern transcontinental railway. It was outside their sphere of influence. How could they line their pockets in Yankee territory?
Secretary of war, Jefferson Davis, also would do his best to gum
up the works.

Major Stevens swore again and then grimaced. On top of
everything else, his painful hernia was giving him fits. Some
mornings, mounting his horse almost was more than he could
manage. Dr. Suckley advised bed rest -- if he didn't take a few
days off his feet he might suffer a strangulated hernia that could
kill him or demand an emergency operation. For a couple of days
he did slow down, but every minute that went by was torture. Time
was precious. He felt as helpless as a worm in an anthill. Already
George McClellan would be in the Northwest, perhaps he even had
discovered a pass through the Cascades. Next step would be to ne-

gotiate for the rights of way with the natives, something he, himself, wanted to do. Stevens gritted his teeth. McClellan would be stealing all the glory while he lay like a ruptured dog in the Rocky Mountains.

Stevens shouted for his assistant. "I want you to go over the organizational chart. Examine every position and piece of equipment. We're running low on funds. Only the devil knows when we'll get more. Terminate every unessential man. Pay them off until the money runs out."

"These people are a long distance from home," the assistant pointed out. "It will mean a hardship for many."

Stevens remained adamant. "Can't help it. It's either that or admit defeat; for certain we're not going to do that."

Among those discharged were Carrot Top O'Flanigan and Raunchy Gray Beard Rankin. They were stunned and objected bitterly, and rightly so. After weeks on the trail the remuda finally was trouble free. Both men had spent many extra hours breaking the mules and keeping them fit.

"Damnation!" the Irishman exploded, his carrot colored hair standing on end like porcupine quills. "So this is the way the Territory of Washington's goin' ta be run. When things git a bit shaky those thet did their bit, workin' ther fingers ta the bone, are cast out like leprous dogs."

"The ol' guv sure took a good place ta turn us loose," Raunchy Rankin observed glumly, "right at the foot of the high mountains. Look't those peaks, yonder. Nuthin' short of a mountain goat kin scale 'em. Maybeso, we's lucky at thet. Kin yuh 'magine a train puffin' its way through these mountains? Could be this whole crew soon'll be turning tail an' headin' home."

"Naw," Carrot Top disagreed. "Ol' Stevens'll find a way. When he's made his mind ta do somethin', he's as stiff-necked as a petrified pelican, but I ain't likin' this even a wee bit. The only reason I jined up was ta git back ta the Willamette Valley. The boss may be short of money, but so am I."

"Yuh made the journey ta Oregon country afore," Raunchy said. "Why don't we mosey on. Cain't be too difficult if these army plodders kin do it."

"Hmm!" the Irishman grunted, scratching his carrot top. "I ain't been over this trail but knew a galoot thet did. Can't say as he's one ta especially trust. We followed the Applegate Trail tagether, endin' up in thet hell hole, Umpqua Canyon. Anyhow, this fella said onct yuh struck buffalo country yuh had it made. Yuh cross the Bitterroot an' follow the river Indians call the Kooskooskie. Fer sure I ain't 'bout ta go back ta Ireland an' take up potato farmin' agin. 'Twas the blinkin' potato famine thet drove me west in '46. I ain't chancin' thet agin."

**

The trek across the continental divide and Lolo Pass was far more demanding than either Carrot Top or Raunchy anticipated, yet, they still were the first members of Stevens' main body of surveyors to arrive in the land of the Nimpau. Looking more dead than alive, the two men were discovered by a horsemen guarding the Kooskooskie Trail. Their bedraggled clothing hung on the gaunt bodies in tatters. Their footwear had been worn through as they had trudged much of the way on foot, having slaughtered and eaten their mules (Donahue going under the knife first) while still on the east slope of the Bitterroots.

Upon arriving in Lapwai, Carrot Top and Raunchy were taken to the lodge of mountain man, Red Craig. He put them up in the log cabin where Joe Jennings had spent the winter of '44-'45, the year Raven Wing stabbed him with a knife, nearly putting out his eye. While Craig went to bring them food, Carrot Top noticed a bundle in the corner with a note attached to the buckskin thong binding. Always inquisitive, he untied the cord and unfolded the paper. "This is the property of Joe Jennings," he read.

"Joe Jennings. Thet name rings a bell. Blimey! Jennings! Thet's the chap thet was tellin' how easy 'twas ta git from buffalo country ta the Nimpau homeland, the lyin' bloke. If I see him agin I'll certainly tell him a thing or two."

"Maybe you'll just have that chance," said Red Craig, who had returned with a hamper of food and stood unnoticed in the doorway. "Joe's Indian relatives live on the hillside above Lapwai village. Why don't you visit with them. They'd be happy to tell you where to find him. I'm sure they would like to visit with a friend of Joe's"

"Ah-ah !" Carrot Top gulped, quickly putting the paper back. "Cain't be the same man. Joe's as white as yuh or me."

"That doesn't signify anything. I have an Indian wife and half Indian kids."

"Yuh-yuh know," Carrot Top stammered. "I'm thinkin' we'll be fit as a fiddle by mornin'. Me pardner an' me should be movin' on. The Willamette Valley still is a good hike."

"Well, that's fine. You may run into Joe Jennings on the trail. When he left here he was going to Cayuse country and that of the Walla Walla, both of which you'll surely pass through."

Carrot Top glanced at his companion and gulped. Raunchy looked away. That crazy Irishman. He should never have hooked up with him. The short skip and jump across the mountains had turned into a grueling journey. Only by eating starving Donahue and his own lean mule, every bite so tough and painful they hardly could choke them down, were they able to pull through. Now, his snooping and big mouth had gotten them crosswise of their red-bearded host, Joe Jennings, and perhaps a family of Indians. At this rate he would get them both killed and scalped.

**

In carrying out McClellan's orders to alert the Cayuse, Joe Jennings and Deacon Walton rode along the west bank of the Columbia, their first destination, Fort Walla Walla. At the Hudson's Bay trading post they stopped to replenish supplies. Joe soon satisfied his needs, but Deacon wasn't able to decide on a gift for his grandson, One Who Kicks. Joe watched his elderly companion absently finger one item after another.

"I'm still a might anxious 'bout things in Lapwai," Deacon remarked. "Thet Raven Wing's like a chancy charge of gun powder. Yuh never know when she's apt ta explode. Look't what she did ta yuh with thet knife. How kin yuh turn yer back on someun like thet?"

"I guess you're planning on rejoining Michael and Morning Star?" Joe asked.

"Yep," Deacon replied. "I'm gittin' tired of wanderin' 'round like a lost hound dog. I'm sure Michael an' Mornin' Star're thinkin' its time ta mosey home. I ain't wantin' ta disappoint 'em. Soon's we hike through Cayuse country, I'll be headin' on."

While they were paying for their purchases, Pambrun, the trading post factor appeared. "Did yuh meet with the Oblate fathers?" he asked.

"Yep, we did thet," Deacon replied. "Treated us right well."

"What's the news up that way?" Pambrun queried. "Did McClellan's surveying party stop by?"

"Why, yes it did," Joe answered, surprised that the Hudson's Bay man was so well informed. "Where did you get your news?"

"You Americans are about as subtle as a herd of elephants thunderin' through a brush patch," Pambrun smirked. "A party under the command of a Lieutenant Saxton just left, going north through Palouse country. I tried to persuade them against it, but you couldn't have changed that young lieutenant's mind without beating him over the head -- stubborn as a mealymouthed mule."

Pambrun wagged his head. "You know the Palouse don't feel kindly toward Blue Coats. 'Member that volunteer outfit under Gilliam thet had a set-to with the Palouse . . . ran off a slew of their horses and plugged a bunch of their braves? I'll tell you they ain't forgot that, not by a long shot."

Joe nodded thoughtfully. He certainly did remember. When they had come to the Indian village he, himself, had gone ahead to determine if the people were friendly or hostile. "It's a Palouse camp," he had told Gilliam. "They're peaceful folk. They had nothing to do with the Whitman Mission tragedy."

"I don't give a hoot what label you give them. They're bloody Redskins," Gilliam had replied. "It's our business to sort them out." He ordered the men into the village. He collared the chief and accused him of harboring fugitives. When the chief claimed his people were innocent, Gilliam became furious. He ordered his men to round up the village horses and drive them away. "If these people won't cooperate, we'll give them a damn good reason to do so," Gilliam had declared.

Joe inwardly groaned. What a terrible mistake that had been. The Palouse loved their horses nearly as much as they did their children. Hardly had Gilliam's volunteers left the village before the Palouse came after them, viciously descending upon the column. The battle lasted all afternoon, through the night and into the following day. His brother-in-law, Macon Laird, who had his big bay shot out from under him, had barely escaped with his life. What a terrible day, and all because the leader of the volunteers was too arrogant to listen to advice.

The former trapping partners rode away from Fort Walla Walla with Pambrun's stinging words ringing in their ears. "I believe thet fella'd love ta see this railroad business go bust," Deacon commented. "Course, he's lookin' out fer hisself. Once those slick eastern traders git planted here Hudson's Bay'll be no more. 'Twouldn't put it past the ornery varmint ta do mischief. He might hev sent thet Saxton bunch right smack dab inta'n' ambush. Maybeso, we should warn 'em."

Joe hesitated. It would be taking them out of their way, but Deacon was right. As McClellan had said, at all costs they had to keep the region peaceful. Spurring their mounts into a lope, the two riders followed the trail of Saxton's supply column. A short while later, Deacon pulled up and pointed.

"Take a gander up yonder. Ther's our Blue Coats surrounded by Injuns. "Oh! Oh!"

Several armed horsemen galloped straight toward them. "Palouse!," Joe muttered, trying to remember the name of the Palouse leader he once had met. Before he could do so the horsemen charged up, brandishing rifles.

The lead rider motioning for them to ride forward to where a large body of men and equipment waited. It was a mixed group, several soldiers in uniform, other white men in homespuns, several in buckskins and a number of Indians, many of whom were mounted and armed. Alongside the trail a dusty column of wagons drawn by mules and oxen had pulled to a halt. From the piles of dung it appeared the animals had stood in place for a considerable while.

Every face in the crowd turned to watch them ride in. Except for the creak of saddles and stomp of impatient animal hooves, the scene was so quiet it gave Joe the shivers. What had they run into? He glanced at Deacon but, from the expression above the bushy, tobacco-stained beard, it appeared the old trapper also was dumbfounded.

A uniformed officer emerged from the crowd. "What message do you bring?" he brusquely asked Joe, ignoring Deacon. "Speak up, my good man. I am in command here."

"I'm not your good man," Joe curtly answered, taken back by the officious reception. Was this fellow in trouble or was he not? He couldn't chance upsetting the Indians until he found out.

"I'm Lieutenant Saxton under orders to deliver supplies to Major Stevens in the Rockies," the officer continued more affably. "I meant no offense. Actually, I'm in a bit of a pickle. These people have held us up. If I understand them, they say it's dangerous to proceed. A band of young braves have torched the vegetation on the far bank of the Snake. I've been trying to tell them we mean them no harm, but it hasn't done any good. If you know your way around these parts, I would welcome your help."

"We'll gladly do what we can," Joe said agreeably. He rode forward to the edge of the crowd and glanced around, looking for a friendly dusky face. Except for Gilliam's disastrous excursion into the Palouse homeland and a brief meeting with one of their leaders, Joe'd had little contact with the Palouse.

Several of the warriors sidled forward, suspiciously eyeing

them. One seized the bridle reins of Joe's mount, another those of Deacon's mule. They made curt motions to dismount. Deacon was slow. The man confronting him grabbed his coat and jerked him to the ground.

Suddenly the name of the Palouse leader he once met, came to Joe's lips. "Kah-lat-toose," he said. "Is the man here?" The two warriors turned to stare at each other. Seeing his advantage, Joe quickly added. "Kat-lat-toose my friend." He removed a ring from his finger and handed it to the nearest warrior. Deacon dusted himself and fished in a pocket, taking out a twist of tobacco which he handed to the man who held his mule. From the crowd came a murmur. Onlookers pushed forward. "Chief Kah-lat-toose friend," someone said. Lieutenant Saxton alertly ordered a pack of gifts taken off a mule and distributed.

All of a sudden everyone was chatting cheerfully. Hardly before the bewildered white men knew what was happening, they were sitting in a circle smoking and eating, as if among lifetime friends. The Indian leader promised to see Saxton's command safely across the Snake River the next day. Boatmen pointed to flimsy craft, motioning how they would ferry supplies and men. A guide took them up river to point to a place for the animals to swim across.

The fires the Palouse had set on the far side of the river had been a mistake, the Indian leader said. They had heard the Blue Coat led party had intended to seize the land. The fire was meant to keep that from happening. Now that they understood they only were passing through, scouts would guide them into the lands of the Colville and Spokan.

The next day Joe and Deacon cut across country toward the Blue Mountains and the homeland of the Cayuse. "Well, ol' friend," Deacon said as the riders neared the foothills. "I should be leavin' yuh. It's still a long piece ta Lapwai an' a longer piece ta the Sweetwater. Besides, fearin' fer Mornin' Star an' her son, me ol' womin'll be gittin' anxious. She hardly kin stand ta let One Who Kicks outta her sight. I tol' her we'd be away a short while, an' here 'tis nigh on six months."

"One more day won't hurt," Joe said. "You should have a good rest before journeying all that way to the Sweetwater. After all, who knows when we'll meet again?"

Thus, it was, as the two riders neared the Cayuse village of Stickus on the upper Umatilla River, they were startled to see Michael Two Feathers ride out to meet them.

"What the tarnation're yuh doin' here?" Deacon demanded. "Didja come by yer lonesome or did Mornin' Star an' the baby come with yuh?"

"They also are here," Michael replied but said no more.

"Tarnation!" Deacon repeated. "Is thet all yuh got ta say? What made yuh leave Lapwai? Heavens, man, I'm yer wife's father. Jest cause yer hitched ta her, don't mean yuh kin leave me in the dark."

Michael told of changing One Who Kick's looks from girl to boy and Raven Wing's reaction and their expulsion.

Deacon removed his muskrat fur cap and ran a hand over his baldness. "I was hopin' the leetle tyke'd take afta me, but he didn't. Right from the start I could see by the square shape of his shoulders an' the length of him, 'twasn't ta happen. Fer certain, he has the cut of his other grandfather, Little Ned. Sure didn't 'spect thet 'twould be held agin him. There's enuff troubles in the Indian world without family squabbles over sech trifles. Yuh did jest right by comin' here. It'll save us time in gittin' ta the Sweetwater. We kin take off in the mornin'."

"I don't think we can do that," Michael said.

"What do yuh mean? What in the blazes is holdin' us here? From the way things're goin' 'twouldn't surprise me none if there'll soon be bloodlettin' all over the whole bloomin' plateau. These Injun people're stewin' in ther juice now, but sooner'n yuh kin say Jack Sprat they're sure ta be talkin' war. I've seen these signs afore, an' it ain't pleasant ta be caught up in an' Injun fracas. Yer brother Joe'll vouch fer thet. Me thinks 'tis best ta git outta these parts as quick as we kin make our ol' nags move."

"Morning Star isn't well," Michael replied. "We carried her all the way from Lapwai on a travois."

Deacon clapped his cap on his head and reached for the bridle reins. "Sakes alive! What the tarnation yuh done ta her? She's been as healthy as a horse all her born days." He kicked the gray mule into a trot and then into a lope, finally into an awkward gallop, heading straight for the columns of smoke rising from tipi lodges in the Cayuse village ruled by Stickus.

Michael glanced at his Boston brother and grimaced. "That man watches over his daughter as if she were the only woman that ever gave birth. Now that she is with child again, he'll be worse than ever."

Joe grinned. "So, you'll soon have another mouth to feed? Aren't you the productive one?" He was as surprised at how calmly he was taking the news as he was by the news itself. The thought that Morning Star was on the verge of adding to her family gave him pleasure rather than pain. But the next morning when he saw how ill she was, his heart felt like it would break. If anything, he was more concerned for her welfare than either her father or husband. In her condition she never would make it to the Sweetwater. Yet, remaining in the Cayuse village was not the answer either.

"You must take her to our sister, Tildy, in the Willamette Valley," Joe said to Michael. "She'll get the best of care there."

"That is a long hard journey," Michael objected. "The trip from Lapwai almost was more than she could endure."

"We can hire a wagon to take her to Fort Walla Walla. From there to Fort Vancouver she can travel down river in one of Hudson's Bay's Mackinaws. At Fort Vancouver another hired wagon can take her the rest of the way to Tildy's."

Michael hesitated. He had no desire to have his second son, for he was certain the newborn would be a boy child, take his first breath in the lodge of a hairy face, but what could he do? The mother of his children deserved the very best treatment he could give her.

IX

There is little in common between us. The ashes of our ances-
tors are sacred and their final resting place is hallowed ground,
while you wander away from the tombs of your
fathers seemingly without regret. . . .
Seattle, Duwamish

O'Flanigan, his carroty hair looking like rats had nested
in it, and his friend, Rankin, whose gray beard bushed out like a
feather duster, arose early to be greeted by their host who presented them with two mules fresh from the pasture. The animals' ears twitched ominously and their eyes had a mean glitter.

"Here are a couple of critters for you," Craig said. "They
may be a bit frisky but being muleteers I'm sure you'll be able to
manage them. News from the plateau isn't especially good. So
if I were you, I'd high-tail it while I could. The way things are
shaping up, who knows what tomorrow may bring."

Carrot Top was incredulous. "Yuh mean these mules're
fer us'ns? How kin we ever repay yuh? Rankin an' meself ain't
got two cents ta rub tagether, an' our prospects're 'bout as good
as a couple of homeless tom cats."

"Well, at one time or another, most of us have been in
such a fix," Red said graciously. "Who knows, maybeso next
year you'll be doing me a similar favor."

"We'll sure enuff take keer of these mule critters," Raunchy Rankin said gratefully, chewing vigorously on a chaw of tobacco that Craig also had gifted him.

"Yeah, you do that," Red said. "Since you're going to the
Willamette Valley I'd like to have you deliver that bag to Joe
Jennings. It's been around so long he's probably forgotten about
it. He has a sister and grandfather living there. The sister married an Englishman named Laird. Macon Laird, I believe is his

full name. If you can't find Joe, leave it with these folks."

The Irishman patted his mule tentatively and quickly swung into the saddle. Just as quickly he went flying to land flat on the ground. He dusted himself off and glared at Red Craig.

"What kinda critters are these buggers, anyhow? Ain't they been rid afore?"

"Well, not much," Craig admitted, smiling to himself. These two tenderfoots talked big, but, like he figured, still had a lot to learn.. "I took it for granted that experienced mule skinners like you could manage them without half trying."

After a short skirmish, during which Raunchy Rankin received a painful kick in the shin, the riders were mounted.

"Have a safe journey" Craig said, still chuckling to himself. "Indian people don't take to mules, so they shouldn't be stealing them."

"Wish he hadn't mentioned Injuns," Raunchy said, rubbing his bruised leg. "The next people we meet up with are the Cayuses, the ones who murdered the Whitmans."

"Aye, but those who committed the crimes was hanged," Carrot Top replied. "A fellow called Meek sure saw ta thet."

"I hear tell they made a mistake an' hanged most of the wrong people. The worst killers got away."

"Aye, thet's what they say," the Irishman agreed. "Wish yuh hadn't brought thet up. Fer sure, now I'll be seein' cutthroats behind every tree, bush an' rock."

As the two riders passed from the forested lands of the Nimpau and into the treeless plains of the Cayuse and Palouse, not an Indian person did they see. Except for long-legged jack rabbits, a lone coyote and a few magpie birds, they saw little wildlife. The lack of living creatures was nearly as threatening as meeting up with hordes of people. The empty, never-ending, open space began to wear on the two riders' nerves.

"I ain't likin' this a bit," Raunchy declared. "Where's all the livin' creatures gone? Surely the sight of these ornery mules ain't sent every human bein' an' wild beast inta hidin'."

They made camp on a creek that was nearly dry and settled in for the night. As dusk fell the silence that made the riders nervous turned into a creeping wave of sound that grew into an ear-shattering crescendo. It began with the chirp of a cricket, to be joined by another and another, growing into a rhythmical chorus. As if to challenge the crickets, deep voices of frogs began to throb. From somewhere lonely yips of coyotes joined in. The men glanced at each other and grimaced, both wishing the silence they complained about would return.

The two men awakened the next morning weary from lack of sleep. O'Flanigan, whose carrot hair was now matted like a skein of unraveled thread, went to collect the mules. The one he had ridden wouldn't budge. Only when he seized a floppy ear and twisted it with all his might would the mule move. "Thet blasted Craig gave us these mules on purpose," he stormed. The Irishman's anger increased as the mule kept shying away while he struggled to load the Jennings' bag. "This bloody packet must weigh two stone. What yuh 'spose the bloody thing holds? I hev half a notion ta leave the cursed thing by the trail."

"Better not," Raunchy advised. "These mountain men're touchy people. Look at thet French Canadian crew the governor hired, tougher than a basket of snakes. We're goin' ta hev enuff trouble dodgin' Injuns, without takin' on mountain men, too."

Raunchy Rankin's fears were soon realized. The riders topped a ridge to see three Indian horsemen waiting in the trail.

**

From his favorite lookout on the hillside, Vision Seeker had watched the two mule riders leave. There was something familiar about that bag behind the lead rider's saddle cantle. It resembled one he had seen years before. He searched his memory. Only one fact came to mind. This bag, or a similar one, had left its mark upon his early life. When he next saw Red Craig he would ask him about the two mule riders and what they might be carrying. He caught himself up short and grimaced. Who the people were and what they possessed was none of his concern.

Besides, he had plenty of things occupying his mind and time.

It was getting so he avoided meeting his sister, Raven Wing. Her surly nature had not changed. In fact it was getting worse. Every time they met her lips seemed to draw back in a snarl, like a wounded wild animal might do. Even her son, Young Wolf, watched her with anxious eyes. Instead of remaining near the log cabin lodge, he had made a brush hut on the hillside where he could keep guard over his mother from a distance.

"Why do you not take your mother back to White Bird country?" Vision Seeker asked Young Wolf one day.

"How do you cage a porcupine without getting a handful of needles?" Young Wolf had asked in return.

More and more, Vision Seeker found himself involved with village and tribal affairs. No longer could Indian people remain isolated in their traditional homelands. Whether they liked it or not, they slowly but surely were being drawn into the wider world. If Indian people were to survive they had to face reality. These invaders from beyond the River of Many Canoes had a mission -- turn the western wilderness into what they called "civilization". The hairy faced ones were as relentless as salmon coming home to spawn. If a few dropped along the way, the rest pushed onward until they reached their goal.

Vision Seeker sighed. He could not shake from his mind thoughts of the awesome swiftness with which the Indian way of life was vanishing before his eyes. It left him feeling hopeless. The future was far too disheartening even to think about.

THE GREAT POWWOW

X

What should it matter that one bowl is dark and the other pale,
if each is of good design and serves its purpose well.

Polingaysi Qoyawayma, Hopi

The Indian horsemen remained motionless in the trail. They were the same Walla Walla men, who days previously, had stopped Joe and Deacon. A similar procedure was to follow. The lead horseman motioned for the hairy faces to ride until they came to the village of Peu-peu-mox-mox. There they were ordered to dismount and ushered up to the leader's tipi lodge. The stately Walla Walla chief studied them. "I don't know why these pale faces believe themselves so special," he thought. "The one has the hair of a mangy red fox and the eyes of a swamp frog, the other a bush and snout of a porcupine."

Peu-peu-mox-mox motioned to one of the outpost guards who had escorted the hairy faced ones to the village. "These people look suspicious," he said in his native tongue. "Where did you find them? Are there any more?"

The guard put his right hand to his chest and thrust it away, a negative sign, while averting his eyes and pinching in his nostrils as though the sight and smell of the two mule riders was more than he could take. "These hairy faces are like sand fleas," he said. "Get rid of two of them and four more appear."

The two hairy faced ones indeed appeared suspicious. They nearly were frightened out of their boots. All the horrid tales of Indian tortures came rushing to their minds. The Irishman glanced wildly around for an avenue of escape. There wasn't any. Two men held their mules and camp people and sniffing dogs had circled around on every side. The way they twitched and perspired made Peu-peu-mox-mox think of trapped weasels. They probably were harmless but in these dark days one could not take chances. He stepped forward and motioned for the visitors to enter his tipi lodge. After he did so, he turned to the guard. "See what these hairy faced ones carry," he ordered. "Keep anything that can do harm."

After the ceremonial pipe had been passed around, Peu-peu-mox-mox carefully placed it back into its special carrier. He had no desire to speak to these hairy people but thought it best to do so. They might say something useful.

"What brings you to the homeland of the Walla Walla?" he asked through his interpreter.

"We-we jest was passin' through," Carrot Top stammered.

Peu-peu-mox-mox remained expressionless. He turned to Rankin. "You have Willamette Valley lodge?" he inquired.

"No-no, jest keepin' this man company," Raunchy replied, tobacco juice running from the sides of his mouth and into his beard. He put a hand up to stop a twitch in his right eyelid.

"Hmm!" the Walla Walla leader grunted. Even if these people did know something, they were too nervous to speak. He wanted them out of his lodge before they dirtied themselves from fright. "You people stay the night. At daybreak you go."

Although the hairy faces were served a cooked meal and treated with silent respect, they were too unnerved to sleep. They were up before dawn waiting for their mules to be brought in. Shortly, their mounts arrived, saddled and bridled. A comely maiden glided out to hand them a pouch of food. The guards who had escorted them into the village, escorted them away. At a bend in the trail the Indian horsemen pulled up. The leader pointed to a range of hills that loomed on the horizon.

"Take Great River ferry," the leader said. "Leave Walla Walla land." The three Indian horsemen stolidly watched until the two riders disappeared over a range of hills.

All morning long the two men pushed ahead, determined to put as much distance between them and the Walla Walla encampment as they could. Only near midday did they stop to let the animals drink and rest. While eating the food the maiden had given them, Carrot Top stopped chewing to swear. "Jumpin' Jeosophat! Those thievin' Injuns kept thet Jennings' pack Red Craig asked us ta deliver."

"Good riddance," Raunchy replied, spitting out a piece of gristle. "We sure ain't goin' back ta fetch it, leastwise I ain't."

"Yeah, but for the Injuns ta steal it, thet pack has ta be of considerable value. Wonder what 'twas? From the heft, could've been gold. We should've looked. What dummies we are."

Peu-peu-mox-mox also was inquisitive. He called to a guard and had the bag brought to him and had it opened. The contents perplexed and saddened him. His son, Elijah Hedding, and the senseless manner in which he had been slain, came to mind. With all of his mission schooling, his son would have known what to do. The thought that never again would he have Elijah in human form by his side was like a spear piercing his heart. Why had he kept this bag, anyway? The sight of it would be a constant reminder of the dreadful way his son had died.

He closed the bag and shoved it away. He wished the two hairy faced ones never had come. Ah! What were they doing with things like this? From their looks, between them they didn't have the brains of a field mouse and from their actions it was obvious they were equally as timid. A sinister thought suddenly struck Peu-peu-mox-mox. The two hairy ones had come from the east. The surveying party also approached from the east. Perhaps these two hairy faces were part of a plot to take over Indian land? The Walla Walla leader called for the guard.

"Mount up and take this bag to the Black Robes at St. Joseph Mission," he ordered. If anyone could tell whether or not these things were evil, it would be Black Robe Pandosy.

**

On November 25, 1853, Governor Stevens arrived in the village of Olympia where he would establish his base of operations. Although bedraggled by muddy travel and soaked to the skin by heavy rain, he still put on a display of enthusiasm for the task ahead.

"With your help," he told the gathering that greeted him, "we will put this new territory on the map."

The citizenry was impressed by the governor's determined manner and the fact that he immediately plunged into the business at hand. There was so much to do. Foremost on his agenda was completion of the railway survey. It was Stevens' dream to see steel tracks linking the Northwest to the eastern seaboard. Successful completion of this project meant making treaties with a host of Indian tribes. There also was the matter of completing the northern boundary with the British. Ownership of the San Juan Islands in Puget Sound was in dispute.

The presence of Hudson's Bay was a thorny problem. The Pierce administration wanted them to disappear in a peaceful manner. This was a ticklish task. Many Americans believed Hudson's Bay had been behind the Whitman Mission massacre. Ignored were the facts that Hudson's Bay had rescued the massacre survivors and the trade goods the company had furnished to satisfy the ransom demands had never been paid for. Thus, bitterness on both sides was like a festering sore.

In February, 1854, Governor Stevens laid out his plans before the legislature. Onlookers came away shaking their heads. The governor's list of needs was so endless and encompassing, it would take decades and gushers of monies to accomplish. In addition to the transcontinental railway, a network of regional roads had to be constructed. An improved mailing service was needed, as were legal, educational and cultural entities. But nothing could be assured until the Indian question was settled.

The latter was bluntly brought home to the governor. In early March, on nearby Widby Island, a white man hacked an intoxicated Indian to death with a sword. The son of the dead Indian tracked the white man down and took his revenge. The dead white's friends seized the killer, but he fought back. In the fracas another white man was killed. The Indian guilty of killing the two white men was traced to a Snohomish village. Stevens demanded the guilty party be surrendered. The villagers refused.

To extract a measure of justice, Stevens burned the Snohomish people's canoes.

It did not take the wisdom of a King Solomon to realize Governor Stevens' ambitious program was far beyond the capabilities and resources of the fledgling territory. The federal government would have to lend a hand. Stevens quickly made up his mind to take his problems to the national capitol. On March 26, 1854, he and a group of hand picked associates boarded a ship bound for the east coast. The party crossed the Panama Isthmus and arrived in New York in May. After collecting his family, who had remained in New England, Stevens journeyed to the nation's capitol to present his problems to congress and various department heads.

Things did not go as Stevens wished. The continental railway survey so close to his heart, immediately ran into trouble. In crossing the Isthmus of Panama an important portion of the report documents had been packed in the baggage and were lost, no one seemed to know where. His request for additional funding was turned down. Secretary of War, Jefferson Davis, looked on the northern route for the continental railroad with disfavor. He wanted it to connect the southern states with the west. The struggle for supremacy between the south and north that would soon result in the Civil War, was the final straw that dashed Stevens' dream of linking the Northwest to the eastern seaboard.

Discord amongst his own party also emerged to frustrate Stevens' attempts to further his ambitious goals. He and McClellan quarreled. McClellan insisted passes through the northern Cascades would not allow year-around traffic. Deep winter snow would block the passages for months at a time. Indirectly, McClellan, whose specialty was engineering, supported Jefferson Davis' plan for a southern route for the railway, causing a rift between Stevens and McClellan that was impossible to bridge. Instead of returning to the Northwest, McClellan chose to cross the Atlantic as an observer of the Crimean War.

While Governor Stevens battled to secure support for his

various projects, Indian tribes in the Northwest continued to make plans for the time when he would return. News from the territorial capital made it clear that upon his arrival Governor Chief Stevens would launch a treaty drive that would lay claims to Indian lands. The government would designate the acreage they wanted -- what was leftover would be for the Indian.

To prepare for this eventuality, tribal leaders got together and mapped out the territories that would make up their homelands. Some claims were modest, others unrealistic. Five Crows of the Cayuse claimed the Grande Ronde Valley, and from the Umatilla river down the Columbia to the John Day River in Oregon. Tuekakas, Old Joseph of the Wellamotkins, made claim to the land drained by the Salmon and Little Salmon rivers, the headwaters of the Weiser, Payette and the Wallowa Valley.

When all the claims were mapped out they included nearly all land between the Rockies and the Cascades, leaving nothing for the white man. Except for Stickus of the Cayuse, Lawyer of Kamiah band of Nimpau and Garry of the Spokans, the leaders vowed to fight rather than give up any of their claims. The land claims were to be kept secret from the hairy faces until Governor Chief Stevens came to make treaties. When he announced the lands he wanted to purchase, Indian leaders would say this land already had been claimed. Since there was no land for sale the council meetings would fail. The governor would leave them in peace.

Unfortunately, there was a traitor in the Indian gathering. Lawyer, of the Kamiah band of Nimpau, who fancied himself a cut above his Indian brethren, informed government authorities of the land claim plan. When Stevens returned late in the year, he knew what he faced. He would be ready for those scallywags. It would take more than a bunch of conniving aborigines to get the best of Governor Isaac I. Stevens.

THE GREAT POWWOW

XI

At last we are face to face with those dreaded people, the
coming of whom was foretold by the old medicine man,
Watumnah, long ago.

Kamiakin, Yakama

Vision Seeker was dispirited. Never a person to reveal his emotions, he continued to conduct himself with his usual aplomb. It was at night, after darkness had fallen, that his countenance took on the look of a troubled man.

Running Turtle, who had the task of watching over the herd at night, was the only one who knew of his brother's distress. One evening, in circling the herd, he came upon Vision Seeker staring into the embers of a dying campfire, lost in thought. Long shadows etched the furrows in his brother's face like marks of a badger's claw. For the first time ever, Running Turtle, realized his brother carried a burden almost too great to bear. Rather than make his presence known, Running Turtle slipped away. "It is Raven Wing. She is making us all old before our time," he thought to himself.

It indeed was Raven Wing who weighed heavily on Vision Seeker's mind. From the day she had driven Michael's family away, he had tried to reason with her. As patriarch, it was his responsibility to hold the family together, but the family was wrenched apart as if sliced with a knife. Raven Wing remained adamant. She was glad her son's family was gone. Never would they darken her door again, she vowed. For days after their departure she remained inside the cabin and wouldn't let anyone in. Speaking to her had to be done through the closed door.

Raven Wing's second son, Young Wolf, was no help. He sided with Raven Wing, guarding her like a mother bear protecting her cub. Vision Seeker was ashamed to admit he never had liked Young Wolf. He could not forget the deceitful manner in which the boy was conceived. While Raven Wing's husband, Little Ned, had been away, she took up with the treacherous French-Canadian trapper, Francois. For days Raven Wing had left her firstborn, Michael, alone in the log cabin while she went to her lover, spending hours with him in a nearby tipi lodge.

Vision Seeker had discovered the clandestine love affair by chance. He happened by the log cabin to hear baby Michael screaming. He entered the cabin to find the baby alone on the buffalo robe covered sleeping pallet, hungry and dirty. After tending to the child, Vision Seeker went in search of the baby's mother. On the creek bank not far away was a newly erected tipi lodge. From within came sounds of . . . "Wagh!" The thought of that moment still made his blood boil.

Upon Little Ned's return Raven Wing acted so brazenly it was sickening. Hardly had she left her lover's embrace before running to her husband, cooing like a mourning dove. Francois had been equally shameless. He continued to hang around. That was too much. He could remain a bystander no longer. In the dark of night Vision Seeker had cut his way into Francois' lodge, sliced off half the man's ear and ordered him to leave Lapwai. If not, the next time they met he would slash Francois' throat.

"Agh!" Vision Seeker groaned. What was the matter with him, recalling old ills when there were so many new ones to face? As mountain man Deacon often said, "let sleeping dogs lie".

**

A few days later the big man from White Bird country came riding up to Vision Seeker's hillside retreat and swung down as calmly as if invited. Vision Seeker inwardly fumed. He liked his privacy. Anyone entering this private place without invitation, irked him, but as usual Vision Seeker concealed his irritation and greeted the man politely.

"Dismount and join me," he invited.

The big man rode a short distance and dropped the horse's reins beside a patch of grass. He loosened the saddle and patted the animal's neck. In few strides he loomed over Vision Seeker, grasping the hand in his enormous paw. "You are a good man. I am a good man," Tall Horse said. "Let us sit and talk."

The big warm brown eyes reminded Vision Seeker of a friendly dog that had been given to him as a child. From the way the big fellow tended to his horse one could tell he was kind . . . perhaps this man called Tall Horse was the answer to temperamental Raven Wing's problems. Vision Seeker reached for his pipe bag. They smoked in companionable silence. After the pipe was cleaned and put away, Tall Horse spoke.

"I come to talk of your sister," he said, his voice soft but echoic. "My lodge and heart are empty. I need a woman to fill them. Your sister needs a man. Young Wolf, says she is unhappy. Let us make a bargain."

Vision Seeker inwardly grimaced. So the big man had spoken to Young Wolf who had told him of his special retreat. His dislike for the scamp went up a notch. "If you want to bargain, do it with Young Wolf." The words were out before he could call them back.

"Young Wolf has no horses," the big man said simply.

Vision Seeker gave him a sharp glance. "How many horses do you need?" Again he had spoken without thinking.

"Maybe 10 - 12 and a few cattle," Tall Horse replied. "You do not wish to shame your sister?"

"Hmm!" Vision Seeker grunted. Perhaps he should agree. He could afford the horses and cattle. Still, he hesitated. He hardly could picture himself match-making through the closed cabin door. "I will think it over," Vision Seeker said.

Vision Seeker had little time to give Tall Horse's proposal much thought. There was growing concern about the approaching Stevens' surveying party. Scouts keeping watch, sent back alarming reports on the size and activities of the hairy faces and their rough French-Canadian employees. The surveyors popped up everywhere. In the north they were seen on Milk River and Bow River. Others had camped on the grassy plains of buffalo country. Scouts tracked another party through Hell Gate Pass and up the Bitterroot River to its source in the high mountains. It was quite apparent the white man would not rest until he found a satisfactory route for the steel tracks of his steam eating, fire belching monster.

Nimpau leaders insisted on holding another roasted beef feast council meeting. Thirty-seven cattle were butchered and grilled and consumed. The elders who addressed the gathering announced the feast was given to unite the hearts of all Indian people in the fight to protect their lands from the hairy faced invaders. Vision Seeker sat in on the meetings, but said little. He did not approve or disapprove. The Nimpau were a peace loving people. They talked war but knew how devastating it could be. The cruelties the Blue Coats inflicted on their Cayuse neighbors had demonstrated the futility of fighting the invaders.

Shortly after the Nimpau feast the Cayuse also held a council meeting. Father Pandosy, who had been visiting the Cayuse homeland during this time, wrote at length about his observations:

"The Indians are like puppies that bark afar off; now, however, hearing what I do, I say the puppy has grown to be a full grown mastiff. I will recount to you what they say. All Indians on the left bank of the Columbia from the Blackfoot to the Chinook inclusive, are to assemble in Cayuse country. All on the right bank, through the same extent of country, are to assemble on the Yakama." Pandosy referred to these assembled groups as part of an overall plan to exterminate the whites who were on the verge of seizing Indian lands.

Regardless of whether Indian tribes were uniting to go to war, the atmosphere was so threatening, plans for establishing a Protestant mission in the area were canceled. Indian agent, Nathan Olney, advised settlers in the Walla Walla and Umatilla valleys to leave and arranged for soldiers to escort them to safety. Thus, as the curtain lifted on the year 1855, the citizenry of the Columbia River basin, whether Indian or invader, faced a bleak New Year.

THE GREAT POWWOW

XII

I came from the land of the white man to the East where the people are thicker than the grass on the hills. Where there are only a few now, others will come with each year until your country will be overrun with them. . . .
Father Pandosy, June, 1854

The Season of Deep Snow ended and the curtain lifted on the Season of New Grass. The beauty and freshness of spring did little to bring cheer to the citizenry of the Columbia River plateau. Indian people were burdened with the threat of losing their lands. The settlers feared the Indians would sneak into their homes and slaughter them while they slept. Matters did not improve when rumors swept across the plateau that the new territorial governor chief had told the Yakama leader, Owhi, if the Indian people did not sell their land, soldiers would force them to leave. Every man, woman and child would be driven to the north where winters lasted nearly the entire year.

By this time Indian statesmen realized Governor Isaac I. Stevens did not mince words. He meant what he said, and, if necessary, had the means to support his statements with force. After all, the White Father in Washington was on his side. There was no way to fight him. If one did, an army of Blue Coats would invade his homeland. This terrifying knowledge hung over the Indian people like a heavily laden rain cloud -- one misstep and a raging downpour might descend to sweep them away.

Yakama leader, Kamiakin, who had resisted previous attempts to draw his people into war with the invaders, finally was aroused into voicing his distrust. "These people make us look like fools," he told Father Pandosy. "They say words sweet as honey. Behind their backs they hold hatchets made of steel. We give them help. They repay us with treachery."

Father Pandosy, who loved the Indian chief like a brother, sadly shook his head. "It is as I feared," he said. "The white man will take your country as they have taken other countries from the Indians. You and your lands will be seized and your people driven from their homes. It has been so with other tribes; it will be so with you. You may fight and delay this invasion for a time, but you cannot avert it."

The words of Governor Chief Stevens and those of Father Pandosy, spread from village to village, making people frightened and furious. How could these invaders steal the land? Like the air one breathed and the water in the streams, the Great Creator made land for everyone to use. To sell land was beyond the Indian peoples' imaginations. Land was not goods to sell or trade. Land was Mother Earth. If we give up our land, how do we eat? All food comes from Mother Earth. Berries, roots, fruits, deer, salmon -- where will we find these good things? Our sacred places, what will become of them? Will the bones of our ancestors be safe, or will they fall under the plow and hoe of the hairy faces?

The people came together seeking solutions to this terrible threat to their livelihood. A gathering of Indian leaders of all the major tribes met in the Grande Ronde Valley. For five days they sat in council. Unanimously, they vowed not to sell their lands. Eloquent orations were made by many present:

"I wonder if this ground has anything to say," asked Weatenatenamy (son of Cayuse Young Chief who had taken the name of his father). "I wonder if it is listening to what we say?"

Yakama Owhi posed the question. "What are we to do, steal this land from Mother Earth and sell it?"

"This land is our mother. Who of us can sell their mother?" said Stickus of the upper Umatilla Cayuse.

"We love our country -- it is composed of the bones of our people, we must not part with it. . . ."

And so the oratory went. Many of the things said at the Grande Ronde Valley council would be repeated when the Indian leaders met with Governor Chief Stevens at the meeting that would become known as The Great Powwow.

**

The year of 1854 had been a special one for the Lone Wolf clan. The illness of Morning Star was over. She gave birth to another sturdy boy. It was an unusual event, unlike what the parents had envisioned. The event occurred in a hairy face's log cabin home -- the midwife a complete stranger. It was rather uncomfortable for all involved. Michael's half sister, Tildy, who had intended to assist at the birth, at the last moment decided she was not up to the task. She had a child of her own but that was about the limit of her birthing knowledge, she explained.

The expectant father, Michael Two Feathers, thought a midwife was unnecessary. For Indian people childbearing was as natural as eating and sleeping -- a woman stopped long enough to give birth, then continued with her duties as usual. His mother, Raven Wing, had given birth to him while riding across the snow covered plains of buffalo country. Besides herself, the only one present was her brother, Vision Seeker.

Michael had not assisted in a human birthing, but was fully prepared to do so. Many a colt and calf he had helped emerge from the womb and watched as it took its first breath. Why should the entry of a human child be any different? However, he and his family were guests at the Willamette Valley home of his half sister and her hairy faced husband. Even though he occasionally disagreed with their decisions, he went along with whatever they suggested. When Tildy's husband, Macon Laird, hitched a team to the spring wagon and set off to fetch a midwife, Michael made no attempt to stop him.

Although he did not reveal it, Macon Laird was as unstrung by the affair as his wife. He knew nothing of midwives nor where to get one, however, the family who had recently settled on the next homestead had been blessed with at least half a dozen kids. All day they could be heard shouting and boisterously brawling. Someone there had to have experience in bringing infants into the world, Macon reasoned. He wheeled the wagon into the drive and announced his need for help almost before the sweat-stained team of horses came to a stop. Shouting kids and barking dogs greeted him. Soon their mother appeared. Immediately, the children fell silent, the dogs cringed and crept away with tails between their legs.

Macon was appalled. He should have listened to brother-in-law, Michael, who insisted there was no need to fetch a midwife. This woman sounded and looked like a harridan. Her faded ginghams, wispy, bedraggled hair and hands and arms covered with soap suds, were evidence she had been interrupted while doing the family wash. That, and, the exasperated expression on her face, which said, "who are you and why the devil are you upsetting my day," made the usually unflappable Englishman hesitate.

"I'm awfully sorry to barge in on you like this," Macon finally stammered. "A lady at the farm next door is about to give birth. We need the help of a person experienced in such things."

"Nuff said." The disheveled woman wiped the suds away with her apron. "I'm the person you need. Let me get my bag of things. I'll be out in two shakes of a lamb's tail."

The rapid drive back was done in silence. The thought that he had made a great mistake occupied Macon. The midwife attempted to tidy herself. She knew little about the neighbors. She had heard the husband was a rich and perhaps titled Englishman who kept his farm as neat and clean as a city park. She and her husband had intended to make themselves known, but since moving into their new home they had been overwhelmed. While trying to keep body and soul together and tending to the needs of six children, there never seemed to be a free moment.

After getting her hair pinned somewhat satisfactorily, the midwife slyly glanced at her neighbor. He was tall and lean. Above a square chin were firm lips, a neat thin mustache and rather prominent nose and eyes as blue as the sky above.

Someone had said Laird was a family black sheep who had fallen out of favor with his father, a lord or earl or some such titled member of British aristocracy. As a punishment for his misdeeds the father had inveigled the government to shunt him off to the New World and give him a minor post. While he was abroad, that administration had been voted out of office, leaving him stranded in America. The midwife glanced at the mysterious neighbor again. What crimes had he committed? He had the looks and bearing of royalty, but looks were only skin deep. Didn't those English kings, dressed in all their finery, nonchalantly lop off the heads of wives? Involuntarily, the midwife shivered.

The spring wagon wheeled into the front drive and slid to a stop in front of the door. Tildy, who had been nervously watching the driveway, gave a sigh of relief and dashed out. The painful birthing pains had reached their peak, making Morning Star gasp with each contraction.

"Hurry! Hurry," Tildy implored. "The time is near." She held out a hand to help the midwife down and stared. "Bithiah! Bithiah Abernathy!" Tildy exclaimed.

"Tildy Jennings!" Bithiah echoed. "Why, we haven't seen each other in years."

Momentarily, the excitement of meeting each other overrode the reason they had come together. More than a decade earlier they had been close neighbors in New England, running in and out of each other's houses on a weekly, sometimes daily, basis. They had attended the same church and schools. Memories of those days came flooding back.

"What wonderful times we used to have," Bithiah exclaimed. "Whoever would have thought we would be neighbors again in far off Oregon?"

"Ladies, you can reminisce after the baby arrives," Macon instructed. He handed the midwife her satchel, took her by the arm and escorted her into the house, motioning toward the doorway that led to the back room where the expectant mother lay. Bithiah entered to find her patient was a dark faced woman. Standing at the bedside was an equally dark complexioned man. Two feathers hung from his hair.

"Goodness sakes!" Bithiah uttered, but quickly recovered. "We must have hot water." She opened her bag to take out a soft cloth and tenderly wiped the perspiration from her patient's face, her thoughts whizzing around like a whirlwind. She could not believe what was happening. To meet her childhood neighbor was shocking enough. Then, to find she had been called in to deliver an Indian child! What in the world were Indian people doing in the home of Tildy Jennings and her aristocratic husband?

Bithiah had little time to solve the mystery. Hardly did she shoo away the husband and turn back the covers, before the expectant mother gave a painful groan and the tiny pink head appeared.

"You have a fine son," Bithiah reported. "Looks as healthy as can be."

The lady on the bed smiled. "That is good," she said.

The three words spoken in impeccable English, deepened the mystery surrounding this strange family. While Bithiah cleaned and wrapped the baby, her brain again became a whirlwind of confusion. The thought that she nearly had become a member of this weird family made her shudder. If Tildy's brother, Joe, had asked for her hand she willingly would have accepted. Perhaps then she would be lying here instead of this Indian woman. But what had happened to Joe? She had not seen nor heard of him for years. As she was finishing the delivery room chores, the dark man with two feathers dashed in. Before she could stop him, he grabbed up the baby and was out again.

The mother smiled. "The father has to make certain his boy child has all of his fingers, toes and male parts," she announced.

"For heaven's sakes!" Bithiah silently exclaimed, but marveled at the quick way her patient had recovered from the travail. These people were beyond belief. She wouldn't have missed this experience for the world. She patted the patient's shoulder and smiled. "I hope your child brings you great joy," she said.

"Thank you. I know he will," Morning Star answered gratefully.

The lady of the house had coffee waiting for the midwife. Dazed by the events that had happened so quickly, Bithiah hesitated in the doorway. The quiet and orderliness of her former New England neighbor's home was as shocking as the bedroom scene. Granddad Jennings, who had been sitting in a rocking chair near the fireplace, stood graciously to greet her. Bithiah acknowledged them with a bob of her head. A boy about seven years of age, who had been sitting in a corner reading a book, also politely stood up. He introduced himself as John. He stepped forward to move a chair and held it for her while she sat down.

The polite manners of her hosts made Bithiah uneasy. At home it was hurry-scurry all day long. No one had time for the niceties. It was everyone for him or herself. How thankful she was that the children had remained home. What in the world would she do if Tildy and her husband invited her family here? The thought of what might happen made her cringe.

The cleanliness and richness of the rooms and their furnishings were a surprise, too. The floor, what she could see, was spic and span. The remainder was covered by a huge colorful rag rug. Framed pictures hung on the walls. In a carved casing a clock, ticking away the seconds, sat on a shelf. Through a doorway she could see polished copper pots hanging in a row above an enamel decorated wood stove. Tildy served her coffee in a fragile porcelain cup with matching saucer. A layer of delicious looking cookies on a matching plate were set before her. She hadn't seen fine chinaware like this since leaving New England.

The more she observed, the more confused she became. There were so many questions she wanted to ask. What had happened to Sandy Sanders, the school teacher who had crossed the plains with the Abernathys in '45? He and Tildy had intended to marry. In fact, Sandy had traveled ahead to prepare a home for Tildy and Granddad Jennings. But where was he now, and how did Tildy come to marry this Englishman? And what about these

Indian people? What in the world were they doing, living in the
home of a cultured European?

Bithiah took a sip of coffee and bit into a cookie. "Ah!"
she thought, "this is the way to live.   Perhaps if I had married
Joe Jennings I would have a beautiful home like this."

"Your brother Joe, what is he doing?" Bithiah blurted.
"The last I saw him was in '45 at the end of the trail. Dad had
talked him into driving the stock over the mountains. Saul and
my husband Luke went with him. We expected to meet up with
him again here in the valley, but Saul said he turned back, had
unfinished business to tend to, he said. You remember my brother
Saul. He's grown into a big man, has a wife and family. Yep, '45
it was. No one who made that terrible crossing of the Oregon
desert will ever forget it."

Before Tildy could answer, the door swung open and a
slender youth in his late teens entered. At the sight of the lady
guest, he whipped off his hat and made a slight bow. "Bithiah,
this is our son, David," Tildy said. "David this is our next door
neighbor, Mrs. Olafson."

"How do you do, it indeed is a pleasure to make your
acquaintance," David said with a charming smile. "We often see
children at play at your house."

Bithiah stared at the young man. Where in the world did
he come from? And what politeness. He had to be the son of the
Englishman, but could he be? His complexion nearly was as dusky
as the Indian couple whose child she just had helped to deliver.
Bithiah was so at a loss, words failed her. To make her even
more speechless, the Indian husband and wife came out of the
back room. The woman who, just an hour ago, had been in such
great pain, seemed completely recovered. She smiled at Bithiah
and thanked her again for her help.

"Yes, it was most kind of you to come over on such short
notice," the feathered father said. His English was even better
than that of his wife. "We would like you to accept this gift as a
token of our gratitude."

Bithiah took the gift, her eyes so blurred she could not tell what it was. It had been years and years since anyone but her mother had treated her with so much kindness.

Noticing the difficulty the lady was having, Michael kindly explained the nature of the gift. "This is what is called a friendship bag. Cayuse people make them of corn husks. They weave the husks together and decorate them with dye."

Bithiah wiped her eyes. "It is beautiful," she said attempting to smile, trying hard not to reveal the name Cayuse made a tremor race up and down her spine. They were the people who had murdered her fellow Presbyterian brethren, missionaries Marcus and Narcissa Whitman. She must never let her father know the origins of the bag. Although a good Christian man, he hated the Indian people who had committed the Whitman Mission massacre almost as much as he did the Devil.

Bithiah got to her feet. "I must get back to the farm," she said firmly. "By now the kids will be climbing the walls and there's the washing to finish." She really did not care if the kids lifted off the roof and the washing never got done, but if she didn't leave at once she was going to break down and bawl. In comparison to Tildy's life, her's was a disaster.

"That's too bad," Tildy said. "We must soon get together and talk about old times."

"Yes, we must," Bithiah agreed, but in her heart she knew meeting again would be a waste of time. No longer did Tildy Jennings Laird and Bithiah Abernathy Olafson have anything in common. "Ah," she inwardly groaned, "how humiliating and ironic." Her parents always had looked down on the Jennings family. She never would admit it to a soul, but it was the attitude of her father and mother that had caused her to question the worth of Joe Jennings. She had been determined to wait for him but, like so many people new to the western wilderness, her parents could not stand to see their grown-up daughter without a husband.

Yet, here were those Indian people . . . they acted like

they belonged. The tall young man named David had to be the Englishman's son . . . A surprising thought suddenly occurred to Bithiah. Instead of avoiding these people, she had to know them better. She would shape up herself and kids and be neighborly. There was no doubt about it, she never could rest easy until the cloud of mystery that cloaked the Macon Lairds was stripped away.

Bithiah would have been shocked to know the mystery that surrounded the Macon Laird family was far more complicated than she possibly could imagine. The family's past history indeed was cloaked in mystery, mainly because they kept to themselves. Some valley residents were prejudiced against Macon Laird because he was British. For a while it was rumored Macon Laird was a spy sent to turn the Indians against American settlers. Why else would Indians be seen coming to and going from the Laird homestead?

For a time there also was the hue and cry that by being British, Laird had no right to the land on which he lived. He should be uprooted and deported back to his homeland. Inspection of land grants in the Oregon City recording office put a stop to this movement. The land had been claimed by Tildy's first husband who had been killed in the Cayuse war. As the slain man's widow she had every legal right to the homestead.

The Laird family had weathered the past with a fair degree of equanimity, but the future looked bleak. Just before Morning Star's birthing pains had started, news arrived that left all of them distraught. That night they had stayed up until the wee hours pondering how best to deal with this unexpected development. Daylight came and still they had no solution. To relieve her distress, Tildy cleaned the house from one end to the other, making it appear spotless to Bithiah. It also so exhausted Tildy she didn't feel up to the midwife duties.

Now, like the Northwest Indian tribes, the Macon Laird-Jennings family also faced a future filled with uncertainties.

THE GREAT POWWOW

XIII

Agreements the Indian makes with the government are like the agreement a buffalo makes with the hunter after it has been pireced by many arrows.

Oray, Ute

Upon returning from the less than satisfactory journey to the nation's capitol, Governor Stevens applied himself to conducting treaties with local Indian tribes. His first attempt at treaty making began with a meeting of the Nisqually and Puyallup on Christmas day, 1854. Dressed in frock coat and black hat, Stevens, stood to deliver a speech that was more or less repeated many times in the next 12 months. A Benjamin F. Shaw, the only non-Indian present who knew the natives' language well, acted as interpreter.

"We come to you as friends," the governor chief began. "This is a day of peace and friendship between our peoples. Last year we journeyed through your lands and saw your numbers and your wants. We traveled east to tell this to the White Father in Washington. The White Father felt for his children and sent me here to make a treaty for your benefit. He wishes for you to have homes, pasture for your horses and fishing places. He wishes to have you learn to farm and have your children go to school. He asks you to sell your land to make all of this possible. I come to you today, to talk about these things."

The message was interpreted into Chinook by Ben Shaw and then into the Puyallap and Nisqually dialects by native interpreters, the entire procedure taking hours. Stevens' address closed with a promise of gifts now, and if his listeners agreed to treaty demands more gifts would be forthcoming. The result was a resounding victory for Governor Chief Stevens. Under this first treaty he had gained control of 2,500,000 valuable acres of land whereas the Indian tribes were left with less than 4,000 acres, much of it isolated wilderness.

However, a meeting with the Clallam, Skokomish, and Chimakum did not proceed as smoothly. When asked if the Indian leaders had anything to say, several stood to deliver eloquent objections.

"Should we sell our land, what shall we eat?" the leader of the Skokomish asked. " Our food is berries, deer, and salmon. Where then shall we find these things? I don't wish to sign away my land. Without land our people will be destitute and die for lack of food."

Others objected to the loss of sacred sights and burial grounds. A Skokomish named Jim said it would make him sick to lose his homeland. Yet, on the following morning for some mysterious reason all the Indian leaders agreed to the treaty terms. Again, Stevens had won the day.

Tribe after tribe fell before Stevens' treaty onslaught. Objections were glibly overcome by assuring the people The Great White Father would look after his children. Those who feared for the loss of their fishing grounds, were promised new fishing equipment that would bring them more fish than ever before. The loss of hunting grounds was countered with the promise of cattle, pigs and other domesticated meat source animals.

Most of the non-Indian community were delighted with the manner in which Stevens freed the land for homesteading and peace to the region. Old timers who had spent years living and trading with Indian people were far less enthusiastic.

"Look at this galoot Stevens, he promises the moon, stars an' everythin' in between," the elderly fox faced recruit stormed. "Does he think he can pick these things off trees? He's makin' a big splash now, but what 'bout tamorra? One of these days these poor creatures're goin' ta wake up an' see what they've given away. Then watch out, all hell's goin' ta pop loose."

Former fur traders and trappers, a number of them with Indian wives, especially were appalled. The governor was looking at today only. Not once had he expressed concern for native traditions, customs, religion, laws -- nothing that related to the Indian way of life. It was inevitable that sooner or later trouble would rear its ugly head. The easy takings realized today would have to be paid for in blood.

East of the Cascades the Indian people were aghast at the easy way their coastal brethren had caved in. "The man is evil. He cast a spell over them," Yakama Kamiakin said to his spiritual advisor, Father Pandosy.

The Catholic father shook his head. "It is turning out exactly as I warned, and perhaps for the best. At least there has been little bloodshed, so far anyway."

"Are you saying we should give our lands away without a struggle?" Skloom, Kamiakin's brother asked.

"No," Pandosy replied. "Hold out for a good trade. You must act wisely, stand together and bargain for the best deal you can. Right now these people are flushed from victory. The man Stevens hates to be bested. When they arrive, they will be few, but you will be many. They will be amazed at your strength in numbers and give much more than they intended. As they say, a bird in the hand is worth two in the bush. That will be their belief and they will act likewise," the black robe concluded.

Skloom, who had more talent as a talker than a thinker, left the mission in a quandary. "What is this thing about birds in hand and birds in bushes?" he asked Kamiakin. "Birds are birds wherever they may be."

"Pay no mind," Kamiakin replied. "The black robe knows many things. People send him messages from many places. Did you see the big black bag the Walla Walla man brought to him?"

"Yes, but what did it hold? The black robe looked inside and shook his head and had the man who brought it put it in the place where he keeps gunpowder and lead."

"It had to be something dangerous. He did not want to have it in the same place where he speaks to the Christian God."

"Hmm!" Skloom grunted. These black robes with their crosses, incense, and bread and blood they said were those of the god, Jesus, always amazed him. They were good people but, oh, how strange. One did not know if they were practicing jokes at the expense of the unlearned Indian people or really believed in what they were doing.

Early on Stevens realized that making satisfactory treaties with tribes east of the Cascades was a far greater challenge than those of the Puget Sound and coastal areas. Like the plains Indians, the natives of the Columbia plateau were roamers. They enjoyed traipsing from place to place: camas fields, salmon streams, buffalo prairies, elk and deer grazing grounds, even the dizzying heights where the coveted mountain sheep lived -- all were home to them. They loved the freedom of this nomadic life. As Missionaries Henry Spalding and Marcus Whitman had discovered, accepting the sedentary life of working with hoe and plow was not to the Indian peoples' liking.

In spring, 1855, Stevens sent a pair of envoys to prepare these nomads for his planned upcoming treaty councils. Andrew Bolon, who Stevens had appointed Indian agent for the tribes, was chosen for the task. Bolon had the reputation of having considerable knowledge of the plateau peoples. A big man with a red beard and a temper to match, he fit right in with Stevens' French Canadian rough and ready recruits. However, Bolon was a dubious choice. He had an abrasive manner and regarded the Indian as an inferior being. Fortunately, Stevens was aware of these shortcomings. To accompany Bolon he chose James Doty, a trusted man who had taken part in the first council meeting with the Puyallup and Nisqually.

Before the envoys left, Stevens took Doty aside. "Bolon and you are a team much like the double edge of a sword. He is the rough cut and you are the smooth edge. If the situation demands a bit of the iron fist, Bolon's the man for the job. If diplomacy will do the trick, that's where you come in. Diplomacy must be tried first. I suggest you begin with the Oblate fathers at St. Joseph mission. If approached properly, I am sure you can win them over. They can be the key to a successful treaty with the Yakamas.

The emissaries arrived on Palm Sunday to be greeted by Father Pandosy who met with them while his brother priest Father Durie was saying High Mass. Doty was chagrined. It was not the time to discuss business. For religious orders Holy Week was one of the busiest times of the year. Doty, mindful of Stevens' emphasis on the need for diplomacy, begged Father Pandosy's pardon for barging in unannounced and asked if they could meet on the morrow to arrange for a meeting with Yakama leaders. The priest agreed. Bolon was irate.

"Why all this pussyfooting? We were sent to bring these Yakamas to heel. I say we get after the business before these savages have a chance to run and hide."

Regardless of Bolon's ire, Doty had his way. The envoys made camp a short distance from the mission. The following day, at the request of Father Pandosy, Skloom arrived. Bolon, who had expected to meet with Kamiakin, again was nettled.

"Where is that brother of yours?" he demanded of Skloom through an interpreter.

Skloom looked away as if he did not understand. These hairy faces had the manners of the pigs they kept, making rude noises all the time. "He has no wish to talk," Skloom said finally.

"Wagh!" Bolon exploded. "This is not getting us any-where. How can we deal with these people if they hide in the brush like a bunch of frightened rabbits? I say we go flush them out."

Finally Kamiakin did arrive, but remained encamped a mile away. Upon Father Pandosy's insistence, other Yakama leaders appeared, Owhi and his brother Teias. Stevens' agent, James Doty, was finally able to deliver his message. He explained the plan to divide up the land.

"It will be best for everyone," he assured. "On the land set aside for your people you may live like you always have. No white man will be allowed to enter your reservations without your permission. Teachers will be provided to teach the children to read, write and learn crafts that will make their lives easier. All these things will be told to you when we meet in council."

Kamiakin who had sat glowering in the background, spoke for the first time. "Will the payment for our lands be fair?"

"Of course," Doty replied. "All things will be agreed on when we meet. When and where do you suggest that be?"

Kamiakin tersely suggested the treaty place be the Walla Walla Valley at the traditional meeting grounds where Indian people had hosted the explorers, Lewis and Clark. He also requested that all peoples of the plateau be present: Cayuse, Nez Perce also called Nimpau, Okanogan, Palouse, Umatilla and Walla Walla. The time for the council would be at Governor Stevens' convenience.

Doty was not certain this would meet with Governor Stevens' approval, but he agreed to Kamiakin's terms. "As they say, a half loaf is better than none," he later said to Bolon. "However, I think someone should remain here and make sure of the half loaf. Since this is your territory, why don't you do that. I'll round up a couple of chaps, trek on, and invite the Nez Perce. They seem to be the key to our problem."

THE GREAT POWWOW

XIV

*From little causes come great difficulties. That is the reason
we speak from small things to big ones.*

Eagle of the Light, Nez Perce

The spring planting was nearly finished. Now, if there
was adequate rainfall and birds and rodents were kept under control, an abundant harvest would be the reward. These were the
thoughts of Red Craig as he leaned on the rail fence and gazed at
the cultivated field. He went to the spring, cleaned himself of the
dirt and sweat of the day's toil, and strode toward his log cabin
home where his wife, Isabel, would have an early evening meal
waiting. The pair of dogs that had raced up to greet him, suddenly swerved to go barking. The sound of muffled hoofbeats
could be heard above the breeze rustling in the trees.

"All right, you've done your duty," Craig said to the two
barking dogs. "Now be quiet." Uttering doubtful growls, the
guardians did as their master ordered, yet remained by his side,
their tails stiff and eyes fixed on the trail that led down the valley
to Lapwai. Craig reached inside the cabin door for the long-barreled Hawken. He didn't believe danger approached, but in these
days when people were as nervous as livestock in fly season, it
didn't pay to take chances.

Around the bend and out of the trees loped three horsemen. The lathered animals and the dusty coated riders made it
clear that these men either were on the run or had come on serious business. Whichever it was, they were heading straight for
Red Craig's farm. Red thumbed back the hammer of the Hawken
and wished for his hand gun.

"That's far enough," he shouted.

"For crying out loud, Craig, what's got into you?" the lead

rider hollered. "We've come on important Indian business. I'm Jim Doty. You remember me. I was with Stevens' survey party."

"Sorry. I don't get many visitors these days," Craig replied, putting away the Hawken.

The riders dismounted. While shaking hands, the cabin door opened to let out a cat. The tantalizing odor of roast meat drifted across the open space. Doty stopped to sniff. "I guess we arrived at a bad time. We can come back later."

"You came at a very good time," Craig said graciously. "My good wife has a proper meal prepared, and I'm sure after your ride you can do it justice." The invitation was given with a degree of trepidation. It was not fair to land these three ravenous strangers upon Isabel. By the time they ate their fill there would be little left for her and the children. But, the code of the west was that regardless of the cost one rendered hospitality to guests.

He helped the men water and tether their horses, showed them where to wash up and ushered them into the cabin. Even he had to draw in his breath at the sight of the table neatly but plainly set and loaded with savory food. His wife always came through. She was one in a million.

For a while there was little talk, mainly because the diners were too busy passing bowls and platters and devouring the delicious ingredients they contained. Also, the guests were somewhat bashful in the presence of the dark but pleasant faced woman who contentedly watched as they devoured everything in sight. They knew Red had an Indian wife, but knowing and seeing were two different things. There was an aura of solidness and tranquility about her that put a person at ease. She had cooked and served a bounteous meal, and must have had to scramble to make ready for three uninvited guests, yet, she appeared as calm and collected as if nothing untoward had occurred.

After the meal Red Craig ushered the men outside to smoke and talk. "Why the big lather to get here?" he asked.

"A big council meeting is to be held in the Walla Walla Valley," Doty replied. "Kamiakin of the Yakama insists all tribes in the Columbia River basin be present, especially the Nez Perce."

"This is the new governor's idea?" Craig queried.

"Actually, Andy Bolon and I agreed to the terms believing that it would be agreeable to Stevens."

"Bolon! His only merit is his red beard."

Doty glanced at Craig's own red bush and chuckled. "You don't like Bolon? Is it because his beard is redder and longer? He and Yakama Skloom seem to get along fairly well."

"They're both rascals. As they say, birds of a feather flock together. Neither Kamiakin nor Father Pandosy can stand Bolon. They don't believe he has the patience to deal with Indians."

"He sure can run," Doty said. "That's why Stevens looks on him with favor. If the Indian's can't be satisfied any other way, he'll have Bolon impress them by outrunning their ponies."

Craig and his visitors laughed. Bolon had earned notoriety by bragging he could outrun a horse and then did so.

"Well, perhaps he will be of use at that," Craig said, his good humor restored. "When is this big confab taking place?"

"About the first of June. In one grand feat of diplomacy Stevens plans to make treaties with all the tribes: Yakama, Cayuse, Palouse, Walla Walla, Umatilla, Nez Perce and others. His idea is to establish two reservations for the whole shebang."

Craig shook his head. "Ah, yes, he put the Skohomish, Clallam and Chimakum on a postage-sized piece of ground and got away with it. He won't be able to seduce the plateau tribes that easily. I can't imagine these people crammed together like a pen of sheep, least not for long."

"Why do you say that?" Doty asked.

"These people are accustomed to freedom. They like to move around. Ordering them to remain on a reservation is the same as locking them in prison. Sooner or later they're going to break away and there'll be hell to pay." Craig puffed on his pipe so fiercely sparks flew out to land in his red beard.

Doty was appalled. He had expected Craig to look on the council meeting with favor. If he was against it the Nez Perce surely would stay away, and their presence was essential. Kamiakin would refuse to attend, and Peu-peu-mox-mox of the Walla Walla probably also would refuse.

"Am I hearing you right?" Doty asked. "Are you against getting these people together? It seems to me it's the sensible thing to do, speaking to them all at once. Much more efficient than taking tribe by tribe. It worked west of the Cascades, why won't it work here?"

Craig's face turned as red as his beard. He jerked the pipe from his mouth and jabbed the stem at his three guests. "I'll tell you why. You are treating these people like they are cattle, putting them out to graze in one pasture or the other. These folks love their homes, their land, their families, and protect them the best way they can. Now, along come officious galoots from the east who can't track a fat pig through a snowdrift telling them where to live and how to live. Come down off your high horses and put yourselves in the shoes of these Indian people."

Doty's eyes bugged out in astonishment. If anyone was on a high horse, it was Red Craig. He was standing by the red savages as though they were civilized beings. His trouble was that he had lived among them too long. Doty rose to his feet and motioned for his companions to do likewise. To remain was a waste of time and energy.

"I thank you for your hospitality," he said stiffly. "Before darkness falls we'd best leave."

"Yep, that's the way you birds from the east face things," Craig said, also rising to his feet. "When the heat in the kitchen gets uncomfortable you get out. Well, write your report to the Great Father in Washington and call for the troops . . . make a mess of things as usual. But if you want to do what is right, sit down and we will discuss the matter. Without the Nez Perce this Walla Walla council meeting of yours will amount to nothing."

Doty glanced as his companions sat back down. "You are right. We need the Nez Perce. Their presence is essential for success," Doty agreed. "What can we do to get your support?"

"First of all you can quit treating Indian people as if they all came out of the same bag of beans. Anyone who understands them knows that each tribe has its own way of looking at the world -- customs, philosophy, feelings . . . Take the Cayuse. They are proud people. They don't want to be thrown in with the Umatilla, Walla Walla, or anyone else. Although their ranks have been decimated by disease, they still think of themselves as a great Indian nation. When you go to make a treaty with the Greeks you don't ask the Irish and Swedes to accept the same terms. Why not treat these people likewise -- give each tribe a feeling of importance . . . dignify them with a treaty of their own."

Harris, a gray beard who had ridden with Colonel Gilliam's volunteers, spoke for the first time. "It's been my experience that unless yuh roast an ox or two, yuh cain't get 'em ta sit down long enuff ta hev a proper gabfest."

"Well, why don't you feed them, then? What provisions have been made for that?"

"We haven't yet decided. Far as I know, everyone is bringing their own grub."

"There you go, invite them to a powwow and expect them to bring their own eats. What kind of hospitality is that?"

Suddenly the dogs leapt up to race around the house to bark. From up the valley came the thunder of hoofbeats. Craig went to the cabin door and returned with his Hawken. Two native horsemen pulled up long enough to shout. "Fire! Fire!"

"Where?" Craig shouted.

"Lapwai village. Lodges burn!" The horsemen were away, pounding down the valley trail. Hurriedly, Craig and his guests mounted up to follow. Although dusk had started to fall, as soon as the riders cleared the trees, smoke could be seen spiralling skyward on the east side of Lapwai village. A slight breeze was blowing it toward a cluster of lodges. Craig spurred ahead. If the wind grew any stronger it would wreak havoc, burn everything in its path, including what remained of the vacant mission compound where Reverend Spalding had held forth.

Toward the fire line where smoke and flames were creeping down the hillside, Craig and his three guests galloped. They soon found themselves among villagers with shovels, hoes, axes -- any weapon to fight the fast spreading fire. Men, women and children began to hack at brush. Shovels of dirt went flying to cover smoldering grass. Mats soaked in the creek, flayed up and down to douse cinders and tongues of flame. Children ran back and forth carrying kettles and pots of precious water. Craig spotted his medicine man father-in-law, Thunder Eyes, beating on a smoking bush with an old pair of buckskin pantaloons. The sight made Craig's heart swell with pride. That was the type of stuff these people were made of, when threats to their existence arose, they joined together as one to face the challenge head-on.

Suddenly the breeze shifted, blowing away from Lapwai village. The fire began to climb up the hillside toward the rocky outcroppings where it could do no harm, leaving behind a trail of blackened brush and scorched trees. What had started this fire? Craig dismounted and studied a mound of ash and smoldering wood. It could not have been a lightening strike. There was not a cloud in the sky. People were very careful about camp fires. They knew too well the dangers of open flames.

A ray of light glittered off a bulge in the ashes that resembled molted glass. Just as he thought, besides the mission house, there was only one glass window in the entire village -- Little Ned's former log cabin home. Craig grimaced. The labor and love that had gone into the building were gone as if wiped away by the hand of God.

"What happened to the occupants -- Little Ned's widow and son, Young Wolf?" Craig wondered aloud. A movement high on the hillside well away from the fire, caught his eye. There stood Raven Wing, gazing down upon the log cabin ruins. Her face appeared to be streaked with black. Had she been caught in the fire? He looked again and then again. He could not be certain, but he would swear she was laughing!!

THE GREAT POWWOW

XV

Only to the white man was nature a "wilderness" and only to him was the land infested with "wild" animals and "savage" people. To us it was tame.

Luther Standing Bear, Oglala Sioux

Before departing for the land of the Nez Perce, James Doty had written a note to Governor Isaac Stevens apprising him of the results of his meetings with the Yakamas and Father Pandosy. Instead of a council meeting to be held with the Yakama, Walla Walla and other tribes of the immediate area, the Cayuse, Umatilla and far away Nez Perce also would be present.

In the comfort of his Olympia home, Stevens thoughtfully studied Doty's brusque missive. In a way the news pleased him and in another way it didn't. The pleasing aspect was that he could save time. Rather than hold half a dozen council meetings he could wrap up the entire Indian population east of the Cascades in one fell swoop. The presence of the Nez Perce would be helpful. They were a peace loving people, and from the time of Lewis and Clark had been friendly and helpful to the whites. In fact Gass, a member of the Lewis and Clark expedition, reported the Chopunnish, as they had named the Nez Perces, were the most friendly, honest and ingenious of all tribes.

Yet, would the other tribes resent their presence? If they showed up en masse they vastly would outnumber the others. Besides, in comparison to the Cayuse, Umatilla and Walla Walla, their problems were less onerous. They had not suffered from the covered wagon invasion, and thus were spared the disastrous plagues of diseases the Cayuse, in particular had suffered.

Stevens seized a map and spread it on the desk. Another problem the enlarged council gathering posed was the fact that large areas of the homelands of the Cayuse, Umatilla, and Nez Perce were located in Oregon Territory. If he made treaties without consulting

Oregon authorities he would find himself in a hornet's nest of red tape and bickering, which he didn't need with irascible Jefferson Davis at the helm of the War Department.

"Get me Joe Jennings," he suddenly shouted to his aide.

Stevens furiously began to plan the trip. At this time of year traveling from Puget Sound to the Walla Walla Valley was not an easy journey and there was so much to be done. "Let's see," he uttered aloud. "Shelters will be needed, gifts to be given, meals to prepare, latrines to . . ." He threw down the quill pen, splattering the paper with ink. It was going to take an army to arrange all the necessities. He still was fuming when Jennings appeared.

"I want you to ride forthwith to the Willamette Valley. The presence of the Oregon Territorial Superintendent of Indian Affairs, Joel Palmer, is required at the Walla Walla council grounds. I'm sure you know him, he's been dealing with this Indian mess for years. Somehow the fellow has wrangled the rank of general, so treat him with proper respect. I don't know what he's done to deserve the rank, but anything goes in the volunteer services. Instead of pay, promotions are promiscuously handed around. I have heard even mess sergeants have been commissioned. Let's see -- what date shall we set for the Walla Walla council?" Stevens paused to consult a calendar.

"May 28th . . . ? Agh! Time! Time! Where does it go? There's not enough of it to do all the things that have to be done. To make the request of General Palmer official I'd best put it on paper. By the time you pack and saddle up I'll have it ready."

Joe was not pleased. Instead of heading to his home on the Sweetwater, his partner, Deacon, had remained behind only to fall ill. During a rain storm he had been soaked to the skin. Shortly afterward the elderly man developed a chest cough and shivering chills. The survey party medico diagnosed pneumonia. Although somewhat recovered, Deacon remained pale and weak. Feeling responsible for his companion Joe hated to leave, but could not take him along. Except for Stillings and Sergeant Coombs, there was no one to watch over his old friend. Joe thought of slipping away, but Deacon never would forgive him and he never would forgive himself if the old fellow should take a bad turn while he was gone.

"The governor has ordered me on a trip to the Willamette Valley," Joe announced as he collected his bedroll and possibles. "Shouldn't be gone more than three or four days."

Deacon struggled to rise from the cot. "Jest what I been waitin' fer, an excuse ta git outta this bloomin' hole. Rain! Rain! It niver lets up. How does a body put up with it? It isn't a fittin' climate fer anythin' but ducks, beaver an' pelicans."

"Listen, partner, you're not fit to ride anywhere," Joe insisted. "For your own good you have to stay. The medico said you need a good long bed rest."

"Bed! People die in bed."

"People also die on the road."

"Thet's better'n lyin' here coughin' meself ta bits."

There was no keeping Deacon put. He struggled into his clothes, and would have plodded to the pasture for his old white mule except that Joe had brought the reluctant animal in himself. Nothing less than tying him to his bunk would keep Deacon in the sick bed. Joe assisted him into the saddle where his friend sat clinging to the bridle reins like a scruffy circus monkey on the back of a camel. Deacon looked so comical that if the poor fellow hadn't been so ill Joe would have laughed. As it was, he reined his mount on the trail and led the way out of camp.

That night they stopped over in a meadow made soggy by the constant drizzle. In dismounting, Deacon nearly fell and made no resistance when Joe laid out his bedroll and insisted he lie down. After a meal of gruel and pan bread, Deacon came alive.

"I been thinkin' 'bout death," he said, his voice amazingly strong. "Now yuh take the Good Book where Job speaks of the hereafter. 'The small and great are there; and the servant is free from his master', thet's what ol' Job said. Then there's the way our Indian friends view death. 'There is no death. Only a changin' of worlds'. Yep, both these thoughts're mighty comfortin'." He pulled the blankets up to his gray, tobacco bespattered bushy beard and fell asleep. In the morning when Joe went to awaken him, he found that his partner had passed into the next world, his face as peaceful as if enjoying a pleasant dream. For a long while Joe stood over the body of his old friend. Besides himself, Deacon was the last member of Buck Stone's trapping brigade. He remembered the first time he had laid eyes upon his old trapping companion at Gimpy's Horse Emporium in St. Louis. It had been one of the lowest periods in Joe's life. He had come from Boston to search for his father and almost had given up when Buck Stone and his gang of trappers appeared. Deacon, his round merry face, cheery smile and bushy beard that fell nearly to his rotund waist, made him think of Robin Hood's Friar Tuck and had brightened his day. When he did find his father, who refused to accept him as his son, it was Deacon who consoled him. After his father's death, the kind man again had stepped in to ease Joe's pain.

"Well, old friend," Joe said gruffly. "What am I to do with you? Do you want to have your bones planted here, or do you want to rest some place else? Trouble is -- no time to take you to your Cheyenne home."

Slowly and carefully, Joe began to bind the body in the blankets. His thoughts went back to the time Deacon had read the final service over his father, Little Ned, deep in the Bighorns. A year later in the Land of Big Smokes, Deacon had conducted grave side services for Buck Stone and Clay Beamer. Who was there to perform the funeral service for Deacon? He, Joe Jennings, couldn't possibly do it. Deacon deserved better.

Joe saddled Deacon's white mule. The animal refused to come near his fallen master. He snorted and drew back. If Joe hadn't snubbed him to a tree trunk the frightened animal would have broken away.

Leading the white mule, Joe jogged disconsolately down the trail. He would leave Deacon's body at Fort Vancouver and hurry on to deliver Stevens' message to Joel Palmer. After carrying out his assignment he would make a fast journey to his twin sister's home in the central valley and inform Michael and Morning Star. They would be heartbroken if they weren't on hand when Deacon was placed in his final earthly resting place.

**

Tildy's log cabin home was ablaze with rays of the fading sun. In the blue soft shadows the barn stood in the background like a brooding cliff. Between house and barn, a copse of evergreens sprang up like a fountain, a breeze making the limbs sway and tremble like falling water. In a fenced pasture a lowing herd of cows plodded toward the barn. Behind them came two lads, one tall and slender, the other short and stocky. The scene was so serene and homey, tears clouded Joe's eyes. To upset the lives of these people with the news of death was cruel.

Joe Jennings' appearance did not bring the show of familial affection he had expected. His twin sister, Tildy, seemed preoccupied. Husband, Macon Laird, greeted him affably enough but, he too, appeared to be troubled. Granddad Jennings perked up long enough to say hello and shake hands, then returned to the rocking chair and promptly fell asleep. Michael and Morning Star proudly introduced him to their new son then, they too, grew quiet and uncommunicative. Only youthful John, Tildy and Macon's blood son, and adopted David Malin Laird seemed glad to see him, insisting he come to the barn, which he diplomatically avoided, and help them milk the cows and put out feed for the horses and pigs.

Except for the chatter of John and David, bursting with youthful energy, the evening meal was eaten in silence. The only other amiable utterances came when Tildy related the frantic efforts to provide a midwife to help deliver Michael's and Morning Star's new son.

"What excitement," Tildy exclaimed. "Macon went tearing down the lane in the buckboard, not knowing where to go or whom to see. And what do you suppose happened? You'd never guess in a million years. He comes flying back with Bithiah Abernathy, our neighbor from back home. I don't know who was more surprised, Bithiah or myself. Neither of us knew we were neighbors. Didn't you and Bithiah have something going? Seems as though Sandy wrote that you and she were . . . Obviously, that's water beneath the dam. You would never know her now. I think she has six kids. She married a fellow named Olafson who, I understand, had some of the youngsters by another woman."

Joe choked down a mouthful of food, stunned by the news. Yet, the mention of Bithiah, who at one time had been the love of his heart, didn't faze him a whit. He actually laughed at the surprised meeting of Tildy and Bithiah!

At the end of the meal Joe politely thanked his hosts and drew Michael aside. Under the copse of evergreens, Joe delivered his sad news. Michael's stolid expression did not change. "I knew the last time he was here he would not last long. Morning Star felt that way, too." He glanced up at the star strewn canopy overhead, his lips barely moving.

Joe glanced away. In spite of his brother's mission school Christian education, for things close to his heart he kept to the old ways. He was praying to the Great Mysterious.

Joe's thoughts turned to Morning Star. Poor girl. She and her father always had been so very close. The thought of her pain brought a mist to his eyes. She would be heartbroken. Life for her never would be the same. Suddenly, Tildy's voice came out of the darkness.

"We must have a serious talk," she said. "There are things that need to be said. I dislike bothering you, but something has come up that can't be pushed aside."

"All right," Joe answered, his mind on Michael and Morning Star and their terrible loss. "We'll talk first thing tomorrow."

However, before he finished rolling out his blankets, a messenger arrived with orders from General Joel Palmer requesting his presence. At first light Palmer and party would be setting out for the Walla Walla Council meeting.

Tildy glanced out her bedroom window just in time to see the riders thunder away to disappear from view. "Oh! He completely forgot me. What are we to do?" she cried to her husband.

THE GREAT POWWOW

XVI

. . . we are members of the sacred hoop of life, along with the trees and rocks, the coyotes and the eagles and fish and toads, that each fulfills its purpose . . .

Wolf Song, Abenaki

Sometimes called "the New York of the Pacific", Fort Vancouver lay situated on the north bank of the Columbia River, 100 miles from the Pacific Ocean and some six miles from the mouth of the Willamette River. For overland travelers new to the region, the first sight of the former Hudson's Bay trading post was a revelation. This was no modest structure like previous forts encountered on the Oregon Trail -- Forts Laramie, Hall, Boise and Walla Walla. On a bluff overlooking the river a huge palisade thrust itself skyward enclosing a courtyard around which ranged a number of substantial, well constructed residences and other buildings. In the center of the courtyard stood a canon bound to a ship's mount, and near it a pyramid of cannon balls.

Spreading outward from the fort were cultivated fields of wheat, oats, barley and row crops of peas, potatoes, corn, squash and other edibles. Barns, granaries, root cellars and housing quarters for workers were spaced along the exterior palisade walls to end at the base of a nearby ridge. The entire area resembled a carefully planned and well tended plantation. For the weary travelers, it was like coming onto a fairyland oasis in the heart of a wild, formidable gray-green desert.

However, the small group of mourners that would come to say farewell to mountain man Deacon Walton, would see none of the site's original beauty because for nearly a decade Americans had been caretakers of Fort Vancouver and its surroundings. The proud palisades had lost their stateliness. Fields, fences and outbuildings were in disrepair. The surrounding forest had begun to reclaim the land. The bountiful livestock and numerous workers were gone. Except for a few sheds and shanties, the plantation effect was gone. For those who had known the fort under the rule of John "White Eagle" McLoughlin, the current dilapidated sight of the formerly neat and thriving settlement was like choking down a bitter pill.

Joe Jennings, riding the ferry across the broad Columbia, had time to study all the disrepair. Even the ridge to the rear of the fort where tall verdant fir and spruce trees had stood in a line like soldiers in review looked ragged, like a picket fence with half the pickets missing. This was where the US army was building its own version of Fort Vancouver and, from all appearances, was doing a sloppy job.

As the ferry approached the north shore, Joe scanned the open area surrounding the fort where previously hundreds of acres of cultivated fields, pastures and orchards had flourished. Again, the neglect made him cringe. Somewhere in the weeds and tall grass was the old cemetery, the place where down-an-out workers and transients had been buried. It was not at all a proper place for Deacon's final resting place, but not being army or a person of importance, where else could the old trapper be laid to rest?

Joe hurriedly led his mount down the landing slip and up the roadway that led to the fort. He had hoped Michael would meet him but, of course, his brother did not know when he would arrive. Actually, he was late. The meeting with General Joel Palmer had taken more time than he had planned. Palmer insisted on learning every detail of the proposed Walla Walla council -- who would be there, how long would the deliberations take, what provisions should he bring. . . ? Many questions Joe could not answer, and this vexed the general.

"How can I prepare to take part when you don't tell me what we need? This is a serious business. If it isn't handled judiciously we could have an Indian uprising on our hands."

Joe had ridden away uncertain that Joel Palmer would attend the council meeting. He should have remained with the

Indian agent but had promised Michael they would meet at Fort Vancouver to arrange Deacon Walton's burial.

As he reined his mount on the dirt road that led to the army post a procession rounded a building and came slowly marching toward him. Leading the column was a team of horses pulling a wheeled vehicle Joe could not identify. The brass of the harness fittings gleamed in the bright sunlight. A squad of soldiers with rifles at trail, marched alongside the two-wheeled vehicle. On a platform between the wheels lay a flag draped container . . . a coffin!

Joe jerked his mount to a stop and whipped off his hat. A member of the fort command was making the journey to his final earthly home. A sergeant in full dress uniform shouted an order. The column came to a halt. The sergeant stepped forward and stood at attention. "Burial party ready for duty," he snapped, the words echoing across the grassy plain.

Joe gasped. "Sergeant Coombs," he managed to sputter. The coffin had to contain mountain man, Deacon Walton. How in the world had the sergeant managed it -- a burial fit for a soldier fallen in the line of duty? Realizing Coombs was standing stiffly awaiting for his approval, Joe quickly nodded. "Thank you, Sergeant Coombs," he said, too flustered to think of anything else. The sergeant did a sharp about face and ordered the procession to move on.

Joe dismounted and stood bareheaded, waiting for the draped coffin to pass and then turned to follow when another surprise awaited him. In addition to mourners Michael and Morning Star, were the sergeant's wife, Lucille, and her parents, Bill and Nancy Morgan. They acknowledged him with a solemn nod as they passed, paying no attention to his open-mouthed stare.

"Tarnation!" The exclamation that Deacon had used so frequently, came unbidden to Joe's lips. The thought of the effort Sergeant Coombs and his extended family had made to take part in the burial of a man they hardly knew, brought tears to his eyes. If Buck Stone and Little Ned, lying in their pitiful, unmarked graves, could see the ceremony honoring their former trapping partner, they would think it a big joke.

The caisson halted beside a recently excavated grave. Upon the sergeant's command, the soldiers stacked their weapons and proceeded to place the coffin at the grave side. From somewhere a man of the cloth appeared.

"There shall be no more death, neither sorrow, nor crying, neither shall there be any more pain: for the former things are passed away," the parson intoned.

The flag was removed from the casket, carefully folded and handed to Morning Star. The casket was lowered. Handfuls of dirt were tossed after it. The honor guard lifted rifle barrels skyward and fired a salute; the service was over. The soldiers shouldered their rifles, the caisson began to move, and slowly the mourners drifted away.

Joe remained behind, too stunned by the rapid chain of events to move. The ceremony had been perfectly organized and executed, but he had the gnawing feeling something had been lacking. Exactly what it was, he could not say. If Deacon had been watching from the spirit world, he would have died again, this time from mortification. He was not a soldier, in fact, often was derisive of them and never had been one to seek the limelight. In his entire life no one fussed over him as they had today. The thought made Joe smile.

"That's good enough for you, you old scallywag. That's what you get for leaving me high and dry on the trail."

THE GREAT POWWOW

XVII

*The red man has ever fled the approach of the white man,
as the changing mists on the summits flee before
the blazing morning sun. . . .*
        Seattle, Duwamish

There had been a heavy shower of rain, but the sun already was shining through breaks in fleecy gray-white clouds. The air was cool. Tree leaves and thick carpets of grass, covered with raindrops, were a sparkling brilliant green. The spring storm filled the creek to overflowing. It gushed merrily along one edge of the willow-fringed meadow. Preparations for the thousands of Indian arrivals were well underway.

At the Walla Walla Council site a line of tents had been erected to house Governor Stevens and his fellow negotiators. In front of the tents a wooden frame had been constructed over which several layers of evergreen tree branches were laid, forming an arbor. Under the arbor stood a series of rough hewn tables. Here, important guests would be welcomed, and when the occasion arose this was where they would sit with their white hosts and partake of a meal served on platters and eaten on tin plates. During negotiations the tables would be used by scribes to record what had been said. Stevens, especially, was anxious to have his statements fully and accurately documented. What happened here could very well go down in history as the start of a great Northwest empire.

In the background, behind the tents and arbor, a hodge-podge of lean-to shelters could be seen, some merely canvas pack coverings laid over low-bending willow boughs. In addition, a small log cabin had been erected to hold and protect provisions, supplies and gifts that would be distributed among heads of participating tribes.

By the time Joe Jennings arrived most of the preparations

had been completed. His tardiness was not looked on with favor by Grasshopper Stillings. "Who do yuh think yuh are, some high-falutin' galoot thet can't dirty his hands?" the gangly mule skinner chided. "We been workin' our fingers ta the bone while yuh been gallivantin' 'round the territory like yuh hadn't a care in the world."

"With you in charge why should I have any worries?" Joe bantered. "Looks to me as if you have everything in apple-pie order."

"'Tain't me. It's the sarge thet did it. He's been drivin' us like we was slaves. Since he finished buryin' yer mountain man friend, he's been stormin' 'round like a dog tryin' ta ketch its tail -- do this -- do that -- get off yer duffer, we're behind schedule. He rousts us out afore daybreak an' we flop in bed with the owls. Can't yuh see the pouches 'neath me eyes, yuh could hide a half-grown shoat in each one."

"Ah, quit complaining. You should be happy you have an efficient noncom. He certainly did us a good turn by organizing Deacon's funeral. No one could have done it better."

"Yeah, 'twas done in style, wasn't it? Didja see me?"

"No, where were you?"

"I was the fella leadin' the team thet drew the caisson. Course duded up in those fancy dress uniforms one wouldn't recognize his own self."

"I'm grateful to you. You certainly sent my old trapping partner off in style. He would have been mighty proud. I still don't understand how Coombs could have pulled it off, or why he would. He was not especially fond of Deacon."

"He had a leetle help -- yep, yuh could say a lot of help. Thet missus of his'ns finally let him know who was boss."

"What do you mean? What part did Lucille play?"

"Yuh 'member the Barlow Road fracas on the Cascade summit? 'Twas '49 when me pal Beamer an' me was near blown ta kingdom come. We was dead meat 'till yer brother, Two Feathers, saved usn's bacon. We'uns was laid low; gut shot like a couple a sheep killin' dogs. A bloody Cayuse was reachin' fer ol' Sarge Coombs' scalp. The Morgans was swearin' an' cursin', Lucille screamin' . . . then stormin' outta the woods came yer brother an' his warriors whoopin' an' hollerin', makin' straight fer the Redskin thet was liftin' the sarge's hair.

"Well, ol' sarge may hev forgot thet fracas but his wife sure ain't. The story I heerd was thet if he didn't arrange a slap-up funeral fer Michael's wife's pa she'd pick up the babies an' head fer home -- split the sheets, as it were. She'd a did it, too. Her folks was visitin' an'd take her home lickety-split. As yuh might know they ain't 'specially taken with the sarjent.

"So, yuh see, the sarge was in a tight fix, 'tween a rock an' a hard spot, yuh could say. By conductin' an official burial party fer a civilian he was goin' agin army rules an' regulations which could land him in the stockade -- maybe worse, or face the wrath of his spouse an' his in-laws."

"Hmm!" Joe grunted, too amazed to speak.

**

An African proverb states that the sting of a fly can launch the end of the world. How the course of a life, or that of a nation can turn on a spoken word, a drawing of a line or some other simple, perhaps unintentional act, is frightening. A map is laid out on a rough hewn table, men pour over it, pointing to this place or that, toying with plains, mountains and streams as though sifting through pieces of a puzzle.

Finally, they come to the people. What do we do with them? If we place them in the mountains will they be happy, or cause trouble? We can't have them wandering around like home-less children. Ah! There's a desert. Why not send them there? These people do not like to plow and cultivate the soil. Why give them anything productive?

The rivers must be set aside. They will be needed for transportation and irrigation. The little streams will do for the people. After all, how much water do aborigines need? After drawing a few straight lines linked with wavy ones that follow undulating terrain -- summits of mountain ranges or streams, the planners' work is done. They roll up the map and sit back to toast themselves. Playing God was exciting.

This, more or less, expressed the random thoughts of Joe Jennings as he watched Isaac Stevens, Joel Palmer, Jim Doty and others pour over the map of the Northwest. When they spoke their thoughts seemed strictly based on how best to develop the region (civilize it) with little thought of the consequences for the native inhabitants. The only Indian tribe that was treated reasonably well was the Nimpau, perhaps because their lands were inaccessible, and the least likely to attract homesteaders and city dwellers. Also, they were the largest of all tribes. The planners agreed the Cayuse, Umatilla, Palouse and Walla Walla, small in numbers, would need very little land.

Hardly were preparations for the council completed when an outpost guard galloped in, shouting, "The Indians are coming. They approach by the thousands!"

Governor Stevens was aghast. He had arrived the previous day and had yet to get acquainted with the physical facilities, discuss the council schedule, study scouting reports, establish council rules, or do the many other things that were needed to conduct an orderly meeting.

"These natives can't charge in whenever it takes their fancy! A certain protocol must be observed," he complained. "Here it is May 24th. They're nearly a week early! What are we to do with them? Who are they, anyway?"

From a vantage point that overlooked the sloping plain leading up to the council grounds, a horde of humanity loomed into view, the column so long the trailing end was lost in a spiral of dust. Leading the column was a body of horsemen, the sun glittering on spear points, rifle barrels and painted naked skin of riders. Behind the horsemen came dozens of pack animals,many dragging tipi poles and travois. Leading the animals and walking beside them were women and children. In the distance plodded a herd of cattle, driven by a group of mounted youth. Trailing them was a vast herd of horses.

"Holy Moses!" Stevens uttered. "You'd think it was the tribe of Israelites fleeing Egypt. Who can they be?" he asked, clapping a spyglass to his eye.

"Has to be the Nez Perce," Andy Bolon replied. "No other tribe has numbers like this."

"Looks to be a white man among the leaders," Stevens observed. "Perhaps you can identify him."

"Man with a red beard like mine," Bolon muttered. "Fer sure, that's Red Craig. The Nez Perces don't go anywhere without him. The Indian beside him looks to be the fellow called Lawyer. He's easy to recognize . . . sits the saddle a bit lopsided. Nearly 20 years ago he was shot up in a fracas at Pierre's Hole. There's Joseph from Wallowa and Thunder Eyes, Red Craig's father-in-law. That's odd. I don't see Old Looking Glass . . . probably a good sign. Looking Glass ain't at all friendly."

Two horsemen broke away from the column and galloped ahead. One rider carried what looked to be a colorfully wrapped parcel. Both riders made straight for the council grounds and the arbor where Indian leaders were to be greeted.

"These people are bringing gifts of some kind," Joel Palmer observed. "We best make ready to receive them."

Stevens and his party barely had time to retreat and meet the two horsemen. The colorful parcel was presented with a flurry of words and signs. Red Craig served as interpreter. "The flag is from the Nimpau -- The People -- to honor the new Governor Chief," he explained, "It is meant to symbolize the friendship that exists between the two nations."

"Hmm!" Stevens uttered, mystified. "I indeed am honored." The parcel proved to be an American flag. How in the world did they get it, purchase it from Hudson's Bay? Joel Palmer provided a plausible explanation.

"If I'm not mistaken that flag was given to Chief Joseph during the Cayuse War. He must have guarded it all these years and thought now was the propitious time to give it back. Actually, it is a very welcome gesture. Not to offend him we had better fly it above the council grounds."

In a flurry of activity a rough makeshift pole was erected and the flag hoisted. Shortly afterward the arriving column leaders rode forward. Self-serving Lawyer led the way followed by Timothy, Joseph, Red Wolf, Thunder Eyes, and other lessor chiefs. Each was greeted. They then were arranged in places of honor on either side of Governor Stevens and General Palmer.

Hardly were the leaders welcomed and introduced when a cry from one of the soldiers rang out, "Whoopee! Watch out! Here they come!" Across the open space charged a phalanx of horsemen, shrieking, waving their weapons, and shooting. Riding barebacked and wearing only breechcloths, the riders swept down so near the horses' eyes shone like polished agates.

The painted and plumed animals, their hoofs throwing up fist-sized clods of dirt, swerved in a tight circle to surround their leaders and their hosts. At a signal the horses abruptly came to a stop. The riders leapt down and began to prance about in a wild dance. Stevens nervously clutched at his hat. "What the devil are these people up to?" he asked, his face turning pale.

To the beat of a drum that had suddenly appeared, the dancers continued to vigorously sway and bound about, waving weapons and shrilly yipping like a band of demented coyotes. The white watchers murmured in astonishment and apprehension. For those with little knowledge of Indian people it was an unnerving experience.

"Pon me word these people're a skeery bunch," Grasshopper Stillings observed. "Fer goodness sakes what's gonna happen when those bloodthirsty Cayuse show up? How kin yuh top this 'less yuh tomahawk an' scalp a few galoots?"

Joe, thinking of his Cayuse friends, glumly agreed. The Nez Perce had arrived intending to show that they were the number one tribe on the plateau. With their overpowering numbers and smooth talking Lawyer in charge, they were certain to be favored over the smaller tribes. But was rascally Lawyer the best negotiator for his people? He had the reputation for thinking only of himself. Stevens was a clever bargainer, probably already had recognized Lawyer's weaknesses and would use them to his advantage.

Joe grimaced. Where was Looking Glass? Where was Vision Seeker? They should be present. Both were thoughtful and levelheaded. They held the people's interests above their own. That night Joe cornered Red Craig, his long time friend.

"Why did you arrive so early? Were you afraid you might not find a place to make camp?" Joe asked jokingly.

"It mostly was Lawyer's doing," Red replied. "When he gets an itch he can't wait to scratch it."

"I'm surprised Looking Glass is not here. What happened to him and Vision Seeker? I would have thought they would have come along. If you ask me, that Lawyer fellow needs a bit of guidance. He's liable to give the whole tribal homeland away."

"Quite so. When we left Looking Glass was in buffalo country. Vision Seeker went to hurry him back -- least-wise that's what I think he did. I guess you know there has been quite an upset in the Lone Wolf family. The cabin your father built burned, a total loss. There was nothing anyone could do to save it. The source of the fire still is a complete mystery."

Joe was stunned. Lapwai never would be the same without Little Ned's log cabin. Since the Lone Wolf clan reunion everything seemed to have gone wrong. Raven Wing had turned Michael Two Feathers' family out in the cold, even though Morning Star was ill -- a most inhuman thing to do. Now the log cabin lodge that had been Michael's youthful home was destroyed. Where had Vision Seeker and Running Turtle been?

"What happened to Raven Wing and Young Wolf?"

"I don't know about Young Wolf but after the fire I saw Raven Wing on the hillside looking a bit disheveled but unharmed. Shortly afterward she disappeared. Where she went, no one seems to know."

"Poor father. He put so much work into that cabin."

Yes, he did," Craig said, shaking his head, "but look at it

this way, that log cabin brought Little Ned nothing but grief. He refused to live in the Lone Wolf family lodge and built the hillside cabin for privacy. I really believe if he had remained in or near the rest of the Lone Wolf family, he and Raven Wing would have led a somewhat normal married life."

"What about yourself? You took a Nez Perce wife and live up the valley away from Lapwai."

"I must admit, Isabel is a bit different than the woman your father married. I am told Raven Wing was a trial as a girl and never really grew up. You should know what kind of gal she was, and is. . . ."

"Yeah! She did have her moments . . . but the last time I saw her she was as kind and motherly as a setting hen. What does Vision Seeker say about the fire? He and Running Turtle keep watch over the cabin like guardian dogs."

"I sat in council with Vision Seeker several times since, but he's never said a word. You know how tight-lipped he is. Getting information is like pulling teeth. He doesn't come forth unless he wants to.

"However, I don't think you should worry. That stepmother of yours has as many lives as a cat. After everything she has been through, a little fire is a small matter. All I can say is that I saw Raven Wing on the hillside after the fire. She appeared alive and reasonably well. I wouldn't be surprised if she hasn't returned to live with her White Bird relatives."

"I suppose you are right," Joe agreed, but he did not sleep well that night. "Where was Vision Seeker?" he kept asking himself. For a lone traveler to make the trek up the Kooskooskie, over the Bitterroots and on to buffalo country was risky at the best of times, but the spring runoffs made it especially tricky. He should know. On the way west after leaving Governor Stevens' surveyors on the upper Big Muddy, he had passed that way himself.

XVIII

*They will be a powerful people, strong, tough. They will fly up
into the sky, they will dig under the earth, they will drain
the earth and kill it. . . .*

Fred Last Bull, Cheyenne

Two days after the Nez Perce arrived, the Cayuse rode in,
300 strong. Whooping and singing, they circled the Nez Perce
camp three times as if to show their disdain, then proceeded to
camp more than a mile away from the council grounds. They
were present but obviously not happy about the whole affair.
While the main body set up camp their leaders met with Governor Stevens. The meeting was cool. Anticipating their distrust,
Stevens attempted to win them over with gifts of provisions and
tobacco. Both were bluntly refused. The proud Cayuse might be
poor, but they still could take care of their own.

"The governor has his work cut out for him," the usually
reticent Red Craig commented to Joe Jennings and Grasshopper
Stillings. "These people have not forgotten the Cayuse War nor
the five men Joe Meek -- the pompous ignoramus -- hanged in
Oregon City. I wonder if he has learned to write anything other
than an X."

"Guess yuh've known him quite a spell?" Grasshopper
Stillings queried.

"Yep, knew Meek when he first hit the west . . . had an
ego as big as all outdoors. First off he joined Sublette's American Fur Company . . . so green behind the ears he couldn't rope or
saddle a mule . . . odd . . . him being a farm lad. But Meek was a
quick learner . . . had to be to stay alive . . . beaver trapping soon
makes men out of boys or plants them six feet under the sod."

"More Indians on the horizon," a member of Stevens' party
announced.

"Looks to be Umatillas and Walla Wallas," Craig, observed. "They aren't looking especially happy to be here, but afraid if they didn't show up they might find themselves left out."

The two bands set up camp near their friends and allies, the Cayuse. There was no show of horsemanship, dancing displays or flag presentation by these people. They were disgruntled and did not care who knew it.

Stevens appeared unperturbed. He expressed optimism. "There is little doubt that the negotiations will be successful," he confided to Andy Bolon. Yet, there were many signs that he should be concerned. The Cayuse made it clear they had not forgotten, nor forgiven, the volunteer army under Colonel H. A. G. Lee for its perfidious actions during and after the Cayuse War -- particularly Lee's opening up Cayuse territory to homesteaders when he had promised not to do so. If the sour mood of the Cayuse persisted they might well be the stumbling block that would wreck the council meeting, Stevens thought.

The outlook became increasingly bleak when word was received from Father Pandosy that Kamiakin of the Yakama was against any treaty that involved land cession. "If the governor speaks hard, I will speak hard, too," Kamiakin was reported to have said.

A rumor also came to Stevens' ears that Cayuse Young Chief, Walla Walla Peu-peu-mox-mox and Yakama Kamiakin were attempting to unite the assembled tribes to oppose any land giveaways. Lawyer, always looking for a way to ingratiate himself, came to Stevens' tent to announce the plot.

"Cayuses wish us to go to their camp and meet with Peu-peu-mox-mox and Kamiakin," he reported. "Why should we council with them? We came to hold council with the Great Chief of the Americans. Our hearts are Nez Perce not Cayuse, not Walla Walla, not Yakama. Our hearts tell us to do what is best for our people, not what is best for other people."

That night there was a long session among the white negotiators hashing over what had been learned. Lawyer, with his overwhelming Nez Perce numbers, they could count on. The ingratiating Lawyer was a pest, but a useful one.

"Perhaps Kamiakin is the key," said Bolon, Indian agent for the region. "He speaks gruff and to the point but has the bearing of a king. If we can get him on our side the Walla Wallas and Palouses will fall in line and then the Cayuse will have to do so, too."

"I am not sure of that," Joel Palmer disagreed. "Young Chief of the Cayuse has a grudge as deep as a ditch, and rightly so. He and his father have been told so many lies by our officials they wouldn't know the truth if it hit them between the eyes."

Red Craig, who knew the hearts and minds of the Indian people better than anyone present, kept silent. In the days to come there would be ample time to speak. The first requirement for dealing with the Indian was patience. When thousands came together, it was important to wait and see which way the wind was blowing before voicing opinions.

"We'll make out fine. With the Nez Perce solidly behind us we have the upper hand," Stevens enthused. "Their numbers and Lawyer's persuasive ability will bring the other tribes in line."

Red Craig shook his head and spoke for the first time. "Don't count your chickens before they're hatched. If Looking Glass and his people show up you will be playing with a different deck of cards."

Thus, on May 29, 1855, the council meeting was launched with misgivings on all sides. Even Mother Nature appeared to believe the outcome would be less than bright. The clouds opened up and a drenching rain deluged the council grounds.

**

In the high country Vision Seeker was thinking much as Red Craig. If he could find Looking Glass and his buffalo hunters and get them to the council grounds in time, Lawyer would have to step aside. Looking Glass was a man the people could trust. Time and again his council and actions had kept the tribe on an even course. Although pressured by everyone to get involved in the Cayuse War, Looking Glass had warned his people to stay clear of the whole affair. He was for peace but not at all costs. Particularly he was not for giving up ground that had been the Nimpau homeland since the time of the ancients.

The trip up the Lolo Trail was a journey into the past. Landmarks along the way reminded Vision Seeker of a myriad of experiences nearly 20 winters earlier crossing the Bitterroots and on the trail beyond. Frequently, he paused to relive those days, some events so vivid they made his heart beat quicken and his eyes tear. People long dead came to life.

For a while his father, Lone Wolf, rode by his side, looking ahead for one last big hunt. Then his brother, Many Horses, was there anxiously watching over his four-legged friends. The White Bird hunter, Rabbit Skin Leggings, appeared. He almost could hear the youth explain the need for the Great Spirit Book which he had crossed the continent to find and for which he had died.

The terrible landslide that pitched two pack animals over the cliff and into the ravine came to mind. Their piercing, frightened cries still seemed to echo from the canyon floor. Near the summit there had been the wind storm that swooped down and felled trees like match sticks. Finally, the Lone Wolf hunting party had come to the springs with water so hot it had burned little baby Weasel Face's fingers.

Vision Seeker wanted to linger at each of these places, but time was against him. He had to find Looking Glass and his buffalo hunters before it was too late. Lawyer and his huge army of horsemen soon would arrive at the council grounds. He would be busy sweet talking the new governor chief, trying to make the most of his position as a leader of the Nimpau.

The thought of the damage Lawyer might do made Vision Seeker quicken his pace. Down the east side of the Bitterroots he went, urging his horse to the limit of its endurance, something he hated to do. On the valley floor he dismounted and walked, extending his strides as far as his legs would stretch.

He passed through Hellgate and up the Blackfoot, finally to emerge on the grassy plains. For a moment he paused to drink in the sight of the green rolling hills where buffalo loved to graze. Even the whisper of the wind filled him with nostalgia. He breathed deeply of the cool crisp air and felt invigorated. How he loved this place where the buffalo made their home. The rustling grass seemed to speak of the many thousands of animals that had passed over this ground. It was spiritual. It was sacred. The spirits of the infinite number of buffalo that had gone to their reward, all rose up at once to greet him. "We are gone, but once we were here by the millions. Do not forget us because this is our land, and someday we will return."

Vision Seeker made camp for the night. Before break of day he pressed on. He came to Sun River where buffalo hunters usually made camp. Two lone tipi lodges met his eye. He rode up to the first one, his heart in his mouth. What had happened to the hunters? Surely they had not broken camp to return to Lapwai. If so, he would have seen them. He called out a greeting. An old man emerged from the first tipi entrance and stolidly stood waiting. A woman joined him.

"It is urgent I see Looking Glass. Where is he?"

"He fight the Blackfeet. They come take horses," the old man said, pointing to the east.

"Oh-hah!" Vision Seeker groaned. Those were the last words he needed to hear. Hunting down Blackfeet raiders could take them miles and miles away. To find the hunting party in the wide wild expanse of Blackfeet country could take days. As the white people liked to say, it would be like finding a needle in a haystack. A saying he really never had understood. Who in his right mind would be sewing in a stack of hay?

He sat down with the old folks. The woman, whose face was as tanned and lined as parchment leather, laid out a light repast. Silently, the two men sat to partake of it, the elder smacking his toothless gums expressing pleasure in eating the food. Vision Seeker barely heard him as he was deep in thought. A groan coming from the next tipi brought him back to the present. "What is that? Who is in the next lodge?" The elder held out his right hand palm down and pulled the index finger toward the ground, the sign of death or grave. "Bad medicine. Wounded in battle," he said.

Vision Seeker leapt to his feet and raced to the next tipi. He started to lift the tipi flap only to collide with a body; a maiden with a tear stained face stood before him. From the darkened interior came the odor of decaying flesh and fever. On a buffalo robe covered pallet lay the form of a young man with a face twisted in pain.

Vision Seeker brushed by the maiden and knelt beside the tortured body. The youth was grievously wounded . . . searing battle wounds made by spear or knife and a ragged tear around the side of his head. Someone had tried to scalp him!

Vision Seeker's thoughts again went back to his youth, this time to the battle at Bear Lake rendezvous when his brother, Many Horses, had been shot, scalped and left for dead. The short, round mountain man named Deacon had pulled him through. This man appeared to be in similar condition as was Many Horses. He could be saved, but how did one do it? If only nephew Michael was here with his healing power and knowledge -- he would save this man. But Michael was far away. It was up to him to do what he could.

"Make hot water," he ordered the maiden. "We'll start by giving our patient a thorough cleaning. Dry your eyes. There will be no more weeping. We are going to make this man well."

Thoughts of the urgent need to find Looking Glass and the buffalo hunters, popped into Vision Seeker's mind. Even as important as it was to find them, the search would have to wait. The saving of human life was far more important than getting to the council meeting on time.

THE GREAT POWWOW

XIX

The whites may travel in all directions through my country.
We shall have nothing to say to them providing they
do not build houses on our land.

Peu-peu-mox-mox, Walla Walla

Before making his way to the council Kamiakin sought out his friend, Father Pandosy. The Yakama leader was reluctant to leave his home lodge. "I see no good coming of meeting with these white people," he told his black robe friend. "They have come for no other reason but to take our land. They don't want it for this thing called "railroad". They want it for the good things Mother Earth provides.

"These white people live by taking everything they can from the plains and mountains. Their wish is to kill our thick forests to build homes, fences and things of wood. They desire to tear our grassy meadows and plains with hoes and plows. They speak of the good these things will do for us. They will make our lives easier? How can anyone feel easy when Mother Earth is being destroyed before one's eyes? Who needs an easy life? That would be the ruin of our people. Because we like to live like our ancestors, they think we are barbarians unable to make our own way in life. Waugh!" Kamiakin glowered.

Father Pandosy frowned. Kamiakin's attitude depressed him. If he attended the council in this frame of mind he would come away with nothing. The man Stevens was not to be denied. He had might on his side. Pandosy thought of the recent wars in Europe when Napoleon Bonaparte went berserk. Fortunately, Indian people did not face a tyrant like that, a man of conquest who took what he wanted straight out . . . no council meetings, no quarter or concessions given, villages sacked, plundered, and burned without regard for human life.

At least here, the invaders came peacefully, willing to talk. Somehow he had to change Kamiakin's attitude. The man was feared, yet respected by Governor Stevens. If Kamiakin managed the situation with care his people might fare much better than Kamiakin anticipated.

"My friend, in a sense we all are barbarians," Pandosy said. "Peoples of all races and walks of life do cruel, senseless things, mainly because they do not understand the world around them. They feel fear without knowing why. They see enemies where there are none at all. They see problems that appear unsolvable, yet upon investigation they are easily overcome.

"For instance, take my own life. When I left my homeland I knew what I wanted to do -- become friends and brothers to the Yakama people and guide them toward a beautiful spiritual life. I had a plan that would take me toward that goal. But when I arrived things were not as I had thought. I had made my plans in a dream world. Now I was faced with carrying them out in the real world -- a world that I knew little about.

"My eastern education did me little good. I had to humble myself and learn all over again because, essentially, I was a barbarian. To touch the peoples' hearts I had to learn your ways, your customs, your religious beliefs, the way you saw the world and the way you managed your lives. When I did so we became friends. We understood each other. We made allowances for each other's thoughts and beliefs."

Father Pandosy paused. Why was he trying to subdue Kamiakin? If Kamiakin went to the council grounds steaming with hate it might bring this shoddy business to an end. Someone had to make Governor Stevens see the light. He had set his mind on claiming Indian land and would resort to every clever trick he had. He was not an evil man, merely an instrument in carrying out the ruthless policy of Manifest Destiny that the American government embraced.

Unfortunately, this evil, as many evils were, had been planned far from where it was to be unleashed. It had been planned by people who had little knowledge of the land or of the people who inhabited it -- in this case what they called the "Western Wilderness" and "heathen Redskin savages". They carried out the atrocious plan with good conscience. They were Christians, civilized, educated people. In their arrogance they knew what was right. In fact they were as destructive as any barbarian . . . treating people far worse than they would their own herd of cattle, brood of hogs or band of sheep.

"Agh!" the good father uttered a sound of disgust. He had to stop thinking this way. He was getting more upset than Kamiakin. Above all, peace had to be maintained. Perhaps Stevens and his cohorts would treat his Indian friends better than he thought. He would pray that it would be so.

His prayers would have to be powerful. For unknown to Father Pandosy, Kamiakin's brother, Skloom, sat in the shadows taking in every word. He also was against making treaties with Governor Chief Stevens, but had his own thoughts on how to block them. Skloom, like a number of Indian leaders, was quick to seize upon any opportunity that might embellish his standing in the tribe.

On May 28th, the day before the council was to open, Stevens was brought word the Yakamas had arrived and had set up camp some distance from the council grounds. He quickly dispatched Agent Bolon to invite the leaders to meet and smoke. Shortly afterward, Kamiakin, Owhi and Skloom of the Yakamas arrived, accompanied by Peu-peu-mox-mox and Father Pandosy, who had ridden in with the Yakamas. As the riders passed by the Nez Perce camp they stared at the great number of tipis and temporary lodges. The entire Nimapu nation seemed to be present. Their numbers were double and triple those of the other tribes at the gathering. Father Pandosy was seen crossing himself. To those who knew him, it was plain the black robe was as disturbed by the sight as were his Yakama friends.

Agent Bolon, who sensed their consternation, attempted to jolly them, but the faces of the leaders remained stern and foreboding. It long had been rumored Lawyer and the whites worked hand in glove. What mischief had they hatched at the expense of the smaller tribes? Nevertheless, the initial meeting with the Governor Chief was cordial. Whites and Indians shook hands and sat to smoke, but the smoldering feeling of ill-will soon emerged. The Indian leaders rejected the offer of tobacco, insisting on smoking their own.

Stevens did not blink an eye. "My friends," he said "We are happy to see you. We have much to say, not only to you but all Indian people gathered here. The good will and prosperity of all Indian people are close to our hearts."

Commissioner Joel Palmer added his greetings. "We come to bring peace and happiness and long life for you and your people. Our words are straight and true. We will speak of many important things, but that will wait until the morrow when all Indian chiefs are present. Does this plan meet with your approval?"

Peu-peu-mox-mox lifted a hand to speak. "I have heard that chiefs and some commissioners say the Walla Walla are unfriendly," he said through an interpreter. "Their hearts are with the Cayuse whose hearts are bad. If this is said, it is not true. We always have been friendly with the whites and are so now. We come to hear straight talk, not to be painted black by people afraid to speak to our face. The Walla Walla accept your council plan but do not know your language well. We want an interpreter who knows how to turn your words into ours without misunderstandings."

The commissioners agreed that at each session two interpreters would be present. Stevens ended the meeting with a sigh of relief. Many dangerous items could have emerged, like the sighting of gold near Fort Colville, which was certain to draw miners like vultures to dead meat. As soon as the news got out this would create a problem of untold dimensions, another reason these negotiations had to be successful and hastily conducted.

Stevens bid the Indian chiefs good-bye with a gracious invitation to partake of the food that soon would be served on the rough hewn tables beneath the arbor. The Indian conferees said nothing, quietly and unhurriedly departing.

That night uneasiness hung over the council grounds and encampments of the smaller tribes. Occupants in the lodges of the Cayuse, Umatilla, Palouse, Yakama and Walla Walla were silent, only an occasional bark of a dog could be heard. Even the coyotes that entertained with their nightly choruses, sounded subdued. In contrast, the Nez Perce encampment vibrated with activity -- drumming, singing and dancing went on far into the night. Only the exhaustion of the performers finally brought relief.

"I fear for the morrow," Red Craig said to no one in particular. "The commissioners had better manage these negotiations with care or . . ." He left the sentence uncompleted.

"What do yuh mean? Are you suggesting we're not going about this the right way?" Agent Bolon bristled. "We've bent over backwards to make these Indians feel at home. We can't be blamed if they turn down everything we offer. What more can we do? What more do they want?"

"They want to keep their homelands, and be treated like respected human beings. That's what they want," Craig answered curtly. "Let me tell you, there's an ache in the heart of every man, woman and child in yonder camps. You can't live as long as I have with these people not to become aware of their hopes and heartaches. Except possibly for the Nez Perce, who have the least to lose, there is bitterness -- a bitterness that if allowed to fester and smoulder can break their hearts or force them into a bloody, impossible conflict."

"Ah," Joe groaned, "that's all we need, another round of bloodshed. When will it ever end?"

"Perhaps, when all Indians are dead and gone," Agent Bolon blandly replied.

"Shut up. We don't need talk like that coming from negotiators. Believe me, in Indian country even the trees have ears." Craig rolled out his blankets, laid down and was still. Joe, who had been watching him, saw that his lips moved. Red was Catholic. Was he saying his beads?

The launching of the council on the following morning also was subdued. After six interpreters had been sworn in, it was decided to call off further proceedings. The weather was overcast and rainy. For Joe, who had been cooling his heels for nearly a week, the delay was hard to bear. He glumly sat beneath the canvas covered lean-to and listened to the monotonous drip of water from tree branches overhead. Although Deacon Walton used to torture him with his constant cackle, now he would give almost anything to hear the old trapper say just one word. He missed Michael, too.

Then, there was his twin sister, Tildy. Why had she and her husband looked distressed? Were they unhappy? . . . Vision Seeker, always on hand for council meetings had gone to buffalo country to search for Looking Glass . . . perhaps something terrible had happened to him.

It was comforting when two of Stevens' dragoons passing by, stopped in front of his lean-to. "Welcome, welcome," he greeted before fully realizing who they were. "Sergeant Coombs! I have been wanting to thank you for the splendid funeral you arranged for my friend, Deacon. I'll bet he's sitting up there proud as punch."

"Think nothing of it," the sergeant gruffly replied. "It was the women's idea. Lucille and her mom were after me like a houseful of hornets. The old man also put in his say. I tell you, it's a grim life with in-laws watching every move you make. You don't know how lucky you are to be single."

"Oh-ho! Are you so henpecked you'd give up your wife and sons?" Joe asked, marveling that he could think of Lucille Morgan without a dull pain striking him in the pit of the stomach.

"Wouldn't trade them for the world," Coombs answered with a chuckle. "Come, Grasshopper, we can't be lolly-gagging around like some people."

"Sarge, I ain't had time to say hello," Grasshopper grumbled.

THE GREAT POWWOW

XX

*Death will come, always out of season. It is the command of
the Great Spirit and all nations and people must obey.*

Big Elk, Omaha

It was one of those mornings when everything started off
badly. Vision Seeker awakened to find a cool misty breeze blowing in from the snow-capped mountains. Hideous nightmares
had kept him awake most of the night. Frightening things happened to him in every one. How many times did he jerk awake to
find his heart pounding like someone was beating on his chest
with a club -- far too many to count.

Shivering in his thin buckskin shirt, he rolled from beneath the blanket. His eyes felt as though they were filled with
sand. "This is no time to feel sorry for one's self," he scolded.
His thoughts turned to the wounded warrior he had left in care of
his mate. He had the feeling he should have stayed. The feverish
man had been half out of his head. Hurriedly he walked to the
tipi and opened the flap.

Fetid air struck him like a slap in the face. Adjusting his
eyes to the semidarkness, he knew the end had come. The
warrior's young mate turned a face to him contorted with grief.
Tears streamed from her eyes, rolling down and dripping from
her cheeks like droplets of rain. Quickly he brushed by her to
examine the man who lay as still as if frozen to the buffalo robe
covered bedding.

"His spirit left in the dark of night," the maiden choked.
Vision Seeker took her by the hand and led her outside.
His own eyes clouded until he barely could see. How clumsy and
helpless he had been, trying to cure this man's wounds the same
as he would tend to a horse or mule. Ah! If only he had paid
more attention to Michael's study of herbs and their applications

this man likely would have survived. He put his arm around the sobbing young woman and held her closely. She had counted on him to pull her man through and he had failed her. With his arm still around her, he half led and half carried the grief stricken girl to the next tipi. The old folks appeared, then the woman took the mourning widow inside.

The old man looked skyward and silently uttered a prayer, then turned his eyes to Vision Seeker.

In spite of the sound of the high-pitched, penetrating keening coming from the tipi, Vision Seeker forced his thoughts to the task ahead. The body would have to be prepared for burial. This was usually done by village womenfolk, but it was doubtful if the two women were up to the task. He and the old man would have to bury the warrior. He glanced at the frail frame thinking the elder would not be much help, but the old man surprised him.

"I . . ." he began walking with determination toward the tipi where the dead man lay. "You . . ." He motioned with his lips and chin toward the rolling grassy plain that extended to the horizon.

Vision Seeker understood. The elder would prepare the body. It was up to him to prepare the grave. Where would the spirit of this man find peace? The bleak landscape brought back painful memories. Only two winters had passed since Lone Wolf, on his last buffalo hunt, had fallen into the deep sleep and had been laid to rest alongside his firstborn, Many Horses. Ah, that would be a fitting place for a warrior. His spirit would not be lonely. He would have the company of a former leader of the Lapwai band of Nimpau and a renown horseman.

Making the decision for the burial place was easy. Making it happen was more difficult. Although he had been over these grasslands many times, every hillock and swale looked alike. A knoll with a rocky top had been a landmark. Even so, it took hours to find the twin graves of Lone Wolf and Many Horses. Then came the laborious task of excavating the grave. The sod was thick and the soil beneath solidly packed. Proper digging tools were unavailable. Vision Seeker resorted to his hunting knife and the old peoples' cast iron kettle . . . the knife to break-through the layers of earth . . . the kettle to scoop the soil away. It took him nearly all day to complete the task.

Finally came the part Vision Seeker dreaded the most, carrying the warrior to the burial place and lowering him into the grave. Vision Seeker entered the death lodge and found the body carefully wrapped and bound. "It is good," he said to the elderly pair. It was apparent in their days they had done this before, probably numerous times.

He glanced at the grieving widow. Her eyes were dry. She appeared to have come to grips with her tragic loss. The warrior's mount, hitched to dragging poles, nervously waited. The widow had painted stripes on the animal's sides and fastened feathers and flowers to its mane and halter. The body, placed on the cradle between the dragging poles, slowly made its way across the grassy plain, carrying the warrior on his last earthly journey.

The burial ceremony went far better than Vision Seeker had envisioned. The elderly man carried with him a small drum. When the body was lowered into the grave, accompanied by the slow beats of the drum, he chanted a death song. Somber notes of the drum and the high notes of the song wafted mournfully over the grass covered plain. Vision Seeker glanced at the slain man's widow. This was the time for her to weep and wail. In-stead, she stood tall and proud. Her man had shown his bravery in battle. What more could a woman ask of her mate?

That night, exhausted from the day's work and drained by the emotional experience, Vision Seeker pulled the blanket up and vainly attempted to sleep. At first dawn he had to saddle up and continue the search for Looking Glass and the hunting party. Already three days had passed on Sun River. The Walla Walla Council probably was underway. Perhaps Lawyer already had decided the fate of the Nimpau, but he had to forge ahead. He could not live with himself if there had been a chance to get Looking Glass to the council grounds and he had not taken it.

Vision Seeker drifted into an uneasy doze. Through a hazy fog, he saw himself lying beneath his blanket. Out of the shadows came the slender figure of a maiden. Her smooth skin gleamed in the dim light like fox fire occasionally seen in the heart of a forest. The beautiful apparition paused beside his prone body and looked down. Vision Seeker's heart beat quickened, pounding in his ears like hoofbeats of a galloping horse. For a long while the entrancing will-o'-the-wisp stood as if waiting for him to speak.

The dream was so vivid, he stretched out a hand to caress this entrancing phantom. The flesh was warm and yielding! He sat upright, his mouth as dry as desert sand. He brushed at his eyes to make certain he was seeing straight. It was no illusion. It was the fallen man's widow. She stooped to pull back the blanket and slid in beside him. Like a trusting child, she turned on her side and went peacefully to sleep.

Vision Seeker lay stunned. He had taken upon himself the task of doctoring the sick and had failed. According to ancient tribal custom the doctor who failed to cure the patient had to pay, often with his life. For him the penalty was taking responsibility for the dead man's mate. . . !

**

The rain had ceased, but the dawn brought with it a feeling of uneasiness. The sun rose like a swollen red ball to hang suspended, its rays trying to penetrate the morning haze. In the west the sky remained dark. An owl flapped out of the grove of willows that grew along the banks of Mill Creek. Joe, who had risen at first light, noticed it fly over the council grounds and shivered with apprehension. The belief among Indian peoples that an owl seen flying in daylight signified death, came to his mind. If he had been omniscient he would have known that within that hour the warrior on Sun River had passed to the other side.

Except for the occasional bark of a dog, the Indian camps lay silent. Gradually, men could be seen trailing out to the herds. A few children followed, playfully tripping and shouting at each other, working off boundless energy that only youth has to spare. Tendrils of smoke began to trail upward in the thinning mist. From the camp of the dragoons came the irritating blare of a bugle. Swallows emerged from hiding places silently swooping across the council grounds. From the tents of the white negotiators, grumbles, grunts, coughing, spitting, mumbled curses, and other noxious sounds that come naturally to outdoor men could be heard.

"I don't know why everybody's in sech a dad-blasted hurry ta git crackin'," Grasshopper Stillings uttered in disgust. "The dad-blamed council meetin' ain't 'sposed ta start 'till noon."

"One o'clock," someone corrected him.

"Fer all the blinkin' good it did yestiday, might as well not start at all," another voice volunteered.

"All right, you dog faces, quit grousing and line up for roll call." The clipped voice of Sergeant Coombs sliced through the air like a hammered anvil.

The second day of the council began with promise. A thousand or more Indian men arrived to hunker down in semi-circles facing the arbor where Stevens and General Palmer waited, seated on a rough hewn bench. Although Stevens was anxious to get down to business, protocol had to be observed. The first half hour or more was spent in the traditional ceremonial smoke. Then Palmer stood to introduce the governor.

Finally, the governor was able to have his say. For two hours he held the floor. He thanked the people for the friendly manner in which they had welcomed the survey parties. He went on to speak of the love the Great White Father in Washington and he had for their children -- the Indian people. He spoke of William Penn and how he and the first Indians grew to love one another like brothers. He told of the White Father, Andrew Jackson, who kindly settled the Cherokee in a homeland called Florida.

Joe Jennings, who watched the proceedings from a distance, listened in amazement. "What fairy tales he tells," he murmured to Grasshopper Stillings. "Is he trying to lull them to sleep?"

"I reckon he's afeared ta jump right in an tell 'em he's here ta take ther land," Grasshopper Stillings replied.

Joe continued to watch and listen. Whether he approved or disapproved, history was being made before his eyes. The encampment had to be the largest assembly of Indian people ever to come together at a single location. And the reason they were present was crucial -- a matter that likely would determine the future of all Indian people in the region.

The immensity of what was taking place on the banks of peaceful Mill Creek was mind boggling . . . but also, humdrum. Stevens would speak and then pause to allow the six interpreters to repeat in the various people's languages what he had said. Stevens would resume speaking and the interpreters were at it again. Stevens' voice hurtled across space like the sharp calls of a crow, then came the gobble of interpreters, like the clucks of a dozen setting hens.

The ancient Tower of Babel could not have been more confusing. At the day's end Joe's brain was in a whirl. If he was battered by the ceaseless din, what had it been like for the Indian people who really did not understand what was going on?

Stevens ended his tiresome speech with more talk of the Great White Father. "The Great White Father said, the white man has his farm, his cattle, and his horses. The red man shall have his farm, his cattle, and his horses. . . . That brings us to the question. What shall we do at this council? We want you and ourselves to agree upon tracts of land where you will live. . . ."

"Ah," Joe sighed. "So he has finally got to the point." He glanced at the rows of leaders' faces. Even after the interpreters finished rattling off their versions of what had been said, there was little change in the stolid dusky expressions.

"What didja expect?" Grasshopper Stillings asked. "These people ain't dumb. They knew what was ta come."

Indian Commissioner Joel Palmer adjourned the session, announcing they would meet again in the morning and would have much more to say, but before they closed did anyone wish to

speak? No one did. The Indian men rose to file silently away.
What they thought or felt only the Great Mysterious knew.

That evening talk around the white contingent's campfires was subdued. What were Indians thinking . . . what was
their mood? These questions were on everyone's mind. Within a
rifle shot thousands of red men were encamped. Should rabble
rousers rise up amongst them and set them aflame they could slay
every white man on the council grounds without half trying.

Activities on the third day began two hours later than the
commissioners wished. Governor Stevens bluntly spoke first:

"My children," he said as if he were the father of them
all, "Yesterday we said we want you to agree to live on tracts of
land which shall be your own and your children's. We want you
to sell the land you do not need to your Great Father. . . ."

Stevens went on to tell them all the good things that would
come to them if they should comply. "We want you to have schools
and mills and shops and farms. We want you to have teachers
and millwrights and farmers and artisans. . . ."

The things the Great Father would help them obtain were
like cornucopia's horn of plenty. "We want in your houses plates
and cups and brass and tin kettles, frying pans to cook your meat
and bake ovens to bake your bread, like white people. . . ."

Even Red Craig forgot his role as official interpreter long
enough to scowl. Stevens might as well tell the gathering to throw
out their old life and begin anew. The freedom they enjoyed would
be confined to one patch of ground. The round tipi the natives
loved would turn into square and rectangular lodges of brick and
stone. Their horses would be harnessed to wagons and plows.
Their children would be locked in schools. Unless camas and
hunting grounds fell within their allocation of land, the glorious
camas harvests and buffalo hunts would be no more.

When Stevens finished with his litany of good things that
would occur, Commissioner Joel Palmer took over. He spoke of
tragic happenings that took place as the white man moved west.

"All experience we have had with Indians . . . shows us

that the white man and the red man cannot live happily together. Although we may live near to each other, there should be a line of demarcation drawn so that the Indian may know where his land is, and the white man where his land is. . . ."

"It's well an' good fer ol' Palmer ta tell these Injuns where they should or should not live, but whose gonna tell the white man?" Grasshopper Stillings queried. "As soon as thet gold strike in the Colville gits 'round, yuh kin bet no line drawn in the sand is gonna stop white men with dollar signs in their eyes. Yuh kin betcher boots like a pack of hounds hot on the trail of a fox gold seekers'll be hightailin' it ta wherever the yeller stuff's found."

"Why are the Indian people so silent?" Joe wondered. "They must know that all these promises of good things are too good to be true. You'd think they would be up in arms."

"Perhaps they're jest waitin' fer the guv ta paint hisself in a corner, then watch him squirm as he tries ta wiggle out," Grasshopper Stillings further speculated.

The meeting adjourned without an Indian spokesman being heard. However, that night Young Chief of the Cayuse did send a message to Governor Stevens requesting to have the following day off. He said his people planned a feast and needed a rest from too much talk. Stevens agreed but was not happy about the delay.

"Those Cayuses are not fooling me," he grumbled. "They're a conniving bunch. They may feast, but they'll be hatching mischief, too."

THE GREAT POWWOW

XXI

Goods and the Earth are not equal; goods are for using on the earth. I do not know where they have given lands for goods.
Peu-peu-mox-mox, Walla Walla

Stevens' two former survey members, Carrot Top O'Flanigan and Raunchy Rankin, pulled their mounts to a stop at the entrance of the lane leading to Macon Laird's Willamette Valley homestead. Before approaching the house they paused to reconnoiter. What they saw nearly made them turn away.

"I say, old man," the Irishman muttered, "these people're gentry, no mistake 'bout thet. I ain't seen diggin's like this outside the old country. Look't. Thet's a coat of arms above the door. I'll be tar'd an' feathered an' ridden on a rail, fer certain thet's somethin' only a bloody British aristocratic blue nose would do, let everybody know they's a peg above the common herd. Sure don't think wagon master Joe Jennings would go fer somethin' like thet. Maybeso, we've been on a wild goose chase."

"'Tis a bit uppity," Raunchy agreed. "But thet woman next door said this was the farm, an' if we was ta find Jennings this was the place ta start. Yuh s'pose we should use the back entrance? We ain't dressed fittin' ta go inta any fancy parlor."

"Fer sure, this ain't the ol' country. We's in the New World where yuh kin do as yuh please."

"Ain't yuh fergittin' the Injuns?"

"They don't count. Yuh don't see any of 'em with domiciles like this."

"Well, we don't need ta go in," the raunchy one said. "But 'twas yer idea ta clear the air -- face the music. Yuh was afeered this fella Joe what's-his-name might come huntin' us'ns down."

"Quite so, since we're here I guess we'd bist git it done."

Tildy Jennings Laird saw the two men stop at the entrance to the lane. Both were astride mules, something one didn't frequently see in the vicinity. She started to call to her Indian brother's wife, Morning Star. At first glance she would have sworn the squat bearded one was Deacon Walton, but that was impossible. He lay buried in the Fort Vancouver cemetery.

Tildy answered the hesitant knocks on the door. Before her stood two men, one tall and one squat, both fumbling with their hats like children caught stealing from a cookie jar. "What may I do for you, gentleman?" Tildy politely asked.

"Well, yuh see," the man with the carrot colored hair stammered. "It's this way. We come with rather ill news. . . ."

"Well, you better come in," Tildy said, with a sinking feeling. How could things get any worse than they already were? She sat the two men down at the table, laying a cup and saucer in front of each one. She poured them coffee and made certain they had cream and sugar, then went outside to call for her husband. Bad news was terrible unless shared with someone else, especially now with the family in such turmoil.

Macon Laird came in, hung his hat on a peg, and sat down across from the strangers. "Well, what are these ill tidings you bring?" he asked in his clipped British accent.

Carrot Top's mouth gaped open. He knew this man. He was the fellow who created such a stink on the journey across the plains, an Englishman through and through. Frantically, he searched his memory. What was that fuss all about? Ah, yes, it had to do with some female, probably this woman who poured the coffee. She had been betrothed to some man in the valley and this fellow came along and upset the apple cart. How could he forget? It was the talk of the wagon train.

"Come, my man, what is this dither all about?" the Englishman insisted. "Whatever it is, spit it out."

Carrot Top collected himself. "Yuh see, we was carrying this stuff fer Joe Jennings an' was attacked by Injuns . . ."

"Yep, thet's the way 'twas," Raunchy cut in. "Those murderin' rascals was on top of us'ns afore yuh could say scat.

Mean as sin they was, caught us an' . . ."

It was Raunchy's turn to let his mouth drop open. From a back room a dusky-faced figure emerged. Two feathers, one white, the other tinged with red, were thrust in his thick dark hair. Behind him came an equally dusky-skinned woman carrying a baby. Then, from between the adults, emerged a small stocky boy holding a lance fashioned from a stick. He stared at the man with the fascinating hair, then darted forward, waving the toy weapon.

"Man, oh, man," Carrot Top muttered when he and his partner were back on the roadway. "If it hadn't been fer the parents, thet kid would've stuck me good an' proper; as it was he near pierced me ear. I niver wanta go through 'nother session like thet again . . . must've aged me 20 years."

"Was a bit dicey as yuh British say, but ain't yuh glad yuh did it? Yer conscience should be white as fresh snow, maybeso yuh won't even havta go ta confession. I still wonder what was in thet bag. Yuh could tell from the looks on their faces these people didn't hev a clue, neither."

Raunchy was right. The Macon Laird-Jennings family was as perplexed as the two mule riders. Late into the night they pondered over the visit of the unexpected visitors. "Are these lost belongings important or are they not? If they are, we should let Joe know," Macon Laird declared.

"Why did it have to come up at this time, when our minds already are in a muddle?" Tildy complained. "Where is Joe, anyway? We can't wait. We must get a hold of him. He's got to know what's in store. . . ."

Michael, who had taken little part in the discussion, finally spoke. "I'll go and tell him, at least about these lost belongings. The other matter should be left for you to explain. Anyway, I should visit Raven Wing and my uncles, Vision Seeker and Running Turtle. Who knows when, or if, we will have the opportunity to get together again."

Macon Laird nodded. "Quite so. Sound thinking. It's time we got this business out in the open. We all will breathe

easier. From what I know of Joe, he'll need a good bit of per-
suading, so the sooner you leave the better."

                              **

On June 2nd, the day after the Cayuse requested holiday,
the council resumed, this time at noon. Commissioner Palmer
started things off by continuing to expound on why the white
man and red man should live in separate lands.

". . . Can you prevent the wind from blowing? Can you
prevent the rain from falling? Can you prevent the whites from
coming? You are answered no. . . .There are few whites here
now. Soon there will be many. Let us, as wise men, act so as to
prevent trouble. . . ."

Palmer spoke of treaties made with the Rogue and the
Umpqua and the good things these tribes had received, not men-
tioning the bloody clashes that had taken place beforehand, nor
the fact the people still were furious by the way they had been
treated. Governor Stevens took up where Palmer left off.

"My children, my brother and myself have opened our
hearts to you, we want you to open your hearts to us," he said.

Five Crows of the Cayuse spoke. "We are tired." These
were the first officially recorded words uttered by an Indian thus
far in the now three day-old council meeting.

When asked if he would speak now or on Monday,
(Stevens claimed the White Father did not wish for them to do
business on the Sabbath) Peu-peu-mox-mox replied, "Why not
speak tomorrow as well as today? We have listened to all you
have to say, and we desire you should listen when Indian speaks."

The Walla Walla leader was clearly unhappy. He surveyed
the crowd, his gaze stopping to rest on the overwhelming number
of Nez Perce: "It appears the Nez Perce have already decided.
They want an answer at once, not giving the rest of us time to
think . . . We require time to think, quietly, slowly. . . ."

The council meeting adjourned, but the day's events had
just begun. That evening Lawyer reported a sinister plot. The
Cayuse had used their requested day off to organize a daring

scheme to murder all white men present, he claimed. It was to be the signal for the Cayuse and their allies to launch an all out campaign to rid the region of every white man. Lawyer's plan to prevent the proposed killing spree was simple. He would set up his lodge next to that of Governor Stevens.

"These people will not attack for fear of killing me, the head chief of the Nez Perce," Lawyer explained boastfully.

The threat of possible bloodshed didn't seem to dampen youthful spirits. That evening a two-mile foot race, which inspired a great amount of wagering, was held in the Nez Perce camp. Afterwards, depending on which man the bettors had wagered on, shouts of glee or disgust rang across the council grounds.

When asked about Lawyer's warning, Red Craig shrugged his shoulders and turned away.

"What did you expect?" a dragoon officer commented to the man who questioned Craig. "The man has lived and slept with these people for so many years he has an Indian heart."

As Stevens had requested, on Monday, June 4th, the Indian delegation assembled, late but orderly. Stevens again asked them "to open their hearts and speak freely". Not one to miss an opportunity to gain the limelight, Lawyer struggled to his feet. His old battle wound was aching like fury. He was ready to pack up and go home. But as long as the council held forth, he had to stay and guard his position as spokesman for the tribe. He launched into a rambling talk supporting what he understood were the plans the Big Chief in the east had made for his people.

Kamiakin then spoke, making it plain he was not with Lawyer. "You say your people will do what is right," he addressed the governor. "Before giving up our land they should do some of the things they promised."

Peu-peu-mox-mox was invited to speak but refused. "I do not wish to speak. I leave it to the old men." There was a titter. The Walla Walla leader had to be in his seventies.

Stickus, Missionary Whitman's friend, also was asked to speak. "Where has all this talk come from?" he asked. "I would wish the Big Chief was here that we might all listen to him. Are the words spoken here straight? Our people do not know."

Peu-Peu-mox-mox finally did speak. "The manner in which you have spoken has made my heart heavy," he said addressing Stevens. "I like you Americans . . . I like Hudson's Bay. I am led this way and that. I do not know what lands these Indians have spoken for, but when they mention the land I shall know."

Stevens finally got down to the lands set aside for the Indian people and the tribes that would occupy them.

"We have thought of two reservations," Stevens announced. "One reservation in Nez Perce country and one in Yakama country -- the reservation in Nez Perce country will extend from the Blue Mountains to the spurs of the Bitterroots and from the Palouse River to part way up the Grande Ronde and Salmon Rivers. On this reservation we wish to place the Spokan, Cayuse, the Walla Walla, as well as the Nez Perce and Umatilla."

The Yakama reservation boundaries and the tribes to reside on it were also presented. Stevens went on to give the reasons for placing the Indian people where he did:

"We can better protect you from bad white men there, we can prevent the trader and the preacher from going there. We can better stop the thief that comes to steal your horses. . . . We want as many tribes together as can be taken care of by one agent. . . . I will speak no more today but will speak again. Think over what I have said and hear the rest tomorrow."

Think it over they did, both whites and Indians. Lawyer was disgusted. The throb of his old wound became more intense. His plans for the Nimpau were going awry. He had no wish to share a homeland with the troublesome Cayuse and certainly not the Walla Walla. He had thought he knew what was in the Governor Chief's heart. Now he was not certain.

The commandant of the dragoons, shook his head in disbelief. How could an amalgamation of Indian tribes with different beliefs and customs be expected to live in harmony on a restricted acreage of land? When news of the Colville gold strike got out, who was going to keep avaricious fortune hunters from crossing imaginary reservation boundaries? Neither the white nor red camp slept easily that night.

While the commissioners mulled over what had been said that afternoon, a lone Indian horseman rode in from the west. Joe Jennings, tired of listening to camp gossip, most of it unsettling, had strolled to a rise in the ground where he had a partial view of the vast array of temporary shelters. He immediately spotted the horseman. Could it be Vision Seeker? If so, what was he doing coming from the west and alone?

The horseman stopped at the Cayuse camp where he briefly visited with Stickus and Young Chief. Afterwards, he passed by the lodge of Peu-peu-mox-mox where he stopped to have words with the Walla Walla leader. Then he wended his way through the camp of the Nez Perce, pausing beside the shelter of Thunder Eyes.

"What the devil do yuh 'spose thet fella's up ta, anyway?" The dragoon sentinel who guarded the approaches to the commissioners' camp asked. "He seems ta know everybody. Yuh 'spose he's a troublemaker? Oh, oh, he's comin' this way. Sure enuff, he's Injun. Look't those feathers. I guess we'll soon find out what he's up to."

"Yep, I know him," Joe said. "He's my brother."

"Oh, go on. He's downright Injun."

"Yep, my Indian brother," Joe said and rode out to meet Michael Two Feathers.

"My dear brother," Joe greeted. "What brings you here? Is something wrong at home?"

"We will talk later," Michael replied, dismounting. "Right now I must take care of my four-legged friend. We have had a long hard journey."

After a scratch meal and a second cup of water, Michael spoke again. "I thought Vision Seeker and Running Turtle would be here. No one seems to know what happened to either one of them. Everyone looks the other way when I mention their names."

"Hmm!" Joe thoughtfully grunted. Apparently Michael
was unaware of the fire that had consumed Little Ned's log cabin
and also the fact that Raven Wing had disappeared. He hesitated,
then asked about the family in the Willamette Valley.

It was Michael's turn to hesitate. He had promised Tildy
to persuade Joe to return to the valley. He remembered her exact
words. "You tell Joe he broke his promise. He said we would
talk and he ran off." Tildy spoke with such desperation he was
worried for her health, but he had no intention of getting involved
in Jennings' family business.

There also was the strange matter of Joe's lost belongings. It was safe to speak of them. He told Joe of the two mule
riders and their confession. To his surprise Joe knew one of the
mule riders but not of the bag they were supposed to deliver and
had lost.

"Funny, Red Craig hasn't said anything," Joe said. "Whatever the bag held it can't have contained anything of value."

Not until they were rolling up in their blankets did Michael
speak of the real reason for his presence. "Sister Tildy is most
anxious for you to speak with her. When you were there you
promised, but you did not do so."

"That's right. I forgot all about it, thought it of minor
importance, the family seemed to be doing well."

"But it was of great importance," Michael insisted.

"Well, tell me about it then."

"I can't. It's a family matter."

"You're family."

"Yes, but this is Boston family business."

"Boston family business? What's got into Tildy, anyway?"
However much Joe entreated, his Indian brother would say no
more. Furious and mystified, Joe rolled up in the blanket and
attempted to sleep. Only when Michael told of the redheaded
Irishman's expression as little One Who Kicks took after him
with his stick lance, did Joe relax.

XXII

My friends, I wish to show you my mind. Interpret right for
me. . . . This is our mother, this country, as if we drew
our living from her.
Stickus, Cayuse

Joe awakened earlier than usual. For a moment he lay
staring at the olive green willow branches that screened out the
sky overhead. Why was he feeling so dull and filled with misgivings? He sat up to see the still sleeping form of his Indian half-
brother. The frustration of yesterday's conversation returned full
force. He had a notion to seize him by the throat and choke the
news out of him. Why was it so urgent that he speak with Tildy?
If the matter had been so important why hadn't she spoken up
when they last met?

Joe got up and made for the nearby creek. He stripped
down to his bare skin and doused himself from head to toe with
the cold, clear water. Afterwards, he shook himself like a wet
dog and pulled on his clothes, then strode toward the pasture where
his big black horse had been staked for the night. He fashioned a
rope halter and rode bareback away from camp. The frisky black
broke into a trot and then a dead run, galloping past the camps of
the Cayuse, Walla Walla and Umatilla. Lodge occupants popped
their heads out like startled ground squirrels. Viciously barking
dogs leapt up to give chase. Into the open where the Indian herds
of horses and cattle grazed, the big black raced. Night guards
shouted and waved their weapons but Joe paid no attention. He
let the horse run itself out.

Finally, he pulled the hard-breathing black to a stop, slid
off the animal's sweaty back to walk. For the first time in days he
really felt alive. Why hadn't he done this every morning rather
than stew around waiting for the Indians to gather at the council

grounds? He suddenly noticed where he was; ahead was the hill that loomed above the old Whitman Mission compound. At the base of the hill was the grave that held the bodies of the murder victims. The thought of their untimely, and gruesome demise made his heart ache. He removed his hat in deference to their memory. As he started to lead the black toward the grave site, a lone coyote emerged from the bushes on the hilltop. Pointing its muzzle skyward, it let out a blood curdling howl that made Joe's flesh crawl. The black jerked the halter rein from his hand and bolted away, running as if fleeing from a thousand demons.

"Whoa! Whoa!" Joe shouted, but there was no stopping the horse until it returned to camp. For a moment Joe lingered by the mass grave and then began retracing his steps. The coolness of the morning soon wore off. The sun beat down unmercifully. The rough soil cut into his moccasin covered feet. He was so thirsty he hardly could wet his lips. The farther he walked the more infuriated he became. It was all his blasted tight-lipped brother's fault. When he saw him again, he would wring his neck. Yet, mid-morning when Michael appeared riding one horse and leading another, Joe could have hugged him for joy. He mounted up and the two of them rode back to camp without saying a word.

By the time the brothers arrived at the Mill Creek council site, the Indian conferees already had begun to gather. Again the commissioners asked Indian leaders to open their hearts. They didn't say so, but they were getting anxious. They had explained everything and still nothing was settled.

The commissioners' hopes brightened when Lawyer of the Nez Perce rose to speak first. If the Nez Perce supported the treaty everyone else soon would fall in line, Governor Stevens reasoned. But Lawyer, in pain from his wound, was not in good form. The aggressive voice was gone. He was mouthing words that had little relevance to the matter at hand. He spoke of how poor his people were . . . of the coming of French and American traders, explorers Lewis and Clark, the laws of the Great Spirit Book, and of the missionaries who taught of the things the Spirit

Book contained. He expressed doubt that a road through his country could be made, but was grateful to the Great White Father who promised to take care of his children. Finally, the Nez Perce leader lowered himself painfully to the ground, exhausted.

Young Chief of the Cayuse followed, speculating on what Mother Earth might say if she were present: "... The Earth says, God has placed me here to produce all that grows upon me, the trees, fruit ... The same way the Earth says it was from her, man was made. The Creator on placing them on earth, desired them to take good care of the earth and do each other no harm. The Creator said, you Indian who take care of a certain portion of the country should not trade it off unless you get a fair price."

Young Chief's colorfully clad neighbor on the Umatilla, Five Crows, spoke. "My heart is just the same as Young Chief's," he said.

Commissioner Palmer asked if Peu-peu-mox-mox had anything to say. In a round about way the Walla Walla leader said he needed more time. He yet had to make up his mind.

"... My heart cried very hard when you first spoke to me, the same as if I was a feather, I flew. ... I thought the same as if you were talking to a feather. I thought what will I do. I have seen everything on both sides of the river. You all are talking together; we all are talking together. Perhaps if we came together at another time and another place we would be of one mind."

Kamiakin of the Yakama was asked to speak but bluntly refused. "I have nothing to say."

His fellow chief, Owhi, said he had nothing to say but once he gained the floor he said a great deal.

"... God named this land to us that is the reason I am afraid to say anything about this land. I am afraid of the laws of the Almighty, this is the reason I am afraid to speak of the land. I am afraid of the Almighty that is the reason I am sad. This is the reason I cannot give you an answer. I am afraid of the Almighty. Shall I steal this land and sell it? Or what should I do? This is the reason I am sad.

"My friends, God made our bodies from the earth as if they were different from the whites. What shall I do? Shall I give the lands that are part of my body and leave myself poor and destitute? . . . I love my friends. I love my life. This the reason why I cannot give you an answer. . . ."

Kamiakin was asked again if he had anything to say.

"What have I got to be talking about?" he retorted, his face a mask of annoyance.

Exasperated by the lack of progress, Commissioner Palmer caustically summed up what he felt had been said by the Indian leaders: "We have heard your chiefs speak. The heart of the Nez Perces and ours are one. The Cayuses, the Walla Wallas, and these other people say they do not understand us. We were in hopes we would be of one heart. Why should we have more than one heart? Young Chief says he does not see what we propose to give them. Peu-peu-mox-mox says much the same. Can we bring these sawmills and gristmills here on our backs to show these people? Can we bring blacksmith shops, the wagons and tools on our backs to show them at this time? Can we cause farms of wheat and corn to spring up in a day that they may see them? . . .

"How long will this people remain blind? We come to open your eyes. They refuse to see the light. . . .We don't come to steal your land; we pay you more than its worth. There is this little valley and the Umatilla Valley that affords a little good land. Between these two streams, and all around it is parched up plain. What is it worth to you or us? Why do we offer you so much? It is because our chief has told us to take care of his red people.

". . . We come to you with his messages to try and do you good. You throw his words behind you. Why do you do it? It is because you have received bad councel. My heart will be glad tomorrow if you come and say we all are of one heart." Palmer retired with the words that he had nothing more to say.

Cayuse Camasspello took the floor, adamant that his people were expected to move to the land of the Nez Perce.

". . .What would I be glad about if I took a thing and then

threw it away? That is the reason my heart cries. If you would show me fine lands and I were to see them, then I would be glad to go to them. How do you show your pity by sending me and my children to a land where there is nothing to eat but wood? That is the kind of land up there. That is the reason I cry. Look at my hands! An old man, I have hurt them by hard work. Then I ask myself, have I labored in vain? What have I to be glad for? . . . Will God think nothing of the labor I have bestowed on my garden? Do you do this to me in pity . . . ? The laws of God are not alone for you, they are for me as well."

Cayuse chief, Howlish Wampo, also spoke bitterly. ". . . The Nez Perces already have given you their land. You want us to go there. What can we think of that? That is the reason I cannot think of leaving this land to go there. Your words since you came here are crooked. That is all I have to say."

As far as Stevens was concerned the day's council meeting was a disaster. Nothing had been agreed upon. Even the Nez Perce had yet to sign on the dotted line. The longer the treaty making was delayed, the more time dissenters had to make excuses. At the rate they were going it would take all summer to get a consensus. He even doubted that was possible. He had to resort to strong arm methods. To begin with he would speak bluntly, let them know he wasn't fooled by their delaying tactics.

"My friends I know you are tired. We all are tired. My brother and I have talked straight but have you? Young Chief, says he's blind. Stickus says his heart is in one of three places -- the Grande Ronde, Touchet or the Tucannon. What's the matter with his old stomping grounds on the Umatilla?

"Then Peu-peu-mox-mox floats around like a feather. Kamiakin won't speak and Ohwi is afraid God will strike him down if he sells his land. Howlish Wampo says we talk crooked. Camasspello says all we offer is wood to eat and Five Crows says his heart is the same as Young Chief who can't see the trees for the forest. . . ."

"Aagh!" Stevens growled after the council grounds had

emptied. These people have made a science of procrastination. Of course that's their nature, never take action today on things that can be put off until tomorrow and then tomorrow never comes. How can they live this way?"

"Seems they've done right well until we white folks came along," Red Craig observed dryly.

The Indian people appeared unperturbed. The evening was spent horse racing. Lieutenant Kip wrote in his diary, "The races tonight were the most exciting we have seen, as the Indians had bet some 16 or 18 blankets on the result and all the passions of their savage nature were called into play."

Stevens was beside himself. "Their way of life is on the line; instead of taking this treaty making seriously, they make a mockery of all that has been said."

The sounds of merriment sent Michael an entirely different message. His Indian friends were showing unconcern because they did not know what else to do. The odds they faced were too overwhelming to accept. For years he had worked at the Cayuse mission at Waiilatpu and attended school there. He had seen first hand how the people handled troubled times. One day they put on a joyous front, the next day they became vicious avengers. Never would he forget the Whitman Mission tragedy. The morning began peacefully. By afternoon the Whitmans and many others were dead or dying. If Stevens didn't bring the council to an end soon, a similar bloodletting could happen here.

Michael glanced at Red Craig. Certainly the former mountain man could sense the mood of the Cayuse, Walla Walla and Yakama. Why didn't he influence the Nez Perce to sign the treaty and leave? Their overwhelming presence augured no good. Was Craig waiting for Looking Glass? And where was Vision Seeker? The two most level heads of the tribe were absent.

When they gathered to eat the communal meal, Joe noticed his Indian brother was deeply disturbed but did not know why. He wondered if Michael knew of the fire that had burned the log cabin and of Raven Wing's disappearance. Apparently not, Craig was not one to gossip and, unless someone in the Nez Perce camp had told Michael, he had no way of finding out. Should he tell him what he knew? Absolutely not. Without knowledge of Raven Wing's fate it would be cruel. Straightway, Michael would ride to Lapwai, probably harm the horse and himself, too.

Sergeant Coombs' usually neat mustache was awry from harassing his cook house underlings. The careless dog faces threw away more than they cooked. Supplies were dwindling. Stevens had expected a relatively short council. More than a week had passed and the end of the treaty making was not in sight.

"Big Chief Stevens claims he's goin' ta sign up the Nez Perces tomorra," Grasshopper said when he dropped by Joe's tent for a visit. "'Bout time, bacon's near gone, scrapin' the bottom of flour barrels, an' bags of beans an' coffee's lookin' thin."

Both encampments were made uneasy by increasing unrest among the Indian youth. To sit placidly all day and listen to the commissioners hammer away followed by the monotonous dirge of interpreters having their say, was more than youthful vigor and high spirits could endure. Early on Camasspello publicly had admonished young men for talking and laughing during council sessions.

"You young men think yourselves very smart," he scolded. "By and by you will learn. Now I am tired of your conduct."

Youth may be censored, but it is hard for young blood to remain still for long. Joe thought back to the days of the Whitman mission tragedy when youthful Cayuse ran wild. Elders watched in horror at the horrible things they did. When asked why he didn't put a stop to the unruliness, band leader Tiloukaikt confessed he had lost control of the young people, even his own sons.

That evening sounds of hilarity again came from the Indian camp. Gambling was in progress. "They are most inveterate gamblers," Kip recorded. "A warrior will sometimes stake on successive games, his arms, and horses, and even his wives so that in a single night he is reduced to a state of primitive poverty and obliged to trust to charity to be remounted for the hunt."

Nevertheless, the night passed peacefully and the sun shone brightly in the morning. Stevens opened the council by reporting the paper for the Nez Perces nearly was ready to sign. He expressed hope that an agreement with the Cayuse, Walla Walla and Yakama also could be finalized.

"We want to know what you want," he said. "We are here for that purpose." But once again Stevens was stymied.

"We do not know our hearts," Young Chief of the Cayuse announced.

"I have already spoken all I have to say," Peu-peu-mox-mox stated.

"I have nothing to talk long about," Kamiakin said. "I am tired. I am anxious to get back to my lodge."

In desperation, Stevens called on Skloom.

"My friends, I have understood what you have said," the brother to Kamiakin responded. "When you give me what is just for my land you shall have it. This is all I have to say."

"Agh!" Stevens muttered. "Getting these people to commit themselves is like flogging a dead horse."

"Don't give up," Palmer cautioned. "They are getting tired. They'll soon give in, pack up and go home. Unfortunately, treaties signed under conditions like this have a good chance of failure. At the moment the people will be happy to get the disagreeable task over with. Later, when they are rested up and have time to think about what they have done . . . well, that will be the time when we find out what has been accomplished here."

In the months to come Governor Stevens would have occasion to look back on Commissioner Palmer's words and kick himself for not paying more attention. More than once he would mutter vehemently to himself, "If the fellow was so apprehensive, why didn't he put a stop to the proceedings there and then?"

To further upset Stevens' mental well being, a messenger arrived with the news that Looking Glass and his buffalo hunters had been sighted. He glanced around in alarm. He had the Nez Perce papers ready for signing but Lawyer was absent. He searched for Kamiakin, who it was said was a close friend of Looking Glass. Perhaps he would sign for Looking Glass, but when approached Kamiakin bluntly refused. Hardly had this taken place when a thunder of hoofbeats announced Looking Glass' arrival. Taking a small party, he had raced ahead, determined to participate in the council. At the forefront of a band of war painted horsemen rode the seventy year-old warrior. From a coup stick glistened a freshly taken scalp. Chanting war cries and waving their weapons, the arrivals stormed into the council grounds.

"Yi!-yi!-yi." Indian youth in the encampment leapt to their feet to voice their approval. Finally, something exciting had happened. All evening the story of the old man's coming was discussed around campfires, including those of the white man. The hunting party had ridden directly from a battle with the Blackfeet. The Blackfeet had raided the Looking Glass camp, stealing some 70 horses. Looking Glass' infuriated hunters trailed them to their lair. In the clash that followed, they rescued the horses and sent two of the raiders to the Great Beyond.

Governor Stevens was not one of those thrilled by Looking Glass' escapades. The arrangement he had made with Lawyer was in jeopardy. Also, upon completing the Walla Walla Council, his intentions were to proceed east and make a treaty with the Blackfeet. After suffering an embarrassing defeat to the Nez Perce, in all likelihood they would not be in a state of mind conducive to signing a treaty of any kind, let alone one that involved making peace with the Nez Perce.

Although Michael and his brother Joe found the tale of Looking Glass' exploits of keen interest, they also were eager to know the whereabouts of their relative, Vision Seeker. The last they knew he had gone to find Looking Glass and his buffalo hunters, but where was he? Strangely, Michael's childhood friend turned foe, Spotted Badger, came to their camp and supplied them with the information. At first Michael did not recognize the war painted youth who stopped in front of their lean-to shelter.

"You wish to know of your uncle?" the young warrior

asked.

"Yes, we do," Michael was quick to answer, as he tried to put a name to the painted face. As boys they once had fought to a standstill. More recently Spotted Badger had made fun of One Who Kicks, calling him his daughter. Why was the troublemaker here? Whatever it was, it could not be good.

"What has happened to Vision Seeker?" he demanded.

Spotted Badger backed away. "You will see," he said. "He makes camp near the lodge of Looking Glass." With a mirthless chuckle, he turned and was gone. Puzzled by the man's strange behavior, Michael stared after him. Why should his former enemy go out of his way to tell him of Vision Seeker's whereabouts?

"It won't hurt to see if what he says is true," Joe said.

Hurriedly, the brothers mounted and rode to the buffalo hunter's camp. Spotted Badger was waiting for them. He motioned toward a campfire. As they rode toward it they saw Vision Seeker sitting beside the flickering flames. He was taking his ease, waiting it seemed, to be served the evening meal. Before the brothers could make themselves known, a slender maiden emerged from the makeshift shelter. She handed Vision Seeker a platter of food and then faded into the background, but not before Michael got a good view of her face. He sucked in his breath and motioned for Joe to turn around and leave.

"I don't believe what I see," Michael said when they had ridden a short way. "Can that really be Vision Seeker? The Vision Seeker I know never was with a woman."

"That's Vision Seeker all right, and he's certainly with a singularly handsome young woman. The way they act she is either his slave or his mate. He never would keep a slave, so he must have taken a wife."

"I don't believe it. I recognized the woman. I went to mission school with her. She is Spotted Badger's sister, nearly 20 years younger than Vision Seeker."

XXIII

Why do you want to separate my children and settle them all
over the country? I do not go into your country
and scatter your children in every direction.

Looking Glass, Nez Perce

Vision Seeker had noticed the two brothers approaching the camp and smiled to himself. He had a good idea of their thoughts. They were appalled. He started to call out to them, but at that moment the food platter came. When he glanced back they had reined away. He chuckled as he ate. He could tell by the way they rode off without looking back, they were confused. If they came to greet him they would not know what to say. The presence of the woman would make them uncomfortable. It was not polite to ask questions, and for certain he was not about to offer any explanation. It was not up to him to do so. Michael and the other members of the family would just have to accept that he had a woman in his lodge and keep their thoughts to themselves.

For that matter they probably wouldn't believe him if he told them about his new mode of life. In fact he couldn't describe it himself. He had taken the young maiden under his protection as he would a motherless colt. That was about the extent of their relationship. Her name was Mu-tu, meaning Down-the-River, for as an eight year-old she had climbed into a canoe which broke free from its mooring and bobbed down the Kooskooskie, the entire village running screaming along the bank.

Yes, Mu-tu did the usual womanly chores, kept the lodge neat and clean, cooked and served the meals and shared his blanket. Other than that they were almost complete strangers. He had made no physical advances and neither had she. He could not forget her as a school girl with snappy brown eyes and a mischievous nature darting about the mission school playgrounds like a sprightly squirrel.

For the first few days and nights she reminded Vision Seeker of a skittish colt. She readily went about the chores, but acted as if any moment she might take flight. At night when she lay by his side often he could see her smooth, glossy skin quiver as if she was reliving the horror of watching her warrior mate suffer and die. Sometimes he heard her quietly crying.

After a few days on the trail she became more composed. She spoke to him now and then, and once played a trick on him by tying his moccasin thongs together making him trip when he hurriedly slipped into them one morning. Then they had come upon the buffalo hunters. She saw her brother and called to him. He galloped up and would have taken her away, but she refused. She had lost one man and now was under the protection of another. She would not leave him until he told her to do so.

Vision Seeker grimaced. He probably should have insisted Mu-tu go with her brother, for now he was beginning to become fond of her. From the way she watched him with those soft brown eyes, he believed Mu-tu returned the feeling.

**

On June 8th Governor Stevens again opened the council with the hope the Cayuse, Yakama and Walla Walla would come to an agreement. Again he was disappointed.

"We have been tiring our hearts for a long time," Young Chief of the Cayuse said. "We do not know our hearts. . . . The reason why we could not understand you was that you selected the country for us to live in without our having any voice in the matter. . . . You embraced all my country. Where was I to go? Was I to be a wanderer like a wolf without a home. . . ? I think the land where my forefathers are buried should be mine. That is the place I am speaking for. . . ."

Late into the night the commissioners had talked of this same matter. The Cayuse were adamantly opposed to moving into the land of the Nez Perce. Somewhere else had to be found to place them, along with the Umatilla and Walla Walla. It was agreed a third reservation was needed, one much nearer to the homelands of the people being displaced. At this point Commissioner Palmer laid out a map. With a stick as a pointer, he showed the gathering where it would be, centered around the headwaters of the Umatilla River, land already occupied by the Cayuse. Although they wished for more, the Cayuse approved. They knew this country. It was good.

Satisfying the Cayuse seemed the answer. The leaders began to fall in line. Walla Walla Peu-peu-mox-mox said when his house (reservation) was ready he and his people would move in. Yakama Kamiakin said all he wished for was a good agent "who will pity the good and bad of us and take care of us."

Red Wolf of the Nez Perce also insisted on a good agent, namely, Red Craig. "I want Mr. Craig to stay in Nez Perce country, and not go away. . . . He understands us . . . he speaks our language. . . . When there is any news that comes into the country we can go to him and hear it straight. . . ."

There was little discord until it came time for Looking Glass to speak. The old warrior, who had been absent when the lines were drawn, was not at all pleased. ". . . Why do you wish to separate my children and settle them all over the country?" he demanded. "I do not go into your country and scatter your children in every direction.

". . . My heart is with the country I live upon and head. That is the reason my heart tells me to say where my children will go. . . . When I hear you talk it goes to my heart. I am not like these people who hang their heads and say nothing. . . ."

The commissioners glanced at each other and grimaced. They had spent days drawing lines on a map in an attempt to satisfy all the tribes and here, at the last moment, Looking Glass wanted the lines redrawn.

Commissioner Palmer rose to object. "If we change the line to where he (Looking Glass) says, we would have to stay here two or three days more to arrange the paper. . . .My heart says yes to the line shown yesterday and today. All things will be done as we told you. . . ."

"Let it be so," Looking Glass said, but later recanted. "I said yes to the line I marked myself, not to your line."

Fed up with the delay, Governor Stevens grimly entered the fray. "I will say to Looking Glass, we cannot agree."

Commissioner Palmer leapt to the governor's support. "The Nez Perces, the Walla Wallas, the Cayuses and the Umatillas agree to the boundaries we have marked. Do you wish to throw all we have said to you behind you? Shall we, like boys, say yes today and no tomorrow . . . ?

"It was my children that spoke yesterday, and now I come to speak," Looking Glass replied. "I asked my children what was their hurry? Why did they run and speak till I came? That is the reason I marked it bigger."

Commissioner Palmer was not backing down. "If we say yes to this line our chief would say no. But if we shall say the line we already have marked is right we believe our chief will say yes. Which will you do, take that line or have it all thrown away?"

"I will not say more today," Looking Glass replied, but it was clear he remained opposed.

In the Indian camps that night and the next day, for the following day was the Sabbath, plenty more was said. Looking Glass was irked. He made no bones about his displeasure, not only for what he considered a bad bargain, but also he was disgusted with his people for not waiting for his counsel. His opposition to the land giveaway gave the Cayuse heart. They, too, refused to sign their land away.

For a while it appeared Looking Glass would carry the day. All of Lawyer's high sounding speeches and his conniving would go for naught. The debate among the Nez Perce became so incensed, Lawyer stalked off and sat sulking in his lodge. But in the end Lawyer won out. He was declared head chief of the Nez Perce and Looking Glass was named second tribal chief.

In the Yakama camp Kamiakin also was upset about the whole business. Giving away his homeland was more than he could stomach. He was determined not to sign. He discussed his decision with Father Pandosy, who also was distressed. He had warned these Americans that if the negotiations were not accepted with good grace there would be serious repercussions. Although peaceful people, when the Yakamas were aroused they could turn into formidable foes, and being their friend he would have to side with them. During the quiet of the night, the good father fingered his beads and said prayers for all Indian people, for it was written as if chiseled in stone, regardless of tribe, the Indian people were taking a trail they never before had traversed.

Finally Kamiakin's friend, Peu-peu-mox-mox, came to call. For a long while they closeted themselves in Kamiakin's lodge. When they reappeared Kamiakin grudgingly announced he would agree to sign the treaty.

Vision Seeker who had attended the day's council meeting, also sat in on the Nez Perce deliberations. In studying the lines drawn on the map, he was appalled by the amount of land the Indian people were asked to give up. "The commissioners are stealing our land," he complained to his friend, Red Craig. "The little they give in return is nothing."

Red Craig nodded. "You are right, but what can one do? The white father in Washington has spoken. He wants this land and he will take it one way or another."

Vision Seeker reluctantly agreed. He had studied the two men who held the future of the Northwest Indian people in their hands. Stevens, particularly, had the look of a man pushed as far as he would go. If the council failed, he very well could call upon the US Army and carry out his demands by force. That would be disastrous for everyone on the Columbia River plateau.

Vision Seeker's assessment of the situation was on the mark. The next day when the Indian leaders still revealed reluctance to sign the proposed treaty papers, Stevens was heard to remark that if they didn't sign they would walk in blood knee-deep.

Lawyer was the first to sign, writing his name with a flourish, the only one to do so. The others marked the agreement with an X, Looking Glass, Joseph . . . in all, 56 did so. To virtually sign away their birthright was so difficult for several, they hardly could bring themselves to do it. Kamiakin, one of the last to sign, after making his X returned to his seat with blood on his lips. In his torment he had bitten them until they bled.

There was little wonder the signing was so tormenting. As a result of it, the Indian peoples agreed to give away the greater portions of their homelands, in several cases all tribal land was lost. The Walla Wallas completely surrendered their ancestral lands. The Klickitats, who had not attended the council, suddenly found themselves dispossessed. In the future they would share a reservation with the Yakama, Palouse and eleven smaller tribes.

Even Mother Earth seemed to voice anguish at the terrible price the Indian people had been forced to pay. The night the council ended a violent wind storm struck the area, hurtling anything not securely anchored across the rolling plain. Not until the next day did the wind subside.

Governor Stevens considered the council meeting a great victory. "Thus ended in most satisfactory manner this great council," he wrote in his diary. ". . . Its influence and difficulty . . . has never been equalled by any council held with Indian tribes. . . ."

Among the many points Stevens made was the assurance that until the treaty was ratified Indian people would be secure in their homelands. Yet, almost immediately after the end of the council newspaper articles over Stevens' and Palmer's signatures announced lands the Indians had forfeited were declared open for settlement. The treaty itself was not ratified by congress until four years later, April 18, 1859. By that time Indian and non-Indian blood had soaked the soil of the disputed lands.

XXIV

From little causes come great difficulties. That is the reason
we speak from small things to big ones.
Eagle from the Light, Nez Perce

"As the saying goes, 'It is an ill wind that blows nobody good'," Red Craig observed the morning after the conclusion of the council meeting.

"Let us hope so," Commissioner Palmer said. "I've just received word the Rogue are acting up again. You put one fire out and another springs up. So I'm off to the Willamette Valley to start this painful business all over again."

Across the council grounds people were packing, loading up, and preparing to leave. No one was in a greater hurry than the Indian people. Their encampments emptied almost as though the wind had blown the occupants and their lodges away. Long trains of horsemen, followed by pack animals, plodding groups of women and children, and herds of extra horses and cattle, advanced toward distant horizons, finally to disappear in the haze.

As soon as he collected himself, Governor Stevens was off to council with the Blackfeet and other tribes in the east. Sergeant Coombs was ordered to return to home base to prepare a supply column that would meet Stevens in two months time at a planned council with the Coeur d'Alene, Spokan, Colville, and Okanagon. Joe Jennings' services were no longer needed, but Grasshopper Stillings continued eastward with the governor.

The abrupt dismissal rankled Joe. Now, he had no choice but to return to the Willamette Valley and meet with Tildy. His Indian half brother would not have it otherwise.

"You must return," Michael kept insisting. "It is a duty you cannot avoid."

"What about you? What are you planning to do?" Joe

asked.

"I'm off to Lapwai to visit Raven Wing and Running Turtle. It may be the last chance to see them for a long while."

"Oh," Joe uttered. "You plan to return to the Sweetwater and live with Morning Star's people?"

"No, I have another place in mind."

"What's the matter with everybody in this Jennings family? All of a sudden they have more secrets than fleas on a scurvy mongrel. Where in the devil are you going?"

"Speak with Tildy and you will find out."

"Aagh!" Joe muttered in disgust, but his Indian brother paid no attention. Instead, he politely invited Joe to go with him to see Vision Seeker who yet had to depart. Involved in endless treaty discussions, Vision Seeker had little opportunity to visit with his nephews. Several times Michael passed by his uncle's tipi only to have the young woman, Mu-tu, say he was away and she had no idea when he would return.

The meetings between Mu-tu and Michael were painful sessions. They both remembered the days they had spent in Eliza Spalding's classroom. They never were friends especially but shared many school day experiences. Michael barely could restrain himself from asking what she was doing boldly traveling with Vision Seeker. Mu-tu wanted to tell, but did not feel it her place to do so. They shuffled their feet and, like dogs meeting after a long period, warily eyed each other, mostly keeping their gazes lowered. At the end of these meetings Michael would mount his horse and Mu-tu disappear into the shadows of the lodge.

This time the meeting was different. Vision Seeker came striding out to greet his nephews. He embraced Michael and shook hands with Joe. "Come," he said. "We have much to say." He motioned for them to sit on a buffalo hide padded log in front of his lodge that stood in the shade of a cluster of locust trees. When he was certain the brothers were comfortable, he called to his woman.

"Mu-tu, we have guests." Mu-tu shyly appeared dressed

in a neat fringed garment decorated with elk teeth, beads and porcupine quills. Michael sucked in his breath. This had been Raven Wing's elk skin dress, the possession she prized over every thing else.

Vision Seeker noticed the surprised look on Michael's face and berated himself. The dress should have gone to Michael for Morning Star. How could he have been so insensitive? The dress hadn't been his to give. The few possessions Raven Wing left should have gone to her sons but Young Wolf had refused to take any of her discarded possessions, and Michael had not been around. Now Michael's feelings were hurt.

Vision Seeker grimaced. He didn't blame Michael for taking affront. Nearly three decades old, the dress still looked much as it did on the Bitterroot, the winter he had been snowed in with Buck Stone's trapping brigade. Night after night Little Ned had fussed over the dress, adding quills and beads. The garment held such poignant memories that when Raven Wing discarded it, he had to save it. Then, on an impulse he had given it to Mu-tu. The poor girl had nothing but old camp clothes. At the time it seemed the right thing to do. The dress changed Mu-tu physically and mentally. It brought out the healthy bloom in her cheeks and lifted her spirits until she nearly appeared as fun loving as he remembered her as a child.

"Sit with us, Mu-tu," Vision Seeker urged. "I know our guests would like to hear what brought us together."

Shyly, Mu-tu sat alongside Michael, her eyes downcast as Vision Seeker told of the death of her wounded mate and then the wild journey into Blackfeet country to track down Looking Glass and his buffalo hunters.

Michael listened but his thoughts were on the elk skin dress. How could Raven Wing give it away? It sickened him to think she had turned against everything his *soyappo* father had stood for. Yet, he loved her. No one discarded his mother.

When the brothers were preparing to leave Vision Seeker took Michael aside and told him of the burned cabin and the disappearance of his mother.

"You think she set fire to the cabin?" Michael asked. "I suppose she did," Michael said when Vision Seeker did not reply. "She hated everything that reminded her of my father, even the precious elk skin dress . . . Poor Raven Wing, where is she now?"

"Back in White Bird country. Perhaps with a new mate called Tall Horse. That is what is rumored, anyway. Sorry about the dress. I should have kept it for Morning Star."

"Does not matter," Michael replied. "I doubt if Morning Star would wear it, and I would not want her to do so. It would remind me of my childhood -- of that terrible night at the Chinook trading center when Francois demanded the dress to wager on a horse race. Raven Wing and he had fought over it until a fisherman came to Raven Wing's aid. Francois slashed the man's throat and we fled in his canoe. . . ." Michael fell silent, and Vision Seeker could think of nothing to say.

The following morning Vision Seeker and Mu-tu broke camp and disappeared over the eastern horizon. Joe and Michael rode west toward the shiny peak called Mount Hood. For hours the brothers rode in silence, each grappling with private thoughts. Over and over in Michael's mind tumbled the news Vision Seeker brought of his mother. How terribly sad to see such a beautiful human lose control of her life. She had so much to live for, but was turning her back on it as if the future had no value at all.

From what he knew of her early years, she always had been a troubled rebel. Lone Wolf loved her more than anyone but perhaps his first son, Many Horses, yet Raven Wing did everything she could to annoy him. She had a husband who did his best to make life easy for her, and she treated him like dirt. Now, she had a beautiful daughter-in-law and two handsome grandsons and burned down her lodge rather than welcome them into her home.

Joe's thoughts were on his brother and sister. Michael could at least give him some hint as to what he was going to face. Was Granddad Jennings terminally ill? The grand old man was getting along in years. No, that couldn't be it. Michael wouldn't be that cruel. It was something else. From all the hints Michael let drop, it sounded like he, perhaps all of them, were planning a journey. Where could that be? Did Macon and Tildy have their fill of homesteading and plan to settle in the east? But if that was so, why should they insist he get involved? It didn't make sense. The farther the brothers rode the greater Joe's agitation increased until he thought he would explode.

Joe did not have long to wait before the conundrum was unraveled. Tildy greeted the brothers at the door with her hair tied in a scarf. Streaks of soot and dust streaked her face and the gingham dress she wore looked as though she had been blackening the stove. A half filled trunk sat with an open lid. On the table were stacks of folded clothes, sheets, towels and a variety of bottles, jars and tins.

"For-crying-out-loud, what's going on?" Joe blurted. Stocky little One Who Kicks darted out, his face flushed with excitement. "We go far on great water," his shrill voice squeaked. "Many days on ship with wings."

Michael grabbed up his son and took him outside. Joe found himself alone facing Tildy, whose white face told him the boy had blurted the truth. Nevertheless, she took him by the arm and walked him out the back door. Joe went along, his brain whirling like a swarm of bees. When they were some distance from the house, Tildy stopped. "As you can see, we are moving. We are going to England. Macon's father died, and now he's what the British call 'laird of the manor'."

Joe stared across the well tended homestead acreage without seeing a thing. England! That was on the other side of the world. It would take weeks to get there. The Jennings family would be split asunder.

"What about Granddad? At his age, a journey like that could be his death warrant."

"That's why I have wanted to talk to you. Granddad can't make the trip, and knows it. But he can't be left here alone. That means someone in the family must stay with him. David Malin is staying, but he's only a kid. Do you now see why we must talk?"

Joe kept his eyes on the horizon. A circling hawk, fluttering its wings, hovered over a tangle of brush. Suddenly, with its claws extended, it swooped down and came up with a struggling rodent and flew away to disappear into the forested hills. Like the rodent, he was caught. With Tildy gone that left only him to take care of Granddad. He would be tied to this Willamette Valley farm until Granddad passed on.

He had an inkling of how the Indian people must feel being forced to live on a patch of ground not of their own choosing. Worst of all must be the realization the freedom they had enjoyed since the beginning of time, was disappearing. It had to be agonizing to see it fade away before their eyes like the morning mist, and there was nothing they could do to prevent it. Little wonder they danced, raced, and gambled. They had to, or go mad.

"What about Michael and Morning Star?" Joe blurted. "They would take excellent care of Granddad and the property."

"Michael and family are going with us."

"Live in England! What are you trying to do to them? They will be like fish out of water. Is this Macon's idea? He can't be thinking straight, taking them out of this land where they have lived all of their lives. What does Michael say?"

"He's enthusiastic. Macon is making plans to enroll him in a medical college."

Joe was shocked. "Ridiculous! Michael's an intelligent young man but ... Does Macon know of Michael's terrible experiences at New England's Fairview Academy? It was disastrous, so awful he never speaks of it."

"Perhaps you should tell that to Macon. You are both educated men and understand these things."

"Yes, I will do so," Joe replied angrily.

They returned to the house where another surprise awaited Joe. The next door neighbor, Bithiah Abernathy Olafson and her brood, came to bid the Laird family Godspeed. It was the first time in nearly 10 years Joe had laid eyes on his former sweet-heart. He greeted her affably enough and was happy to find that his heart didn't lurch at the sight of her as it had in former years. It was what she said that made him cringe.

"How wonderful 'tis to know we'll be neighbors as we were in Middlesex County," Bithiah gushed to Joe. "We must visit often. My boys would like to know of your many exciting adventures -- how you got that mysterious scar fighting the Blackfeet or whoever 'twas. Next to Daniel Boone and Davy Crockett, they think you're the greatest hero that ever was."

Joe glanced at the boys, who had to be 11 or 12. They had the eyes of twin devils. Instead of emitting hero worship, the yellow flecked blue orbs issued a challenge. They would test this "courageous frontiersman". He would find that fighting Indians was nothing compared to encountering a gang of Olafson kids.

The next day Joe got his brother-in-law aside, no easy task as the head of the house inspected each item packed to make certain it was needed and safely would make the passage.

"Do I call you lord, duke or something of that nature, be-ing laird of the manor and all?" Joe jokingly asked, but Macon was not amused.

"Don't talk nonsense. All we need is to get a rumor like that started," he answered curtly.

"Quite so," Joe said apologetically. The last thing he wanted was to arouse Macon's ire. "I understand from Tildy that you plan to enter Michael in medical school. Is that wise, him being Indian? I took him east in the attempt to give him an edu-cation, but he didn't fit in. His fellow students picked on him, bullied him until he revolted. He nearly killed one kid and badly hurt another. The locals were so up in arms, he was lucky to escape with a whole skin."

The question seemed to hit a nerve. "Listen," Macon snapped, "we British are a lot more civilized than you Yankees think. For centuries we have dealt with natives of all kinds. Ac-tually, Michael and family will be treated there far better than here. Look at that rabid redhead Short, who came across the plains with us -- he settled nearby. He hated Indians then and still does. He lays traps for them as if they were thieving wolves."

"Well, there's often a bad apple in a barrel."

"Bad apples have a way of spoiling the lot. Take the trial of the five Indians accused of murdering the Whitmans. That was a put up job if I ever saw one. Right from the start, judges, jury and spectators had made up their minds all five were going to hang, and they did.

"While we're on the subject, let me give you more examples. Your Protestant missionaries arrive dripping with good will. They are going to pave the pathway to heaven for the Indian people. When they get them properly hooked, there is no room for them in the church. To hear the service they have to crouch on the stoop or stand outside in the rain. If you don't believe me, go to church one of these Sundays and find out for yourself."

"Well," Joe gulped, groping for an answer.

"I'm not finished yet," Macon said curtly. "What burns me up more than anything is the way American settlers have treated Doctor John McLoughlin, the former Hudson's Bay head man at Fort Vancouver. No one did more to help incoming settlers than did he. Yet, Americans dispute his claim to land and would take every stick he owned if they could. McLoughlin is everything they hate. He married an Indian wife, has half-breed children, he's British and he's Catholic.

"I know these things because we have been treated much the same. Anytime we go to the market, town hall meetings or anywhere else, people turn their backs and whisper. Of course I am British, but it's mostly because we have Indian people living in our home. That's just not cricket. We are not playing the game by the rules these narrow-minded American settlers have set down. Before you speak of British prejudice, you had better take a long, careful look at your own people."

THE GREAT POWWOW

XXV

Is there not something worthy of perpetuation in our Indian
spirit of democracy, where Earth, our mother, was free to all
and no one sought to impoverish or enslave their neighbor?
                                        Ohiyesa, Santee Sioux

The days of June became days of July and then August. Pastures turned from verdant green to brown. The gurgling creeks became a mere trickle. From the high country deer and elk drifted into the valley to drink from pools of remaining water. In early mornings killdeers emerged to dart from place to place, searching for worms. During the heat of the day flocks of scolding magpies flew from one copse of trees to the next. At dusk it was swallows that silently appeared, gliding in sweeping circles over the fields in the daily quest for food.

Joe watched this ever-changing tableau with a restlessness that he hardly could control. The departure of his sister's and brother's families left a vacuum that was impossible to fill. Granddad Jennings barely moved from his rocking chair, and when he did it was to relieve himself or drop on his bed. David Malin Laird, Tildy's and Macon's adopted son, kept to the fields, cultivating, repairing and tending to the animals. Although Joe often went along to lend a hand, he soon discovered he was about as handy doing farm chores as the three-legged mongrel that romped around, getting in the way. Thus, for the most part Joe, idled about the house, watching his failing grandfather slowly decline.

News from the high country also added to Joe's depressed state of mind. A former member of Governor Stevens' survey party stopped by to report treaty negotiations had run into a snag. Anxious to get on to Blackfeet country, Stevens had quarreled with Victor, the Flathead chief, calling him an old woman who was as dumb as a dog. Finally, after closing negotiations with the

Flathead, Pend d'Oreille and Kutenai, Stevens hurried eastward to stop at Fort Benton on the upper Missouri River where he expected supplies from the east awaited him. But, instead of having docked at Fort Benton, the boat carrying the supplies had discharged the shipment at Fort Union near the mouth of the Yellowstone, more than 300 miles down river. The mistake infuriated Stevens, leading to a bitter quarrel with fellow commissioners and delaying the council with the Blackfeet indefinitely.

"Knowing Governor S, yuh kin imagine he's fit to be tied, an' he has a good right to be so. The Injuns still're waitin' fer the good things he promised at the Walla Walla Council. If he doesn't watch out every tribe in the region'll be on the warpath. All of his councilin'll go up in smoke," reported the messenger whose long ears moved up and down like signal flags when he spoke.

"Hmm!" Joe thoughtfully nodded. "Trouble with Stevens is that he pushed ahead without thinking of the consequences. He should have taken time to follow through with the promises he already had made. You can't blame the Indian people for getting antsy. They've seen too many promises go unfulfilled."

When the messenger took his leave, Joe felt as though a weight had been lifted from his shoulders. At the time Stevens had dismissed him, he had been rankled, believing his efforts had been belittled. Now, with all the troubles Stevens was having, the dismissal seemed a blessing. He even welcomed the appearance of Bithiah and her brood who came to ask if he had news of the departed Macon Laird family. The first hour of the visit was spent looking back on days when they had been neighbors in Middlesex County, Massachusetts. Even Granddad Jennings came alive to report on students who he had tutored there. Joe found himself remembering those pleasant New England days.

"Good heavens!" he exclaimed. He counted back over the years. He had been 16 at the time. Where had the time gone? He was now 32. More than half of his life had disappeared, and what had he accomplished? Not very much. His possessions were few; he had no wife, no offspring and no promise of either. Joe glanced at Bithiah with respect. The lines in her face and sprinkle of gray in her hair were badges of sacrifice, the producing of children and endless giving of tireless love and care. She seemed happy, and he was glad. If Bithiah and he had married, with his restless nature, for certain, they would have been mismatched. When Olafson drove up to collect his family and take them home, Joe walked out and invited him in. He actually felt friendly toward the man he long had envied. Olafson had made Bithiah happy, something he never could have done.

The days slowly ground by. After the Olafson family's visit Granddad momentarily perked up. He pulled out an old atlas and attempted to trace the route Tildy and family had taken. He drew a line down the west coasts of North and South America, across the Atlantic and had them docking at the great port of Liverpool on the west side of England.

"By now they should have had ample time to arrive, don't you think?" he asked. "How do you suppose the Old Country struck them, especially our Indian relatives?"

Joe had been asking himself the same questions. He, too, thought they should have arrived . . . probably already inspected their new home. Was the manor house like a castle? He couldn't imagine Tildy as mistress of the sprawling stone structure Macon had described. The upkeep must be awesome. Of course there would be housekeeping help and the like, but still it would be unlike any challenge Tildy ever before had encountered. But Sis had grit. During the past few months as he watched Granddad slowly fade away Joe had gained a greater appreciation of her worth. She had cared for Granny through her declining months, heard the rasping sounds the poor woman made as she painfully struggled through the final days on earth. Afterwards, Tildy had carried on, keeping the New England farm going, making a home for Granddad, fighting off bill collectors until finally she had to give in.

The knowledge of what she had to put up with, shamed him. He had been out west working trap lines, living a carefree life. He barely had given Tildy and the grandparents a moment's thought. Even when Tildy wrote and begged him to come home, he had made the excuse he hadn't a bean to his name. Aagh! What an insensitive creature he had been. He hoped Tildy would be happy as mistress of her English manor and had a half a dozen more youngsters. She deserved the best life had to offer.

Joe's thoughts also often dwelt on his Indian brother and his family. Before their departure Michael and he had paced the deck of the four-masted schooner, stopping on what was called the ship's fantail to watch the stevedores loading and off-loading cargo. The stiff manner in which Michael watched each load come and go made Joe wonder if his brother wasn't having second thoughts. He was taking his wife and two sons into lands where few, if any, American Indians ever had gone. They would live cheek to jowl with people of a different race, different customs, different traditions, and most of all, a far different attitude toward life itself. Even now, as Joe sat in the comfortable log home with his grandfather, and with Macon's scornful words on prejudice still ringing in his ears, he wondered if Michael had made the right choice.

A sharp rap on the door jerked Joe out of his reverie. David Malin, who had been reading, jumped up to pull the curtain aside and peer out. "It's a white man. Gee! He's all arms and legs," he reported.

"Hey!" came the voice from outside, "Anybody home? I'm lookin' fer a galoot named Joe. Stillings is the moniker, Grasshopper Stillings."

Joe leapt up to fling the door open. "What are you doing here?" Joe demanded after the two exchanged ribald greetings.

"Me enlistment was up so I decided ta look fer a new line a work. Sojerin's all right, but not under Governor Isaac Stevens. Servin' 'neath him's like livin' with a rattler, 'cept he niver gives warnin' when he's goin' ta strike. When thet shipment of supplies got dumped at Fort Union 'stead of Fort Benton, thet guy went ta pieces.

"Things was goin' good 'til we hit Flathead country. Then Stevens got crosswise with Catholic priests at Ravalli's mission -- claimed they was causin' the Injuns ta upset his treaty makin'. Thet kept him in a bad mood all the way ta Fort Benton. Then the missin' supplies hit him. Thet was like a slap in the face. Why, things got so bad the commissioners wouldn't talk ta each other, even argued over who was boss. Then news of the Colville gold strike hit town. People lit out like ther pants was afire, crossin' every reservation boundary thet lie in ther path."

Stillings stayed the night, the next day and the night after that. He got along well with Granddad, and David was fascinated with his tales of army life. Neither one wanted him to leave. Joe didn't mind. He enjoyed his presence as it took him back to the days of '49 when Grasshopper and he were members of the Mounted Riflemen, the summer everyone and his dog had crossed the "Big Open" heading for the gold fields of California.

Five days after Stillings arrived, one of his cohorts, a man named Pinky Thompson, stopped by. In addition to being nearly as tall and gangly as Grasshopper Stillings, he had a pink nose and the distracting habit of twitching it like a rabbit. Pinky brought more news of happenings in the high country. Indian Agent Andy Bolon had been killed. The news came as a shock to Joe and Grasshopper; both of them had spent a number of campfire evenings with the murdered Indian Agent. Just weeks previously Bolon had been robust and energetic. It was hard to grasp that this bright flame of life had been extinguished.

"What's suddenly happenin' up there, anyway?" Stillings demanded. "Has everybody gone nuts? How and where did this terrible murder take place?"

"Well," Pinky answered, twitching his nose as he took a cautious sip of the coffee Joe had placed before him. "Seem's ol' Andy was headin' outta Fort Dalles on his way ta Spokane when he got word of killin's up Yakama way. On the trail he met a friendly Yakama who told him he'd git killed if he went any farther. As yuh probably know, Bolon wasn't perzactly close buddies with either Kamiakin or Father Pandosy. From what we can figure, Bolon took the man's advice an' turned back. That night he camped on the trail an' somebody jumped him, cut his throat an' then threw his body, saddle an' bridle inta the campfire --

could only been Injuns. Anyway, thet's the story thet's bein' told in Fort Dalles."

Pinky twitched his nose and took another sip of coffee. "They's all sorts of rumors makin' the rounds. Some say the Mormons in the Salt Lake region're givin' Injuns powder, lead and muskets. It's said they've got the idea of killin' off all whites in the area so they kin take over. Then, upon the Ahtanum thet pesky Father Pandosy's irkin' the power's ta be. They say he's eggin' on Kamiakin an' his brother Skloom. They've vowed to shoot any pale face thet enters the Yakama homeland. Yep, I'm tellin' yuh fer sure there's plenty of trouble brewin'.

"When the Injuns signed the treaty papers in the valley of the Walla Walla, they said they was of one heart. They was one heart all right, but it wasn't filled with good will. The commissioners should've know'd the way ol' Kamiakin bit his lip when he signed the treaty he wasn't goin' ta sit in his lodge an' take his ease. No siree, he's out ther talkin' up anybody he kin git ta listen. He smoked with a bunch from west of the Cascades. Afterward, Kamiakin an' his braves set up signal posts on mountain tops. When pale faces're spotted crossin' inta Yakama land, smoke signals warn of ther comin'.

"Yep, Kamiakin is a silent one, but he's stirrin' up a hornets nest. He's talked ta the Palouse, Spokan an' Coeur d'Alenes, preparin' those folks fer the comin' of the gold seekers. Afore yuh kin say Jack Sprat they'll be picked off like clay pigeons. In fact already it's beginin'. A Yakama warrior named Qual-chan, or a name somethin' like thet, caught half dozen white folks tryin' ta ford the Yakama River. Straight off, they knocked off four of 'em. Two got away, but they didn't last long. Qual-chan and his warriors caught up an' blasted 'em inta kingdom come. Then a brave with the name of Charley Nason an' 'nother Yakama gunned down two white men in the Ump-tan-um hills.

"Yep, yuh could say since the treaty signin' the Injuns hev really showed what's in ther hearts. Fer all the good he done, ol' Guv Stevens might as well hev stayed in bed. Everybody would've been much better off. The way I see it, all those good things he promised laid the groundwork fer the next Indian war, which I'm afeered's already beginin'."

Unbeknownst to Joe, the Olafson's two older boys, attracted by their neighbor's strange visitors, sneaked up to a window and listened in on their conversations. Soon the news Grasshopper and Pinky brought had circulated throughout the community. Fear of an Indian uprising struck like a thunderclap. Flaming bearded settler, Joshua Short, and his gabby wife, both professed Indian haters, insisted that a town hall meeting should be held: the subject, the looming Indian crisis. Pinky and Grasshopper and Joe were requested to attend but had no desire to get involved and bluntly said so.

The citizenry would not take no for an answer. A delegation, led by Short, marched down the lane, surrounded the porch and called out to the occupants they wanted to talk business. Pinky and Grasshopper primed their rifles, and Joe took down the old scatter gun he had inherited from Buck Stone. He stepped outside, holding the gun carelessly in the crook of his elbow, the barrel slanting down toward Short's protruding belly.

"What's all the fuss about?" Joe asked tersely. It had been five years since he last had seen the flaming bearded man. Age had not enhanced his looks or manners, Joe thought. The pouches beneath his eyes sagged like canvas water bags. His red hair was beginning to show streaks of white and his mouth caved in from loss of teeth. He was a far different man from the feisty firebrand who had clashed with Deacon and his Cheyenne friends at the wagon train camp on the Sweetwater. Joe almost felt sorry for him. Like nearly everyone else, conquering the western wilderness had taken the starch out of the poor fellow.

"I know we ain't always hit it off," Short said in a voice as raspy as a rusty barn door hinge, "but we's here on community business. People want'ta know straight out 'bout this Injun trouble north of the Columbia River. Hevin' Injuns in yer family, an' all these sojers comin' an' goin', yuh must know somethin'. . ."

At that moment Grasshopper thrust his rifle barrel out the window. "I'll betcha I could trim thet redhead's sideburns without half tryin'," he said loud enough for those outside to hear.

"Yuh trim one side an' I'll trim t'other," Pinky, his nose twitching furiously, replied. He thrust his rifle barrel through a second window. The snap of cocking rifles stopped Short in mid-sentence. Uttering exclamations of protest, the men around him alertly moved away.

"I told yuh this wasn't goin' ta work," a voice said.

"Yeah! These people're 'bout as civic minded as a den of skunks."

As it turned out, the two men could not have attended the town hall meeting. That afternoon they were recalled to duty. Pinky's furlough had been cut short, and Grasshopper's enlistment period had been extended for emergency reasons. The messenger who brought the summons reported more Indian trouble.

"Guess yuh heard 'bout the Yakamas takin' pot shots at our boys," the courier said. "Yuh kin betcher life those skirmishes really got the attention of the powers ta be. A fella named Haller an' a company or so of Blue Coats went scootin' up ta teach Kamiakin an' his Yakamas a lesson, caught 'em on the Toppinish. The Injuns began shootin' like fury. Our boys charged after 'em, answerin' 'em shot fer shot, but those cussed Injuns wasn't 'bout ta give in.

"Fer a day or so it looked like a draw. Then, from somewhere a horde of fresh warriors came thunderin' out of the hills. They near beat ol' Haller's outfit inta the ground, but when night come the Injuns took time off ta snooze. Haller took advantage an' hightailed lickety-split inta Fort Dalles.

"I guess now we're fixin' ta hand 'em lesson number two. I wish yuh galoots luck. Those Injuns're puttin' up a mighty good scrap. Fer certain, if'n they's callin' back ugly bustards like yuh two, yuh kin see things'er gittin' desperate."

XXVI

*My people, the Great Spirit has his eyes upon us. He will be
angry if, like cowardly dogs, we give our lands to the whites.
Better to die like brave warriors on the battlefield . . .*
Kamiakin, Yakama

During the fall of 1855, it seemed the pain of the whole
world was centered on the Northwest plateau. Rumors of all kinds
drifted across the land in bits and pieces, and no one knew how to
fit the pieces together. Although not directly involved in the flare-
ups that were taking place, Nez Perce scouts kept close watch.
Each report of killings, whether Indian or non-Indian, was like a
sharp pin prick. If enough of them struck they would draw blood.

To prepare for the worst, council meetings were called.
Leaders met in long wordy sessions. What was the cause of this
sudden wave of bloodshed? Where was it going? What effect
would it have on the inhabitants of the region? These and many
more questions were discussed and rediscussed.

Vision Seeker sat alongside the leaders of the council sessions and, as usual, listened carefully but said little. He was
alarmed by the reports, yet felt any action his people took only
would make matters worse. At the moment the hostilities were
occurring far from the Nez Perce homelands. If everyone kept
his head, the whole business might blow over without affecting
them at all. Again, Looking Glass had saved them from disaster.
He had insisted on having Red Craig as their agent, a man people
respected and trusted whether Indian or non-Indian. He watched
over them far better than did either Governor Chief Stevens or
the White Father who promised to protect them from harm.

The Yakama had not trusted Agent Bolon. Kamiakin disliked him intensely. Even Catholic Father Pandosy had asked
Bolon be replaced. The fact that he had been killed would not

make either Kamiakin or Pandosy unhappy, but killing an agent of the American government was disastrous. The Yakamas should have known the Blue Coats would swarm into their lands like salmon returning home to spawn. Everyone agreed, the Yakama were in for a very hard time.

Vision Seeker's home life also was the talk around village campfires. Here was a man who had lived a celibate life. Except for concern over his sister and mother, for all anyone knew, he never had given any woman a second glance. He spent more time away from his home lodge than he did in it. The forests, hillsides, distant valleys and ravines had been his domain. Suddenly, except for council meetings, he was keeping as close to his lodge as if he had lost all desire to see the outside world.

Looking Glass' band of buffalo hunters had spread the news of the couple's unusual coming together. Some thought Vision Seeker had done right. The poor widowed girl needed protection and he protected her. Others said he had taken advantage of her, a lustful, middle-aged man preying on a young maiden's innocence. At a village feast when Mu-tu wore the elaborately decorated elk skin dress, those who spoke despairingly of his actions, were aghast. Not only was Vision Seeker taking advantage of her, he was displaying her as if she was a person of consequence, on a higher plain than other village women. Only a few of Raven Wing's old time friends, like Small Goat, knew the story of the elk skin dress. Only she came up to press Mu-tu's hands and told her how wonderfully well she looked.

Vision Seeker took no note of village gossip. If he knew of it, he wasn't bothered. He enjoyed the beauty Mu-tu brought into his life. Restlessness that had driven him into the forests and hillsides was gone. He loved to sit by the fire in the evenings to hear his woman stirring around in the lodge. When one night Mu-tu whispered she was with child, he smiled. He mentally counted the days until he truly would become a father.

However, events that were taking place among the neighbors of the Nez Perce could not be shut out like closing a door.

Almost every day riders came pounding up the Kooskooskie Trail and in to Lapwai village with warlike news. The Blue Coats were on the march with monstrous guns capable of cutting down a dozen warriors in one blast. One thousand or more Yakama warriors were gathering at Indian Gap to face this advancing army. Hairy faces throughout the region were fleeing for their lives. Oregon Governor Curry had declared a state of emergency, calling for volunteers. Hundreds of Willamette Valley homesteaders soon would invade the plateau.

Vision Seeker collected the news and stored it away as squirrels did edibles for the winter. One never knew when a small bit of information could be the clue that might lead to victory or defeat. The old tenseness that Vision Seeker had shed, returned to weigh on him greater than ever. Now that he was on the verge of becoming a father, he had a very personal stake in whatever the future held.

**

Early in the fall Joe Jennings also found events crowding in on him. A courier arrived requesting him to present himself for duty. A volunteer army was being organized to support a force of regular army troops under the command of a Major Gabriel Rains. The troop was to march along the north bank of the Columbia until it arrived at the junction of the Yakama River. The object of the campaign was to punish the Yakama, the courier explained. The inexperienced volunteers needed a man with knowledge of the terrain and people of plateau country, the courier went on to say. The man chosen -- Joe Jennings.

Joe shook his head. He had no desire to have any part in fighting the Yakamas. The Gilliam led campaign in '48 had sickened him of the whole business. Besides, he had promised Tildy he would watch over Granddad. The old fellow seemed to be doing well, but at his advanced age one never knew how he would feel on the morrow. Tildy would never forgive him if he didn't keep his promise, but the courier was insistent. If the Indians were not put down every white person in the region was at risk.

"You had better do as the man asks," Granddad said. "You can't shirk your duty to flag and country. David and I'll make out fine." He gave Macon Laird's adopted son a pat on the back.

Why did Granddad put it that way, making him look disloyal if he didn't go? "All right," he reluctantly said to the courier. "I'll be along shortly."

Joe made certain the larder was filled, instructed youthful David Malin on the medicine Granddad should take, and rode down the road to ask Bithiah Olafson if every so often she would look in on Granddad. When he was satisfied he had done everything he could for Granddad's care, he said good-bye. Granddad hugged him and David followed him to the lane, assuring him all would be well. All he had to do was keep himself alive.

Late in the evening Joe arrived in Oregon City, a volunteer assembly point, to find the town in chaos. Tents were pitched in open spaces; horses and mules were tethered to every hitching post; buggies, wagons, and three-wheeled mule killers were parked higgledy-piggledy. Street corners were crowded with men of every age and ilk. Farmers, innkeepers, soldiers, mill hands, lumberjacks, even sailors from ships docked in Canemah, the village below the Willamette River falls, were present, smoking, chewing, spitting, bragging and cursing the Indians who threatened their lives and property.

Public houses rang with the tinkle of pianos and plunking of banjos. The music, if one could call it that, barely could be heard above shouts, curses and the high pitched laughter of ladies of the evening. After the peace and quiet of farm life, the noise struck Joe's ear drums like a flock of quarreling blue jays. "Why was it the thought of going to war made grown men act like boisterous youngsters?" he wondered.

The wait in Oregon City was short. Orders arrived for the volunteers to move north in the hopes of catching Major Rains' command of regular soldiers. The volunteers straggled forward in ragged disorganized groups that reminded Joe of Gillliam's disastrous '48 campaign.

Among the volunteers he was surprised to see a few men he knew, the obnoxious, bigoted Joshua Short and a redheaded Irishman, whose name he could not remember, but the talkative man quickly put him straight. He was Patrick O'Flanigan who had crossed the plains with Joe in '46. There was something furtive about the fellow that aroused Joe's curiosity. He sensed he and his scraggly bearded companion were trying to avoid him.

The second evening the volunteers bivouacked in a sheltered glen at the base of a sheer cliff. The rocky overhang gave limited protection from the ever present misty rain. All day the men rode and tramped along a muddy roadway in a penetrating drizzle. Everyone from officers on down were soaked through. To make matters worse, a chilling breeze kicked up, sweeping through the Columbia River Gorge. Fires were difficult to start. Dry fuel was impossible to find.

Through some miracle Joe discovered an old dry magpie nest that made perfect kindling to start a blaze. His campfire blazed brightly while, from what he could see, others merely produced smoke. Soon he found himself hugging the fire with the Irishman, his scraggly companion, who said his name was Rankin, and the irascible flaming bearded Joshua Short. Short eyed him with distaste. The Irishman and sidekick Rankin, remained as far away as they could and still warm themselves.

The sight of all three irritated Joe. "What's the matter with you two?" he said addressing the carrot topped Irishman and his companion. "Every time I come near you act like a couple of rabbits that chanced onto a rattlesnake."

"Maybeso, they smell the scent of Injun on yuh," Short, rasped.

Joe seized the man's flaming beard, his fury giving him extraordinary strength. He pulled him so close the stench of the repulsive fellow's breath nearly made him gag. "You oversized ferret. When sharing my fire, you keep your bloody mouth shut."

For a while there was uneasy silence as the men rubbed their hands above and thrust their behinds toward the warmth.

Finally Carrot Top O'Flanigan, timidly spoke. "What kind of magic did yuh perform ta git a fire like this goin'?" he asked.

Short, couldn't keep quiet any longer. "Larned it from his Injun relatives -- thet's what," he rasped.

"No, a mountain man named Buck Stone taught me, or perhaps it was a trapper called Little Ned. I can't exactly remember," Joe calmly replied. He was not about to allow Joshua Short to get under his skin again.

Whoever 'twas, larned yuh well," Raunchy Rankin chimed in. "I ain't 'preciated a fire like this in a coon's age."

In spite of the weather and disorganization, the volunteers made good time. Outside Fort Dalles they caught up with Major Rains' regulars. The major, a West Point graduate with service in the Seminole and Mexican campaigns, was not at all pleased.

"These country bumpkins are going to be far more trouble than they're worth," he complained to Lieutenant Phil Sheridan who would go on to make a name for himself in the Civil War. "Unfortunately, that Oregon Governor wished them on us and we'll have to put up with them one way or the other."

In spite of the Major's ill feeling toward the volunteers, he asked to have a local guide assigned to the lead company commanded by a youthful officer. Thus, Joe found himself reporting to brash Lieutenant Webster, fresh out of West Point. From the first he sensed trouble. After introducing himself, Joe respectfully awaited his orders. Webster looked him up and down as if he found the sight repulsive.

"Are you a soldier or a vagrant? If you're a soldier when you report to an officer you salute."

"Yes, sir," Joe drew himself up and tossed a half salute. "Scout and guide Jennings reporting for duty."

"Hmm," Webster grunted. "You know your way around these parts?"

"I've trapped and traveled this country for nearly 15 years."

"Well, we'll soon see," the lieutenant said skeptically, and turned away.

XXVII

We Indians have a spiritual tie with the earth, a reverence for it that whites don't share and hardly can understand.

Harriett Pierce, Seneca

The first day on the trail everything went well. By nightfall Joe felt somewhat better about Lieutenant Webster. However, an incident the following morning dampened his optimism. While saddling his horse he caught a fleeting glimpse of Flaming Beard Short furtively leaving camp.

"What's that fellow doing here?" he asked the guard who had just come off duty. "He's supposed to be with the volunteers that are a day's march to the rear."

"He came with some kind of message -- had to speak with the lieutenant, he claimed," the sleepy-eyed guard replied.

At that moment Lieutenant Webster appeared with boots polished and brass spurs jingling. After a curt nod to acknowledge Joe's presence, he mounted the horse a private held for him and the day's march began. Everything went well until they came upon two draws that looked similar. However, one appeared more passable than the other. When Joe motioned toward the less inviting one, Webster called the column to a halt. "Why choose that one? This one looks better."

"That one leads nowhere. This one takes us through the mountains," Joe replied.

Webster called his sergeants forward. There was a short discussion, then he turned to Joe. "The consensus is we should take the more accessible one."

"Yes, sir," Joe said. "I'll wait here until you return."

"Soldier! . . ." The lieutenant snapped. Then held his tongue. Major Rains was right. These volunteers were about as worthless as a bucket of spit. Why waste your breath on them.

He wheeled about and waved the column forward. The troopers passed by until swallowed by the forest.

Joe tethered his horse and leaned against a tree trunk. It would take a half a day for Webster to find his way blocked by boulders as large as small houses. Just as he was about to snooze the sound of hoofbeats came from the south trail. A captain rode up, noticing Joe, he pulled his mount to a halt.

"Aren't you Jennings, A Company's guide?"

"Yes, sir. I am waiting for A Company to return. The lieutenant wanted to explore this side canyon."

The captain swore. "What the devil. This is no time to go gandering about." He swiveled his mount around to follow the trail Company A had taken.

"This may get interesting," Joe said to Blackie, his horse.

Shortly the sound of marching men came drifting up the trail. The column of volunteers appeared. Out front was a huge man on an equally large white horse.

"Hello, Jennings. What're doing here, waitin' fer the cows ta come home?"

Joe gaped. He had marched with this man during Gilliam's campaign. He searched for the name.

"Don't recognize me, huh? Name's Walsh -- Tiny Walsh. Since we marched tagether me ol' belly's stretched bigger'n a hoop on a barrel of hooch. Well, I better git movin'. Nice talkin' ta yuh, 'cept I ain't heerd yuh say a word."

Hardly did Walsh and the volunteer column pass when Company A appeared. Both Captain and Lieutenant looked grim. Joe said nothing but led the way up the proper canyon.

**

Major Rains was furious. "What have you been doing? It took you four days to get to the Yakama when you should have done it in two. What the hell went wrong? From what I hear you ignored your guide's instructions and took off on your own."

"Yes sir, but-but I couldn't trust the guide," Lieutenant Webster stammered. "I was told by a reliable source he's got

Indian family -- he's on the side of the Indian, not the US Army."

"What reliable source?" Rains demanded.

"Fellow by the name of Short -- swore on a Bible . . ."

"Rubbish! Report back to your company."

The trip into the blocked canyon wasn't the only time waster. When the volunteers and regulars came together, animals carrying supplies of the two forces became entangled. The avaricious volunteers snapped up army goods like hungry vultures. Even mules were shanghaied. Before the march ended the regulars had lost 30 animals and untold supplies.

To add to the Major's ire, from every side painted warriors sniped at the troopers with well aimed arrows. This was the last straw for Major Rains. He would subdue these Indians or else. He shouted for the heavy guns. For hours howitzers pounded the Indians who were holed up behind an intervening ridge.

"'Pon me soul," Carrot Top uttered. "Those poor folk ain't got a chance. I feel downright sorry fer 'em."

Joe agreed. Every howitzer boom made the nerve ends in his stomach bounce and burn as though his insides were aflame.

The howitzers barely fell quiet before two companies of regulars and volunteers, whooping and shouting, charged up the slope. "You bloody Redskins we're goin' ta kill yuh ta the last man," a voice rang out above the rest. Joe was not at all surprised to see that the words came from flaming bearded, Joshua Short. Out-gunned and outmanned, Kamiakin, leader of the besieged warriors, wisely withdrew his forces.

Rather than pursue the enemy, Rains ordered his troop to halt. Actually, his heart was not in the fight. He had no love for Governor Stevens who had created the Indian unrest. Also, Rains was against the idea of a northern transcontinental railway. Along with Secretary of War, Jefferson Davis, he felt that if there was to be a railway linking east with the west, it should be the southern route. In six year's time he would resign his commission and fight for the Confederacy.

The troop was ordered to make camp on Ahtanum Creek

near St. Joseph Mission. Fearing a possible ambush, the troopers cautiously advanced through the canyon toward the mission. A scattering of Indians could be seen fleeing. A straggler on a lame horse fell behind. An Indian guide named Cut-mouth John (so named because part of his mouth had been shot away) raced ahead to chop the fleeing man down and take his scalp.

After making camp, both regulars and volunteers, heated by the skirmish, strode around bragging. From somewhere a jug of booze emerged. With victory and liquor under their belts, the high-spirited men, particularly, the volunteers, began to seek ways to work off pent up energy. Someone spotted the buildings at St. Joseph Mission. "Let's give these traitorous black robes a good scare," belligerent Short suggested.

A group led by the bigoted man advanced toward the mission. Short, like many homesteaders, had a hatred for Catholics. The fact that the priests at St. Joseph were thick with the Yakamas, increased the group's ire. "Let's teach 'em a lesson they'll never fergit," a Falls City farmer yelled. "We ain't toleratin' traitors, 'specially ones thet consort with murderous Injuns."

With the butt of his rifle, Short pounded on the mission door. There was no answer. He lifted a heavy boot and kicked the door in. There was no one inside. A low fire burned in the fireplace. Two cats crouched on the hearth. Somewhere a clock could be heard ticking away the seconds. Account books and ledgers and a letter addressed to the American soldiers lay on a table. Hanging from hooks were the priests' colorful vestments. From all appearances the mission occupants had fled with the Indians, taking with them only what they could carry.

The peaceful scene enraged Joshua Short. "The dadblasted Injun lovers hev got clean away," he shouted, knocking down a painting of the Virgin Mary. A noncom swept the account books, ledgers and letter into a bag.

The mission grounds appeared just as peaceful. Pigs in a pigsty grunted contentedly. In a fenced garden cabbages and withered tops of potato plants lay in neat rows. The volunteers, who

had been existing on salted meat and mouldy bread, quickly saw
the possibility of a tasty change of menu.

The Fall City farmer fired a bullet into a pig's head, a
butcher from North Plains sliced the throat of another. The mad
rush was on. The volunteers went down garden rows, collecting
every edible in view. Potato diggers sent dirt and buried tubers
flying until a Champoeg man's digging tool struck something solid.
He clawed away the dirt to expose a barrel.

"These cursed priests hev buried ther valuables in the
ground." A number of men dropped what they were doing to dig.
Carrot Top O'Flanigan, who had been examining the barrel that
had been uncovered, suddenly swore. "Blimey! Thet's a keg of
gunpowder. I've handled enuff of 'em ta spot 'em anywhere."

The disclosure brought more diggers into the garden. For
certain the blasted pious priests were in league with the murderous Indians. More hidden items were uncovered. Guns, lead,
another half keg of powder, and a heavy weatherproof bag fastened with a thong of leather. The diggers cheered. Here was
what they sought. Only the most valuable of possessions would
be so well protected. The rich Catholics kept their wine in gold
jugs and drank it from chalices of silver and gold. A dozen knives
appeared. They would have slashed at the protective covering,
but Short held up his hand.

"Hold on fellas," he said. "mustn't damage the goods.
Who knows how many thousands this here bag holds." He cut
the binding cord and opened the bag to lift out an object enclosed
in a small canvas sack. He carefully slit it open and swore.

"It's a blasted book! He threw it aside and took out another canvas sack which also contained a book. He withdrew
one sack after another, more than a half dozen in all. "Trash,
furrin', yuh cain't even read the blasted things. Maybeso, spy
writin'. These furriners'll do anythin' ta take this land from us'ns."

"Let's give these priests a lesson -- burn down the whole
shebang," someone suggested. The mission buildings were
torched. The bag of books would have been thrown into the fire,

too, but Carrot Top jerked the bag out of bellowing Short's hands. "Yuh imbecile, could be evidence. Save the bloody stuff . . . hand it over to someun who kin read," he said.

Even into the next morning the celebrations continued. Lieutenant Phil Sheridan later wrote a report of the occasion:

". . . The first thing I saw when I put my head out from my blankets was 'Cut-mouth John', already mounted and parading himself through the camp. The scalp of the Indian he had dispatched the day before was tied to the cross bar of his bridle bit, the hair dangling almost to the ground, and John was decked out in the sacred vestments of Father Pandosy . . ."

The savagery displayed by Cut-mouth John was even more than Indian and Catholic haters could stomach. The scalp and vestments were taken from Cut-mouth, and then the man was run out of camp and told never to show his ugly face again.

It was the letter found on the table, however, that made Major Rains grind his teeth and swear. Supposedly written by Pandosy at Kamiakin's request, it accused the Americans of great injustice: ". . . We know perfectly the heart of the Americans. For a long time they hanged us without knowing if we did right or wrong, but they have never killed or hanged one American, though there is no place where Americans have not killed Indians. We are therefore as dogs. . . . You have fired the first shot. Our hearts are broken. There only is one breath left in us; we did not have the strength to answer. Then we took common cause with our enemies to defend all together our nationality and our country. . . If we lose the men who keep the camp in which are wives and children we will kill them rather see them fall into the hands of the Americans . . . For we have hearts and self-respect."

Later Rains wrote a terse response addressed to Kamiakin: "We will wage war forever, until not a Yakama breathes in the land he calls his own. My kind advice to you is to scatter yourselves among the Indian tribes more peaceful and forget you were ever Yakamas." The letter, written on silk oilcloth was hung on a pole where it could be carried away by any passing horseman.

XXVIII

Respect your enemy for one day the differences that separate
you may pass away and make you friends.
Anonymous

Before the volunteers broke camp on Ahtanum Creek, Carrot Top O'Flanigan and Raunchy Rankin, who had taken no part in Cut-mouth's chastisement, spent the morning searching for Joe Jennings. Finally, the monkey was off their backs. They now had the lost goods to deliver to its rightful owner. The two men went through the volunteer camp and then that of the regulars. Joe was not to be found. Hardly anyone remembered seeing him, and no one knew where he had gone.

"What're we ta do now?" Raunchy asked. "This bag's as heavy as lead an' we'uns got ta lug it 'round, is thet what yuh're figurin'? Hey, there's thet grasshopper mule skinner, let's turn it over ta him."

But Grasshopper took one look and shook his head. "I'd like ta help yuh fellas, but an officer see's thet thing he'll be askin' what's in it. When I tell him, he'll say git the hell rid of it."

Once again Raunchy and Carrot Top were stuck with the cumbersome bag, but now they knew what it contained. How it mysteriously reappeared in Father Pandosy's garden would puzzle them for the remainder of their days.

Since the Webster wrong way canyon debacle, as far as Company A was concerned, Joe Jennings was persona non grata. Lieutenant Webster was too chagrined to seek his services. Other officers, including Major Rains, also avoided him, feeling tarnished by the incompetence of their fellow officer. After the bombardment, Joe had slipped out of camp and went scouting on his own. He wanted to see first hand what havoc the heavy guns had created. As dawn broke he circled the ridge that the Indians, had for a while, successfully defended. Behind it they had erected a stone wall for protection. Howitzer missiles had knocked it to pieces. Boulders had been sent flying. Ugly craters had been cut out of the sod. Personal items and weapons lay broken and useless. It was obvious, the warriors had made a hasty retreat. Ill-equipped and outmanned, the Yakamas had been severely beaten.

When Joe reported in at Fort Dalles, more grim news of the Yakama retreat was received. Scouts following Kamiakin's forces related accounts of great suffering. Many Yakamas, including women and children, had been forced to swim the icy waters of the Columbia River. Exposure and cold had claimed many lives. Uncertain of where to find safe haven, the fleeing people scattered in all directions from Puget Sound in the west to homelands of the Nez Perce in the east. Many traveled north to huddle in camps near the Canadian border where bitter cold weather and scarcity of food had them dying by the dozens.

Joe, who had spent many winter months trapping in the Bitterroots, the Bighorns and on the Yellowstone, knew the terrible conditions under which the homeless Indian people were forced to live. During the immigration of '46 he nearly had frozen his feet. Now, almost a decade later, the affected areas still burned and tingled when cold. The horrendous suffering the Yakamas were enduring and the rising hatred against them, made him glad Michael and his family were safely in Europe where they could live peacefully and be respected. Joe ruefully had to admit, Macon Laird's decision to take them there had been a very wise move.

Word also drifted in of the St. Joseph priests. They had followed the banks of the Columbia northward to Colville to be received by Jesuit Fathers stationed there. But their friendliness with the natives had earned them the enmity of Governor Stevens. He issued a missive forbidding Father Pandosy to reenter the Yakama homeland until hostilities were over.

The arms and gun powder discovered in St. Joseph's garden fueled an anti-Catholic movement among all whites. Father

Pandosy and his fellow priests were accused of supplying the Yakamas with powder, lead and guns. However, on close study of mission account books, only 100 pounds of gun powder had been purchased by the priests in the previous four years, an amount hardly sufficient to keep hunting parties supplied.

Joe's days at Fort Dalles were short. Fear ran high among white communities everywhere. News of Indian uprisings came from the Puget Sound area, Yakama Valley and Rogue River country. To make matters more threatening, Peu-peu-mox-mox was said to be gathering a massive force of warriors in the Walla Walla Valley. If this army of warriors swept through the high country it well could be the death warrant for every non-Indian person in the region. More volunteers urgently were called for. A detachment under the command of Major Mark Chinn received orders to reinforce Fort Walla Walla. Joe Jennings was assigned as scout and guide.

The normal confusion in launching a long march took place. The wake-up bugle call came while still dark. Excited dogs barked, a brace of mules hee-hawed, officers bellowed and noncoms did likewise. Soldiers awakened cursing and grumbling. Tents were struck and baggage packed. Horses and mules were saddled and loaded. A steamboat that plowed the navigable waters of the Columbia whistled its arrival and docked. A mad dash to unload supplies followed. A noncom with countless service stripes on his sleeve issued strident orders.

Joe, already prepared for the march, watched the preparations with an amused expression. The hustle and bustle reminded him of a disturbed ant hill. Except for the noncom supervising the unloading of the steamboat, everyone ran hither and thither as if their pants were on fire. It suddenly dawned on Joe the noncom in charge of the unloading was none other than his old antagonist, Sergeant Algernon Coombs. Strangely, the sight of the irascible taskmaster boosted his spirits. This was one man who certainly knew the rigors of campaigning. By now the old soldier had put in over 25 years of service.

The column forded the Deschutes and crossed the John Day. For Joe every landmark brought memories of the past -- former journeys made along the very same route. There was the trip in '43 when obnoxious Indian Agent Elijah White attempted to force his code of laws on the Cayuse. In '48 he rode with Gilliam's volunteers on the way to apprehend the Whitman Mission murderers. In '49 he passed this way while marching west with the Mounted Riflemen. Joe grimaced. As far as he was concerned every trip had ended in disaster. He fervently hoped this one would have a happier conclusion, but doubted it.

The column made camp at Wells Springs within an arrow flight of Sand Hollows where, in '48, seven years previously, the first battle of the Gilliam led campaign was fought. Before the camp had settled for the night, Joe rode out in an attempt to locate the site where Sandy Sanders, Tildy's first husband, had been killed. He was surprised to see Sergeant Coombs closely follow. Joe drew up until the two were riding side by side. The old soldier was the first to speak.

"Riding alone these days can be dangerous," he said. "A courier from up river reports the Walla Wallas have captured Fort Walla Walla and are watching our every move."

"So, Peu-peu-mox-mox finally is going to revenge his dead son," Joe mused. "'For, as thou urgest justice, be assured Thou shalt have justice, more than thou desirest'," he quoted. Abruptly he pulled his horse to a stop and dismounted.

"Right here in this sand dune the battle we called Sand Hollows took place." Joe removed his hat, knelt down to take a handful of sand and let it sift through his fingers. To his surprise his companion also dismounted, stood at attention and, for a full minute, held a salute.

"I am not especially religious but to me battlefields are hallowed ground," the sergeant explained. "The men who met here, whether friend or foe, did so with courage. They fought, defending what to them was something precious -- their possessions, their loved ones or even their way of life. How can you fault anyone who does that?"

Joe was stunned. He never before had seen this side of
the rough, gruff noncom. Companionably, they rode side by side
back to camp. On the way the old soldier asked after the health
and whereabouts of the Michael Two Feathers family. When informed they had gone to England, the sergeant pulled his horse to
a halt to exclaim.

"What in the world is he going to do there?"

"Plans to study doctoring."

"Dr. Two Feathers. Damn me, but I think he can do it.
Anyone with the brains to study at Fairview Academy can go
anywhere. Good for him. I wish him success."

Joe mentally shook his head. He was more impressed by
the transformation of Sergeant Coombs than his brother's academic ability. "How did you know about Fairview Academy?"

"Oh, your brother and I once had a long, interesting talk.
You should remember it. It was the time I was unhorsed out in
nowhere. It caused such a stink that to this day I haven't outlived
it. After we had crossed the Kansas River I went back to check
on the Morgans. Upon leaving them the horse had bolted, pitch-
ing me off. The next day Two Feathers came looking for me. At
the time I could have shot him, picking his way through the brush
as if taking a Sunday stroll through the park. Glad I didn't. He
sure saved my bacon in that shoot-out on the mountain. . . ."

The old soldier fell silent until they parted near camp.
"By the way, the next time we're both in Vancouver, why don't
you have dinner with Lucille and me? After all, we Mounted
Riflemen, who marched 2,000 miles across the 'Big Open' together, have a tradition to maintain, don't you think?"

Joe was so surprised he did not answer. The change in his
former adversary was more than he could comprehend.

The next day the march continued, but this time it was
toward Umatilla Crossing where it was feared Peu-peu-mox-mox
and his warriors would attack next. The route followed was the
same one Gilliam and his volunteers had taken after the Battle of

Sand Hollows. More familiar landmarks emerged. At Butter Creek Joe searched the banks for signs of the Cayuse camp where Five Crows and his warriors had stopped to nurse their wounds.

After the column made camp Joe rode north to a point that overlooked the homeland of Stickus. Almost as soon as he appeared two armed riders alertly rode up to challenge him. He raised his hand in the sign of friend. The two riders advanced. He knew them -- Cut Lip and Willakin. They stared unabashedly.

"You come visit Stickus?" Willakin asked.

"No, I ride with the Blue Coats."

"You go. Blue Coats no good," Cut Lip said.

The next few days were spent building a stockade and two livestock corrals at Umatilla Crossing. After some deliberations, the fortification was named Fort Henrietta after Major Haller's wife. Why she was honored, Joe never discovered. Her husband had led the initial attack on the Yakamas, a foray which the Indian warriors met and turned back.

While construction of the fort continued, Joe and other scouts fanned over the countryside to determine the location, size, and makeup of the Indian force. Gradually, the pieces of information collected provided a good idea of the enemy numbers and identities. Besides his own warriors, it was estimated Peu-peu-mox-mox had recruited 400 Cayuse, 400 Yakama, 300 Klickitats, 200 Teninos and 200 Palouse. When apprised of the numbers, Major Chinn called his officers together.

"Men, we cannot afford to lose the upper hand," he said. "As the old saying goes, an ounce of prudence is worth a pound of gold. Prudence tells me we need more men and guns. So I'm sending a courier to Fort Dalles requesting two more companies and all the artillery they can spare. Until then we wait and watch."

Noncom Coombs, who was privy to the information, passed it on to Joe who shook his head sadly. "I fear for Peu-peu-mox-mox. The old fellow deserves a better fate than he is certain to receive. These people will not stop until they have either broken his spirit or taken his life, perhaps both.

XXIX

They must yield or perish . . . the time shall come that the roving tribes are reduced to complete dependence and submission. . . . This is the true permanent policy of the Government.
Report, United States Secretary of the Interior

Late in November, the reinforcements Major Chinn requested arrived at Fort Henreitta. Instead of two companies, three appeared with Lieutenant Colonel James K. Kelly in command. On December 2nd, Kelly and his men marched on Fort Walla Walla.

"I'm going to put the fear of God into these recalcitrant Indians or my name isn't Kelly," he vowed. He set out in the evening expecting to march through the night and surprise the enemy at first light of dawn. The elements were against him. A heavy rain began to fall. The sage and buckbrush covered land could not absorb the downpour. Creeks, dry since the spring rains, filled and overflowed. Low areas became muddy swamps. Blinded by darkness and blowing rain, the men could not see where they were going. Soaked to the skin, they stumbled into creeks, fought through unseen tangles of brush and bogged down in the swamps. The element of surprise was lost.

It was nearly noon before they arrived at Fort Walla Walla. Again they were thwarted. The fort was deserted. The buildings had been ransacked. Everything of value had been carried away. The exhausted men spent the evening there, trying to dry out and recover their strength. Kelly called for his scouts, ordering them to locate the slippery enemy.

This was almost home country for Joe Jennings. He had traveled through this land more times than he could count. The track up the Walla Walla River led to Waiilatpu and the old Whitman Mission. Again memories of the past returned to haunt him. He longed for those former tense days leading up to the Whitman Mission tragedy. Then the troubles Indian people faced seemed overwhelming, but nothing like those they faced today. The nearer the column approached the stream called Touchet, the more Indian sign Joe spotted. He had the distinct feeling he was being watched, not by one pair of eyes but many. He pulled his mount to a halt. The sound of hoofbeats drifted to his ears. Who made them and where were they coming from? A feathered crested head bobbed above the nearby brush covered ridge, and then another and another appeared. The Indian horsemen pulled their mounts to a stop to peer down, their expressionless faces glistening under the weak winter sun.

Joe signaled the column to halt. He couldn't tell if the Indians were friendly or hostile. From their actions, he had to assume they were hostile. Peu-peu-mox-mox had suffered all he could stand. He had lost his son and his homeland to the whites. Now, at this late date, he was going to fight back. He loved this Walla Walla Valley. His people had lived there as long as Walla Walla tribesmen could remember. But the Indian horsemen retreated. If they were going to fight it would be at their choosing.

The following morning Colonel Kelly ordered the column to march toward the Touchet River, determined to make contact with the enemy. Baggage, rations and surplus horses were left behind. At the opening of a defile in the hills, Kelly ordered a halt. Out of the canyon emerged six Indian horsemen. Joe who was out front, let out a low whistle. One of the horsemen he knew. He would recognize the straight figure anywhere. It was the Walla Walla leader, himself, Peu-peu-mox-mox. Equally surprising was that from an upright stick he carried a white flag.

"The Old Chief wants a peaceful parley," Joe muttered to no one in particular. What was the matter with him? It was too late for that. He had an urge to shout, "Stop! You are walking into a trap." Kelly was in no mood to talk peace. He wanted to rid the region of all Indians or force them into submission, which now was the policy of the Great Father in Washington. His children had rejected his benevolence and either had to behave or face extermination.

"Won't do any harm to listen to the old boy," Joe heard John McBean the interpreter to say.

"I suppose so," Colonel Kelly replied. "After all he is under a white flag."

"Why do you come with many soldiers?" Peu-peu-mox-mox asked. "My people have done nothing. We are peaceful."

"If you are peaceful why did you attack and sack Fort Walla Walla?" Kelly demanded.

"Our people do not harm Hudson's Bay trading place. The Yakamas make war. Maybe them."

"If that is so, why do your men carry Hudson's Bay things?" Kelly demanded, for behind the chief a large group of horsemen appeared. On a signal they stopped, dismounted and stood by their horses. Within their ranks new blankets and wearing apparel was noticeable which could have been removed recently from trading post shelves.

"Ah! The young men, they not know what they do," the Walla Walla leader replied. "They will give back all that is taken."

Kelly shook his head. "Your warriors also must come to us and give up their weapons and ammunition."

"We can do that. I will return and tell my people."

"No, we will go with you and see it is done," Kelly said. Now that he had the great Walla Walla chief in his hands, he was not about to let him go. As long as he kept the chief hostage the Walla Wallas would not attack, Kelly reasoned.

Peu-peu-mox-mox listened carefully as the interpreter explained. After a moment of hesitation, he made a sign that he was agreeable. "Yes, come with us. My people will butcher many cows and make a big feast."

Kelly ordered his men forward. The band of waiting warriors turned about and retreated, disappearing through the cut in the hills. Suddenly, Kelly had second thoughts and called a halt. The pass they were about to enter was a perfect place for ambush. He was not going chance it. As Major Chinn had said, an ounce of prudence was worth a pound of gold. The company, without baggage and provisions, made a cold, hungry camp. Joe, who also had traveled light, suffered along with the rest, as did the Indian men who had come waving the white flag.

When the camp halted for the night, Peu-peu-mox-mox requested he be allowed to go and prepare his people for the soldiers' arrival. Colonel Kelly refused, believing it was a trick. However, he did allow the Walla Walla leader to send a messenger to make ready the promised feast on the morrow. Before sending the messenger away, the stately Indian leader spoke to him in a language listeners could not understand. Colonel Kelly asked an interpreter what he said, but McBean shook his head.

"The wily fellow's as slick as a barnyard weasel," Kelly muttered. "He and his cohorts came under the white flag with the idea of delaying our march. Old Peu-peu had hoped to save his herds and his people. Now, he instructs his man to hurry and abandon camp. He has delayed us as long as he can."

"Either that or sends orders for his warriors to prepare for the warpath," McBean added.

Besides the cruel elements and hunger gnawing at their innards, a dark, foreboding feeling gripped Kelly's command. Conversation around campfires was sparse and subdued. Although the prisoners were weaponless and watched over by heavily armed guards, still the dark faced Indian men struck fear in the pale faces' hearts.

Peu-peu-mox-mox ignored the soldiers as if they were not worthy of his attention. Other prisoners watched every move they made, their unblinking eyes staring at them like those of night owls. A warrior named Wolf Skin bothered the soldiers the most. Like his namesake, his eyes had a yellow cast and were almost luminous. The watchful orbs even made Joe, who was sympathetic to their cause, turn away. Was this man evil? The thought made him shiver. Through most of the night Indian activity could be heard on all sides of the Blue Coat camp.

"Those damn Injuns is gittin' no more sleep than we is," a middle-aged farmer from Rickreall complained. "They's circlin' 'round like a pack of wolves, lickin' ther chops thinkin' of the fine feed they'll be havin' when daylight comes. Me hopes it's roasted beef they'll be feastin' on 'stead we'uns ."

Finally, the cold light of dawn emerged. On the surrounding high ground warriors watched the miserable soldiers try to pull themselves together. Joe was surprised to see they were led by the Cayuse leader, Five Crows. His flamboyant attire made him attract attention wherever he went. It was said he was related to Peu-peu-mox-mox by marriage Although a disciple of Missionary Henry Spalding, Five Crows had a long history of rebellious deeds committed against hairy faced invaders. Joe passed the information on to Colonel Kelly, who nodded.

"We'd best keep the hostages up front where they can be seen. I shouldn't think they'd attack and put their leaders at risk. Anyway, we're all hungry. Let's go see if our Walla Walla friends have prepared the feast they promised."

The column passed through the defile. Indian sign was everywhere. They came upon a recently deserted camp -- no lodges, no campfires, no pits with roasting beef. The famished soldiers kicked at the debris left behind and cursed. Joe was neither surprised nor disappointed. Peu-peu-mox-mox had learned his lesson well. The white man had practiced deception on him and his people, now he was returning the favor. Rather than feel anger at the man, Joe applauded his actions. Peu-peu-mox-mox would make an outstanding military leader for any army.

The soldiers left the deserted Indian camp and set out to meet up with Major Chinn's command at the mouth of the Touchet, 15 miles distant, grumbling all the way. Once there, Kelly's tired and ravenous men gratefully filled their bellies, but again faced a nearly sleepless night. Barely did they roll up in their blankets when they were aroused by Wolf Skin who made a wild dash for freedom. The guards could not fire their weapons for fear of shooting one of their own. A young trooper leapt to his feet and gave chase. Before Wolf Skin could clear camp, the youth caught up and wrestled him to the ground. To prevent another such occurrence, the prisoners were tied hand and foot, Wolf Skin snarling and glowering like a cornered badger.

On December 7th, 1855, the Battle of Walla Walla was launched. Colonel Kelly, as frustrated and irritated as any of his men, threw caution to the winds. A force of Indian horsemen came within rifle range. A single shot rang out. Immediately, the Blue Coat troopers charged, shooting and yelling as they went. Backed up against the Walla Walla River, the warriors turned on them with vengeance, their numbers far greater than the Blue Coats. Peu-peu-mox-mox and fellow hostages shouted to their comrades to take courage -- they were winning the fray. The troopers were furious. Their anger doubled when an officer rode in with his arm limp, his shoulder shattered by enemy rifle fire.

"What're we to do with these damned prisoners," a volunteer shouted to Colonel Kelly.

"Tie them or kill them, I don't give a damn which. . . ."

"Get the rope an' we'll bind 'em like shoats ready for the market," ordered the butcher who had stabbed one of the St. Joseph pigs. "If they don't like it, we'll cut their throats."

The hostages were seized but before they all could be bound, Wolf Skin seized the North Plains' butcher's knife. Howling like a banshee, he sliced away at his captors. Except for a Nez Perce youth who already had been tied, the rest of the captives began to run. Every one either was shot or clubbed to death, including the great Walla Walla leader, Peu-peu-mox-mox.

The battle continued until sunset when the forward wave of warriors retreated. However, the Blue Coats were given little rest. Indian riflemen kept sniping away at their camp. For Joe Jennings the disastrous day and night was made even worse when David Malin, who had miraculously crossed through the enemy lines, arrived to report that Granddad Jennings had been given only a few weeks to live.

XXX

*Beauty, in our eyes, is always fresh and living, even as God,
the Great Mystery, dresses the world anew at each
season of the year.*
Ohiyesa, Santee Sioux

The first heavy snow covered Lapwai Valley. Vision Seeker awakened to look out at the shimmering landscape. Even as a boy, the first snow of the winter he had greeted with joy. In his youthful mind, Father Sky had painted over all the evil on Mother Earth, making her pure and clean, preparing the way for the promise of spring when the bounty of Mother Earth would emerge new again in all of its color and freshness.

In later years, came the disappointing realization that this wondrous magic he believed in did not always hold true. Winter snow did not erase evil from the surface of Mother Earth. Evil, which came in many forms, was like hibernating snakes and sleeping bears. It lay in wait to catch people like himself unawares.

He thought back to his youth. He had been such a disappointment to his father, Lone Wolf. Perhaps it was because he could see things other people couldn't, or was it because all his life he had been a loner, kept to himself? After he returned from his first vision quests without finding *Wyakin*, Lone Wolf was baffled. Again he sent Second Son to search for the spirit that would guide him through life, and again he returned empty handed. A third time also was a failure, even though he remained in the mountains for a full week

Lone Wolf gave up. He had to accept the fact that Second Son was unlike other boys. He had no time for play or games. He preferred to be alone, studying, searching -- always seeking knowledge -- always coming up with unusual thoughts of future happenings, most of them dire predictions which, unfortunately, often came to pass. Vision Seeker grimaced. Poor Lone Wolf. He never understood the strange power his second son possessed. However, after the last quest the look in his father's eyes . . . The sudden thought struck Vision Seeker -- perhaps Lone Wolf did understand and never let on because so many of his son's predictions were too awful to face.

The Winter of the Circled Moon was an example, the year the first hairy faces Vision Seeker ever saw, appeared. While Lone Wolf and his hunters sat smoking in the snow, the awesome vision of untimely death had come to him like a bolt out of the gray sky above. Lone Wolf thought he had gone mad, but the death he predicted came to pass -- not one death but two! First it was Toohool, the son of Weasel Face, pierced with arrows by Blackfeet raiders. The following winter it was his own brother, Many Horses, who had gone into the white fury that howled down from the north to rescue the herd. He never returned.

"Aagh!" Vision Seeker brushed the awesome memories from his mind. Thankfully, over the years fewer and fewer dire predictions came to him. Yet, more and more terrible things were happening. This year details of the Walla Walla War and Peupeu-mox-mox's death came drifting in. Some accounts were so grisly men would not speak of them in front of family members. How much of the reports was true and how much false, Vision Seeker could not ascertain. On this day of falling snow he intended to find out. He had seen riders going up and coming down the valley. There was only one possible stopping place there, the home of his friend, mountain man Red Craig.

Vision Seeker gave Mu-tu a warm embrace, fastened on his snow shoes and started up the valley leaving a trail through the fresh snow that quickly became smoothed over by more frozen flakes falling from above. In spite of the dark thoughts that crowded his mind, he took pleasure in the swish-swish of the snow shoes and twitter of snow birds that announced his coming from bushes alongside the trail.

A cool breeze stiffened, blowing burning snowflakes into his eyes and into his nose, making him glad when Red Craig's log cabin lodge came into view. A sleepy dog came to greet him, uttering a obligatory bark, it then withdrew to the comfort of its kennel made out of a wooden barrel. Craig's son, Joe, opened the door and hustled him inside. The warmth was so pleasing Vision Seeker's usual taciturn expression broke into a smile.

"Heaven's sake! What brings you out on a day like this?" Craig greeted, surprised by Vision Seeker's unexpected presence.

Vision Seeker removed his snowshoes and outerwear before answering. He was taken aback by the homey scene that met his eyes. He had known this man since he had arrived in 1840, 15 years previously. In all that time he not once had entered Red Craig's home. Curtains were at the windows, pictures and framed embroidery work hung on the walls, as did a cross draped with holly. What attracted him most was a small fir tree in a corner decorated with burning candles and packages beneath wrapped in bright cloth or paper, he couldn't tell which. Red Craig was Catholic. Was this one of the mysteries of his religion?

"Is this the holy day you call Christmas?" Vision Seeker asked, the first words he had spoken.

"No, tomorrow is Christmas, the day we celebrate the birth of Jesus," Craig answered.

"Yes, I know," Vision Seeker said. His thoughts darting back to the time he first had learned of the holy occasion. "Many winters ago I spent Christmas with Buck Stone's trapping brigade in the Bitterroots."

Craig nodded. "Ah, yes, good stout fellows. I guess they all are gone now. I was sorry to hear of Deacon Walton's death. Well, there's still Little Ned's son, Joe. If I remember correctly, he was with them when Buck was killed -- right after the last rendezvous. I wonder if Joe received the bag of goods I sent him. Funny, he didn't say a word about it at the Walla Walla council."

Vision Seeker remained silent. He still was reliving that first Christmas day on the Bitterroot. On Christmas morning Deacon had awakened them beating on a kettle. A bright red cloth covered his hairless head and his beard was whitened with a dusting of flour.

"Wake up," he had shouted, "'tis Santa wishin' yuh a Merry Christmas." From a pouch on his back he began to distribute gifts. All three of the trappers had given him presents. From Little Ned he received a buckskin pouch decorated with porcupine quills. Deacon had given him an Appaloosa pony carved from wood and carefully marked with dots of colored clay to resemble his own Appaloosa. Buck gave him a knife that opened and closed, hiding the blade inside its handle. He, himself, shamefully had had no gifts for his hairy faced friends. Memory of that long ago day was so real and poignant he choked on the hot drink Craig's wife, Isabel, handed him.

"I'm sure you didn't come to speak of Christmas," Craig said, breaking the silence. If everyone will excuse us, we'll retire to the back room and talk business."

This room was far different but equally interesting. A stout desk covered with ledgers and stacks of papers, stood near the back wall. In a corner was a gun cabinet. In the opposite corner two saddles were stacked one on top of the other. Coils of rope hung from pegs on the wall, as did a brace of heavy traps that one set for wolves. On another wall was spread the hide of a mountain sheep, complete with head and tail. Boots, riding clothes, bridles, halters, snow shoes, heavy coats and other outdoor paraphernalia either was scattered about on the floor or hanging from the walls.

"I hope you don't mind the mess," Craig said, clearing off a chair for Vision Seeker. "I'm a regular pack rat, collect everything I can lay my hands on and never throw anything away."

Vision Seeker did not comment. He was impressed by the vast display of possessions and at the same time appalled. If the man had to pack up and leave how ever would he manage? Of course, the hairy faces lived far differently than Indian people. When they built lodges of wood and stone they settled in and remained there. They did not traipse off to the camas fields or buffalo hunting grounds as did the Indian.

"I suppose you have come to speak of the conflicts taking

place on the plateau?" Craig asked.

"We hear terrible things about the death of our friend, Peu-peu-mox-mox. We cannot believe these things are true."

Craig studied the Nimpau friend he had come to respect and trust. How could he break the brutal truth? Even thoughts of the shocking reports that came in made him sick.

After a period of silence Vision Seeker, looking straight ahead, continued, "It is said he was captive . . . they killed . . . they scalped . . . they cut off his ears . . ." Vision Seeker swallowed. "They put his ears in a bottle of whiskey . . . a bottle for all to see." Vision Seek took smaller, shorter breaths. "They cut strips from his body to make razor straps . . ." Vision Seeker lowered his eyes. "They crushed his skull and made buttons out of the pieces . . ." Vision Seeker paused, breathing hard. He glanced directly at Craig. "Tell us these things are not so. How can we face any white man knowing they do these awful things?"

Craig, with sadness in his voice and eyes, shook his head. "I have heard much the same. I fear much of it is true . . ." It was Craig's turn to pause and swallow hard. "I don't know what makes human beings carry out these terrible atrocities. Yet, they have been going on since people lived in caves. Every so often we humans seem to lose control of our emotions -- run amuck, slashing out, killing and maiming like demons. They say there is good and evil in each of us. . . . At times like these evil rises up and overwhelms good. . . . That's about the only explanation I can think of. Perhaps the only way one can accept evil is to consider it as an ordered part of the universe. It cannot be ignored. It's just there for us to deal with the best we can."

Vision Seeker carefully thought over what his old friend had said. He did not know what to believe about evil and good. It was something Indian people normally did not discuss or think about. A thing or person was either good or bad and treated accordingly. Even enemies were looked on with respect. It was the hairy faced missionaries who spoke of good and evil while teaching Indian people of the wonders of heaven and the tortures of hell. But how even evil men could do these terrible things to the body of a respected foe like Peu-peu-mox-mox was totally beyond his imagination.

Vision Seeker slowly got to his feet as if in a daze. His mind was numb. He thanked Craig for taking him into his home and did the same to his wife, Isabel, who was fussing with the Christmas tree. She turned to hand him a plump, colorfully wrapped package.

"Merry Christmas," she said in a bright, cheery voice, the salutation being echoed by her children and husband. Vision Seeker mumbled a thank you in reply. He felt much as he did on that long ago first Christmas when, like now, he had received gifts and had nothing to give in return. All the way home it bothered him. What did he have that he possibly could give these people who seemed to possess everything?

Upon arriving home Vision Seeker handed the present to Mu-tu. "A Christmas gift," he told her, "tomorrow is Christmas day, the time Christians celebrate the birthday of the God, Jesus."

"Yes, Missionary Woman Spalding always told us when this special day was coming. We cut down an evergreen tree, put all kinds of decorations on it, and drew names for gifts. One time I drew the name of your relative, Michael Two Feathers. I wonder if he remembers. I gave him a tie made of cedar wood for his long hair. He said thank you but I never saw him wear it."

Mu-tu's Christmas knowledge and mission school experiences gave Vision Seeker food for thought. Although half his age, she knew more about the Christian way of life than did he. The realization made him feel uncomfortable. All along he, more or less, had thought of her and treated her as an unenlightened child. To discover there were areas where she had greater knowledge than he, was humbling indeed. From now on he had to treat her as an intelligent adult.

Sometimes, as now, it bothered him that he never had been to school. His knowledge had been acquired around evening campfires, wandering over the plains and through the forests, or at camas field gatherings, working beaver streams and watching over, and caring for horses and cattle. Of course, he had good teachers: his father, Lone Wolf; his brother, Many Horses; the three trappers, Buck Stone, Deacon Walton and Little Ned; the old warrior, Two Kill; his good friend, Red Craig; the village storyteller, Man of Many Words; even his nephew, Michael. Now he was learning from Mu-tu. He suddenly remembered a proverb Buck Stone once had said: "Learning makes a good man better and an ill man worse."

On Christmas day they unwrapped the gift from Isabel Craig. Mu-tu clapped her hands in joy. "Baby clothes," she exclaimed. She took out little jackets, pantaloons, baby moccasins and small blankets. She was so overwhelmed she fell into Vision Seeker's arms. A tear dripped down her cheek to spot Vision Seeker's buckskin shirt.

Vision Seeker was equally moved. Isabel had saved the clothes from the time her children had been babies. To have her give them to Mu-tu for their firstborn made him feel like crying, too. Another quotation learned from his former mountain men teachers flashed into his mind: "Be not overcome by evil, but overcome evil with good." The Craig family certainly had made these words come alive.

We have not seen the light of your speeches; as if there was a post between us; . . . as if the Almighty came down upon us here this day; as if He would say, What are you saying? . . .

Peu-peu-mox-mox, Walla Walla

**HERE STOOD
ST. ROSE MISSION
ALSO KNOWN AS
FRENCHTOWN
1850 ----------- 1900
LAND DONATION CLAIM
OF NARCISSE REYMOND
CEMETERY ON HILL NORTH
OREGON VOLUNTEERS FOUGHT
INDIANS DEC. 7, 8, 9, 1855
CHIEF PEU-PEU-MOX-MOX
OF WALLA WALLA'S SLAIN.**

Erected by home economic
clubs of Walla Walla Co.

On Washington State Highway 12, approximately six miles from Whitman Mission Monument, stands this granite block marking the approximate site of Peu-peu-mox-mox's demise.

Peu-peu-mox-mox sketch by G. Sohon courtesy Washington State Historical Society Marker photograph by B.J. Hunt

THE GREAT POWWOW

XXXI

Hope, like the gleaming taper's light,
Adorns and cheers our way; And still as darker grows the
night, Emits a brighter ray.
Oliver Goldsmith, Irish poet

Joe Jennings and David Malin arrived at the Macon Laird
homestead to find neighbor, Bithiah Abernathy Olafson, tending
to the needs of Granddad Jennings. The oldster looked far from
being on his deathbed. It was quick to see why. He loved the
attention Bithiah bestowed on him. From a flighty girl with stars
in her eyes, she had become a fine, sensitive, caring woman. Joe
was so relieved by his grandfather's good health, he couldn't resist giving his former girl friend a bear-like hug. For a moment
she stood still, seemingly returning the embrace, then jerked away.

"That's enough of that," Bithiah said crossly, her cheeks
aflame. "If you're going to stay a while, take off your boots and
quit messing up the floor, that goes for you, too, David. It's hard
enough to keep house without a couple of lunkheads wiping their
muddy boots on the carpets."

"Yes, mam," Joe said, and quickly did her bidding. It felt
good to be cracked around like Granny had done when Tildy and
he were kids on the Middlesex farm.

Soon, they were sitting at the table feasting on the casse-
role that Bithiah had baked at home and put into Tildy's oven to
warm. The talk was mostly of farm topics: the past harvest, health
of the livestock, the threat of wolves, and repairs to fences and
buildings. Before the meal was over Bithiah's two boys appeared
to escort her home. Joe was pleased to see they had developed
into mannerly, handsome young men. At the doorway they carefully cleaned their shoes, took off their caps, warmly
greeted Granddad and gave David and himself firm handshakes.

What impressed Joe even more, was to learn they had been taking care of the livestock. They gave him an account of the grain and fodder the animals had consumed and the quantities that remained.

"I'll look in tomorrow," Bithiah said as she took her leave. "Now, you be good, Granddad, don't let these rascals give you any wooden nickels."

"Bithiah, we can't keep imposing on you like this," Joe protested. "You already have performed miracles."

"Joe, just because you're home doesn't mean you can take over," Granddad scolded. "I can't tell you how lonesome it gets not having a woman around the house."

"Listen to your grandfather," Bithiah said tartly. "He knows what's best." With that she was gone, leaving Granddad snorting with satisfaction and Joe grimacing.

"Don't worry your head about it," Granddad said. "The girl loves to come over here, and I love having her. I shouldn't wonder but what she needs the diversion. From the little I can glean, she's little better than a slave in her own home. Not that Olafson is a wife beater, or anything like that. It's just that he comes from the old country where the man is boss, and you had better know it. I certainly hope that isn't what Tildy is experiencing. Those British are said to be cold as frozen fish."

Joe was so pleased to see his grandfather strong enough to assert his will that he didn't argue. In fact, he had enjoyed the afternoon immensely. Granddad was right. There was nothing like having a woman around the house. Joe put on his boots and went out to inspect the outbuildings and livestock. He could not let the Olafsons take over completely.

Neighbors dropped in to enquire about Indian troubles in Washington Territory. Joe told them as little as he could truthfully do. The terrible night of the captives' deaths haunted him. He, too, had heard about and seen a few of the demonic things that had been done to the slain prisoners, especially the illustrious Peu-peu-mox-mox. Never would he forget that horrible night.

Granddad did not question him, and he said nothing. Joe pushed the Indian problem from his mind and attempted to keep it there. Perhaps that was the cowardly thing to do, but the way matters stood he did not know what else to do and remain sane. The dishonorable manner in which treaties with the Indian people were made and enforced, was established government policy. It would take an act of Congress to change the policy, and with the slow pace they conducted business it would take years to make that happen.

Joe found relief from his worries through the arrival of two thick letters -- one from Tildy, the other from Michael. Granddad immediately seized Tildy's letter and searched frantically for his glasses, which he could not find. He tossed the letter to Joe. "Hurry! Tell me what she says," he implored.

"Dear . . ."

" Never mind that," Granddad interrupted. "Read it quickly, and tell me when she's coming home. Except for Bithiah's visits, this place is like a morgue."

Joe did his best to comply. Page after page he read but most of it was a description of the docking at Liverpool and wonders of her new home. "Tildy's place has 20 bedrooms, a dining room that seats 36 people, 16 house servants and a dozen gardeners and field hands," he finally reported. "Oh yes, they own a pack of fox hounds."

"Never mind about Tildy and her domicile," Granddad said impatiently. "What does Michael have to say?"

Joe had to admit Michael's letter made better reading. Actually, he was surprised at how well his Indian brother expressed himself. "We had what sailors said was a 'smooth voyage'. Although I must say, it took a while for we 'landlubbers' to get our 'sea legs'. Tildy kept to her bunk most of the time. Morning Star did much better. Little One Who Kicks was the best sailor of all. He wanted to be on deck where he could see the wild white seahorses ride the waves.

"Often at night we would stay on deck to watch the crests

approach like ghosts, and then fade away into the darkness. One Who Kicks kept asking, 'where did they go'? I kept telling him they got tired and went home to their lodges, but he didn't accept that. After we rounded Cape Horn a stiff breeze the sailors called a 'gale' came up. That was when things became exciting. The ship pitched like a bucking horse. The crested waves rose up as high as treetops. The rigging overhead creaked and moaned like an animal in great pain. Needless to say, we did not go out on deck in weather like that."

"What an adventure," Granddad commented. "What stories they will have to tell when they get back. What about Michael's schooling. Being an old teacher, I'm interested in that."

"He doesn't say much. After all, he barely has got there," Joe said.

"Well, read what he says," Granddad said petulantly.

"I still have hopes for becoming a doctor, but school here is far different than I expected. Teachers are called 'masters' and wear long black gowns like Catholic fathers. They are very strong on things like Latin and Greek. A tutor comes every day to teach these and other subjects that I must know before enrolling in university. We get along well, but he seems afraid of me. He keeps questioning about my tomahawk and scalping knife and is trying to get me to put away my feathers and cut my hair.

"Morning Star is well . . ."

"Is that all he has to say about his schooling?" Granddad interrupted. "I could've tutored him in Latin. In Greek I was not good. The poor lad, I'm afraid it will be ages before he finishes medical school. One needs a sound academic foundation to tackle something like that."

"I fear you are right," Joe said, folding the letter and putting it on the mantle. "We may not see Michael for a long while." He glanced at Granddad and wished he hadn't spoken. The brightness of his eyes had clouded. He sank back in the chair and pulled the blanket up to his chin.

"If Michael won't return for years and years, I suppose

Tildy won't either."

"You know what we're going to do, Granddad?" Joe asked brightly. "Christmas is just around the corner. We are going to throw the biggest party you ever saw. We'll have the neighbors in, the parson's family, the hired hands, and whomever else you would like to invite. We'll roast a pig or a calf, have a woman in to cook and bake. It'll be the biggest thing to hit this part of the valley. Why, I think I'll invite old sarge Coombs and family. What do you think of that?"

Granddad perked up. "I say, that's a great idea," he enthused. "Why don't we hire a fiddler and banjo player, roll up the rugs and have a dance."

David joined in. "Yeah, we'll hang up mistletoe and kiss the girls. There are a couple who live up the road that have been giving me the eye. Me thinks, without half trying, I could make an arrangement with one of them."

"Whoa! We aren't going to have any hanky-panky," Granddad warned. "Christmas is a holy time of the year. Besides, the parson will be here."

"Well, he can't object to bit of courting, can he?" David replied. "As they say, 'Christmas only comes once a year. We should make the most of it while it's here'."

"Hey, Joe, see what you have started. This kid has completely lost his reason."

"Granddad you only have yourself to blame," Joe accused. "You said you wanted a woman around the house. David is trying to make it happen."

"You fellows are too much for me," Granddad complained, getting to his feet. "It's time for my nap. If I listen to you two any longer, you'll have me dreaming of sugar plums and dancing girls. I'm too old for either."

"You sure brightened him up," David said after Granddad left. "It would be nice to have a party, but maybe it isn't right, with all of the troubles the country is having."

"Yeah," Joe said thoughtfully, "but who knows what tomorrow will bring? Perhaps a miracle. After all, Christmas is the season for miracles to happen. Let's get busy. Time is wasting. I wish we had a few more hands. There's a lot to be done."

As if to answer to his wish, Joe opened the door to see two mule riders coming down the lane leading a pack animal. Carrot Top O'Flanigan and his sidekick, Raunchy Rankin, had finally come to deliver the bag that had been lost and then unearthed in Father Pandosy's garden.

"Thank heavens, we finally hev caught up with yuh," O'Flanigan said, a thatch of his carroty hair peaking through a ragged hole in his battered hat. "This here bag of yers' been a' albatross hangin' 'round our necks, near chokin' us ta death." He pulled the waterproof covered bundle from the pack animal's back and dropped it at Joe's feet where it landed with a thud.

"What is it?" Joe asked. "Sounds like it's full of rocks."

"Books. Thet's what," Carrot Top replied. "Big tomes written in some furrin language. No one kin make head ner tail of most of 'em."

Joe scratched his head. They couldn't possibly be his . . . Oh, they were Buck Stone's! After the fight with the Blackfeet during which Buck Stone and Clay Beamer had been killed, Joe had packed and carried away Buck's precious books, hoping to give them to a school or library. Then on that fateful day in Lapwai when Michael's cruel stepfather, Francois, had been slain, Red Craig had hustled him away, fearful the villagers might do him harm. He had left the books with Craig and never again given them a thought. Now he took each one from the bag, dusted it off and placed all upright on the mantle. Buck's journals and sketch pads had to be laid flat. He didn't have time to go through them now. Nearly 15 years had passed since Buck's death. If the books held any secrets, they would have to remain hidden a few days longer, Joe decided.

"Thank you fellows, I appreciate what you've done. If you're not doing anything special, why don't you stick around. We are planning a bang-up Christmas party." Joe eyed

Carrot Top's rotund figure and round rosy face. "We need a jolly Santa Claus. You're just the man for the job."

Joe's unusual invitation took the two men by surprise, but they accepted with alacrity. They had been wandering around like lost dogs, and this looked like a wonderful place to bed down.

**

The Christmas party came and went. It was the talk of the valley. Momentarily, the fear that hovered over the land disappeared under a heavy blanket of snow. Sledding outings and hay wagon rides brought back memories of Christmases before coming west. On one of these romantic nights, David Malin popped "the question" to a girl who lived up the road. Early in the spring the two were properly spliced. Proudly, the couple came to make their home at the Jennings-Macon Laird homestead.

"Now that you have a woman in the house, you should be happy," David said to Granddad.

"Yep, looking forward to little ones calling me Grandpa."

"You glutton, you are never satisfied," David joked.

"Why should I be? As an ancient philosopher once said, 'Those who want much, are always much in need'."

Carrot Top O'Flanigan and Raunchy Rankin stayed on to help care for the livestock and work the fields. With temporary peace in the high country and the excitement of the Christmas party and David's wedding over, Joe found himself increasingly restless. Everything was going so well, he felt unneeded.

"I feel about as useless as a dog howling at the moon," he complained to Granddad.

"Why don't you study some of those books on the mantle," Granddad suggested. "I can teach you a little Latin. Then there's Plato's *Republic* in Greek. Perhaps we could study that together."

Joe glanced at the row of books. Except for placing them on the mantle, he hadn't touched them. They were painful reminders of the tragic day Buck Stone and Clay Beamer had been killed. He picked up Buck's journal. Almost every evening after returning from the trap line, before doing anything else, Buck would take out his journal and write down the happenings of the day, sometimes sketching a bird, tree or merely a cloud.

Joe lifted the cover and began to read, amazed how well Buck's beautiful script had endured through the years. On the fly sheet was a special note: "To whom it may concern. In the event of my death I wish to have this forwarded to Miss Mary Blackstone, Harvard Campus, Cambridge, Massachusetts, my daughter whom I love more than anyone on earth. Signed, Buck."

Joe stared at the note. Not once had Buck mentioned a family. Except for revealing he had attended Harvard College, Buck never discussed what he had done before coming west.

Joe turned the page. "Holy Moses," he blurted. "It's a story of Buck's life -- journal of a mountain man." He opened a second ledger. "Ah-ha, here are all the Indian legends he collected along the way. More than once Buck had said when he had gathered enough of them he would put them in a book and publish them for all to enjoy. He wanted the world to know of the Indian people's rich heritage -- their customs, religion and beliefs. He said if white people would take time to understand Indian people, fear, prejudice and distrust of them wouldn't exist."

"Why not do as your friend wished, edit the information he collected and publish it in a book?" Granddad suggested.

"Perhaps I should. First, I must get permission from Buck's daughter . . . hmm . . . Blackstone . . . Buck Blackstone? Mountain men were notorious for taking new names. There was a Professor Blackstone at Harvard College . . . wonder if he could be Mary's and Buck's kin?"

"There's only one way to find out," Granddad said. "Find this Mary girl. If she's single, handy and a bit pretty, bring her back. It's time you had a woman in your life."

"You old fox. David is right. You're never satisfied." But the thought intrigued him. How exciting, to meet Buck Stone's wonderful daughter, to visit with her and perhaps . . . Ah! The old trapper would pop out of his grave.

ABOUT THE AUTHORS

Bonnie Jo Hunt (*Wicahpi Win* - Star Woman) is Lakota (Standing Rock Sioux) and the great-great granddaughter of both Chief Francis Mad Bear, prominent Teton Lakota leader, and Major James McLaughlin, Indian agent and Chief Inspector for the Bureau of Indian Affairs. Early in life Bonnie Jo set her heart on helping others. In 1980 she founded Artists of Indian America, Inc. (AIA), a nonprofit organization established to stimulate cultural and social improvement among American Indian youth. To record and preserve her native heritage, in 1997 Bonnie Jo launched Mad Bear Press which publishes historical fiction depicting the role American Indian played in the "making of the West". These publications include the Lone Wolf Clan series: *THE LONE WOLF CLAN, RAVEN WING, THE LAST RENDEZVOUS, CAYUSE COUNTRY, LAND WITHOUT A COUNTRY, DEATH ON THE UMATILLA, A DIFFICULT PASSAGE, THE CRY OF THE COYOTE,* and *THE GREAT POWWOW.*

#

Lawrence J. Hunt, a former university professor, works actively with Artists of Indian America, Inc. In addition to coauthoring the Lone Wolf Clan historical series, he has coauthored an international textbook (Harrap: London) and authored four mystery novels (Funk and Wagnalls), one of which, *SECRET OF THE HAUNTED CRAGS*, received a special Edgar Allan Poe Award from Mystery Writers of America.

*- an historical series in the style of
Storyteller depicting the role
American Indians played in the
"Making of the West"*

Lone Wolf Clan Book Sequence

The Lone Wolf Clan
An awesome vision launches the Lone Wolf Clan
on a journey that changes their lives forever.

Raven Wing
A tale of love and spiritual seeking embroiled
in a clash of cultures.

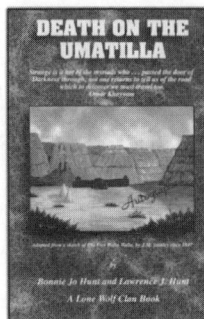

The Last Rendevous
A tale of high adventure and tragedy in the final
days when mountain men reigned supreme.

Cayuse Country
A flood of emigrants cross the "Big Open"
threatening to overwhelm the Cayuse homeland.

Land Without A Country
It was a great land coveted by many but held by
none. Who would have the courage to claim it
as theirs?

Death On The Umatilla
Whitman Mission murderers remain at large; a
Regiment of Mounted Riflemen is ordered to
bring them in.

Cry of the Coyote
The antelope are gone; buffalo wallows are
empty. Only the cry of the coyote can be heard.